To Marie-Josée

The Lord came down to see the city and the tower, which mortals had built. And the Lord said, 'Look, they are one people, and they have all one language; and this is only the beginning of what they will do; nothing that they propose to do will now be impossible for them. Come, let us go down, and confuse their language there, so that they will not understand one another's speech.

Genesis 11, 5-7

I

The crowd in the gym spills out into the hallway. A roar of voices climbs towards the ceiling: the students, amazed to leave their desks and notebooks behind, chatter in a frenzy. Twenty-five minutes have already passed and the air is getting stale. To the right, all the way at the back, one of the basketball nets has been raised and in its place is the familiar black podium used only for the principal's speeches. Everything is ready: the microphone, the speakers, a stool with a pitcher of water and a glass. The hall monitors hurry along the stragglers, push everybody inside, lock the doors with a slam and take up their positions at the front: arms crossed, legs spread. Students are standing on tiptoe, looking around with impatient glances. At Polyvalente Saint-Luc, it's a well-known fact that the principal likes to keep them waiting.

At the opposite end of the gym, near the mats and nets, where the crowd isn't so thick, a squabble breaks out. Two monitors, with their scarlet vests and armbands, chase two boys. The culprits cut a path through the crowd, knocking over two girls who let out sharp shrieks. One of them gets up, rushes one of the boys and grabs him by the collar. What the fuck . . . ? Does he think he can get away with that? No way! The monitors jump them and break it up, then they tell the boys to go kneel down and face the wall, in the left corner, got it? The two of them curse each other under their breath and slouch to the wall. One of the monitors grabs the girl by the shoulders and holds her still: are you gonna settle down or what? She looks at him, startled, like she's paralyzed, then with a brusque movement, shakes herself loose.

Then it's done: the principal takes the three steps leading to the podium in a single stride. Applause and boos rise from the rabble below. The commotion echoes off the walls. The principal stands at the microphone, taking in the sea of heads with a lively look. He pushes back a lock of grey hair and pulls at the knot on his tie. In quick succession, "Barbeau, you asshole!", and "Fucking jerk!" shoot up from the crowd, loud and clear. He opens his mouth, but, knowing better, closes it again. He smiles and ceremoniously raises his arms: "My friends . . ." The gym begins to quiver! The conversations stop, but in the back a girl bursts out laughing: hilarity shakes her flabby stomach and double chin, while another girl tries to help her get a grip. A monitor with a crewcut rushes them, grabs their arms and backs them up against the wall. The principal's smile has faded and he is waving and waving his hand: "Hello, my friends."

With his hand over his mouth, he coughs once, twice. Immediately, dozens of little coughs explode. "Please!" he says, his face tense. He slowly lowers his big, open hands to encourage self-control in his audience. "I want to talk to you about some serious matters. . . ." He takes a sip of water and puffs out his cheeks as though he's gargling. "As you know, over the past few months acts of violence have been committed in our school." He squints his eyes for a moment, as if to measure the effect of his words. "I've already told you that such acts will never be tolerated here." His grandstanding tone surprises the students: contagious joy takes over part of the crowd. "We're here to learn, aren't we? Aren't we?"

A "yes" rings out in unison from the front rows, then a few shouts of "no" crop up here and there, setting off more crazy laughter. It's obvious that the principal only takes in the first answer, "That's right! That's what I thought!"

In the middle of the gym, two boys start to move out of the crowd. They're wearing fluorescent T-shirts and roll their shoulders as they walk. They head for the door, glancing around them. A monitor in the doorway blocks them with his arm.

"And where are you two going?"

He has a big grin. The boys exchange a nervous look, then the taller one's eyes dip low and he gives a bored sigh.

"To the washroom. Where do you think we're going?"

The monitor doesn't answer, his smile widens. The boy puts his hand on his hips and, again, he sighs.

"Don't be stupid, Gino. You're afraid we'll take off, right?"

"You got it, you wuss."

Gino's eyes dart from one boy to the other. Their faces become impassive. The monitor draws closer to the taller one and, tapping on his cheek as if he were a baby, says, "What are you up to this time, Pato?"

The boy ducks away from his hand and pretends to be exasperated. "Can't you see we have to piss! Stop hassling us!"

Gino's face relaxes. He looks both hesitant and slightly ashamed. Here we go, thinks Pato. Yep, he's the easiest of the monitors. No doubt, he'll give in. Gino looks at his watch then he looks Pato straight in the eye.

"Okay," he mutters. "But make it fast. If you're not back in three minutes, I'll cut off your dicks!"

Both boys smile.

"I don't want to have the principal on my ass," explains the monitor. "*Capito?*"

"Yeah, yeah, we get it," says Pato. "You're a good guy, Gino."

The monitor opens the door and, as they go by, the boys give him a few pats on the back. "Okay, okay," says Gino. It's not like

9

he's letting them go out of Christian charity or anything! They hug the wall, certain that Gino's watching them with his piggy eyes and, as soon as they turn the corner, they start to run. As fast as he can, Pato speeds by the boys' washroom. Each of his steps kicks up oversized echoes. He hisses, "¡Apúrate, Alfonso!" They travel down several long hallways that end at metal doors. The farther they go on, the longer Pato's strides become and the more he outdistances the other boy. "Hey," shouts Alfonso, panting, "not too fast!" Behind one door, Pato runs into two Black boys sitting on the ground, moving their heads to the rhythm of their Walkmans. A cloud of smoke surrounds them, a gentle lethargy crowns their movements and reddens their eyes. They don't seem surprised by his sudden appearance. Nonetheless, Pato slows down. When Alfonso catches up, without lowering the volume of his music, one of the Black boys shouts at the top of his lungs, "Look at that, man! Two Latinos playing tag!"

"That is so cute!" yells his neighbour.

The two Latinos hurry away. Behind them they hear the Black boys' tired laughter. Pato's heart rips a drum solo, he turns around: the two Black boys blow him kisses and snigger. Are they going to follow them? Probably not, they're too stoned. Haitians are all the same, always high.

"The problem is the small number of students who are not here to learn, but just to have fun. Of course, I know, everyone likes to have fun. Including me. But that cannot be all a student thinks about. That's where things get dangerous . . ." The students are now listening to the principal without grumbling. It looks like he's taking it easy on them. The last time he talked to them like this, he'd announced that after three suspensions expulsion was automatic.

The two boys push through the last two doors before the basement and run down the stairs four at a time. They arrive at last among the billiard tables and, farther along, the long rows of lockers forming sinister corridors, with dozens of cones of light filtering in at an angle through the dirty window panes. Pato crosses the room, stops in front of one of the lockers and quickly dials the combination on the lock. Never again. They'll never again be able to say that I'm just a good-for-nothing little shit, that I'm scared, that I'm too young. Never again . . . Soaked in sweat, Alfonso drifts over. Pato opens the locker door and grabs a metal tool. When he sees the set of red bolt cutters almost a metre long, Alfonso panics and looks around: there's nobody there.

"Pato? What if you wait and do this some other day?"

The question startles Pato. He notices that Alfonso's eyes are wide and staring, his lips trembling. No way, he's going to cry! The same second, he realizes his heart is pounding inside his chest. Now Alfonso lowers his head and covers his eyes with his forearm.

"Relax," Pato whispers. "The important thing is not to panic. That's what Flaco always says. Right? Tell me that's right."

Alfonso nods his head: yes. They stand there for a moment without talking. Alfonso's tears and his innocent face are irritating Pato more and more, the odour of his sweat nips at his nostrils. Pato's upset at himself for choosing Alfonso for the job. But now isn't the time to get mad. He motions for him to follow and starts running again. A moment goes by before the echo of Alfonso's steps can be heard, as if his heart wasn't in it.

"Every Friday," continues the principal, "for the last three months, I've been meeting with the monitors. They give me a summary of what's gone on during the week. Which individuals have got the most detentions? What did they do? Who did they do it to? Where do they commit these acts of aggression? And do you know what we've realized? Most offences happen during recess." He stops and wipes his mouth with the back of his hand. Yes, the time has come, he's going to spill the beans, they can feel it. "It wasn't an easy decision to make, my friends. And don't forget: you can't be angry with us, just with the few bad apples who

11

are ruining the atmosphere at this school. So, to ensure that these unfortunate incidents no longer occur, we – the administration, the monitors, and I – have decided to eliminate afternoon recess."

At first, a grumbling hovers over the crowd, as if they're not sure they've really understood, then a rumble arises. At last protests shower down on the principal: the crowd is shouting at the top of their voices, here and there students raise their middle fingers. Standing rigid behind the microphone, the principal shrugs his shoulders. His pretending he doesn't care makes the booing louder.

They've finally made it: they're in front of the most famous locker in the school. It's covered with black, red, green, purple graffiti: *Propriété des Bad Boys*, *Public Enemy Number 1*, *Cop Killer*, *Fuck Barbeau*, *Sex, drugs and rap* . . . In the centre, the Bad Boys' symbol: a panther seen from behind, with its head turned back and its mouth wide open. Alfonso's the lookout, his face scarlet. Pato takes a deep breath, snares the lock with the bolt cutters and, with his eyes shut as if he's trying to forget what he's doing, forces it. He can already see Flaco's and his brother's astonished, delighted faces: no way! Not CB's locker! You? You're the one who ripped him off? Really? C'mon, spit it out, tell us how you did it. And he would tell them everything. Flaco would put an arm around his shoulders: I can see CB's face when he finds out a little grade-seven kid broke into his locker! He wouldn't miss it for anything! The lock hits the ground and Pato rushes to open the locker.

Spit wads beat down on the principal's suit vest. He glances at the teachers lined up like soldiers near the podium then lets out a long breath into the microphone. "My friends, please . . . we made this decision for your own good." Now some groups are slow-clapping, stamping their feet. Speaking over the din, he starts again, "One last thing, my friends . . . listen to me, please . . ." With one voice, the room chants, "Nooo, noooo,

12

nooooo!" Despite it all, he continues, "I'm told the tension is caused by supposed ethnic conflicts . . . On that matter, I have only one thing to say . . . listen to me, for heaven's sake!" Again, he turns his head towards the teachers, puckers his lips and angrily runs a hand through his hair. For an instant, he sways, as if dizzy: he is the loneliest man in the world. Then, in a low voice, he grumbles, "Little bastards. . . ."

The teachers exchange shocked looks. The students laugh helplessly, slapping their thighs: that's a good one! Ah! Ah! Ah! Barbeau tries to explain himself: "For several months, a few individuals have been trying to divide us into ghettos . . . We won't let them do that to us . . . The important thing, my friends, is that there are no Italians . . . no Haitians . . . no Latinos . . . no Jews . . . no Asians . . . not even any Québécois, do you hear me? . . . There's no one here except students, students who will persevere, who are hungry for knowledge! Deep down inside, we're all brothers!" At one end of the gym, an entire row pretends to coax long wails out of imaginary violins. Some hug each other melodramatically, others shout, "Brother!" and pretend to sob convulsively. The principal leaves the podium without looking back. The students shout in victory. Ah! Ah!

The quantity of items in the locker leaves them speechless. It's papered with pictures of rappers and Black women in bikinis. On the door, a mirror, and, once again, the Bad Boys' symbol. On the upper shelf, a long-toothed comb, sunglasses and a cap. Pato grabs the glasses and the cap, something falls to the ground. It's a little chain with a silver bird. The bird's beak is twisted and its heavy wings are spread as if it's just taking flight. Pato recognizes it – it's a condor. His father has told him about the intelligence and cruelty of this bird that is feared throughout South America. But what's a Haitian doing with a condor? Something that belongs to a Latino! Flaco and his brother are going to be happy, he's just recovered a stolen article. Quickly, he stuffs the condor inside his shorts and feels the animal come into icy contact with his testicles. *¡Vámonos!*

The students are all blabbing with one another, not in the least hurry to move on. Two monitors open the doors: "C'mon, everybody, show's over!" Perched on a stool, his feet on the cross-bar, Gino watches the students flow by, but his mind is elsewhere. He steals a glance at his digital watch: it's four-thirty-five, ten minutes have already gone by since the Latinos went to the washroom. Deep down, he knew they'd take off. The school has become impossible. The kids do whatever they feel like. Today Barbeau definitely lost it. There's no excuse. . . . It's not the first time a principal or teacher has lost control like that. In class it happens all the time. Pfff, personally, as long as he gets his cheque every Thursday, he doesn't really give a shit. . . . The crowd spills out into the hallway.

In the distance, steps echo like in a church. Pato rushes to his locker and dials the combination so quickly he makes a mistake. Alfonso's face twists like he has cramps. Finally, the lock opens. Flaco and his brother cross his mind again: You're a first-class thief, Pato! That was something else! Robbing the leader of the Bad Boys gang! That'll show that fucking Haitian! You're the kind of guy we need in Latino Power, Pato! He can't hold back a smile. He leaves the cap, the sunglasses and the bolt cutters in his locker, then he closes it. After everyone leaves, he'll put each item in his school bag and that'll be that. He suddenly feels a hand on his shoulder. He turns around: it's the two Haitians from before. No way! What does this mean? They're older and taller by at least a head. A shiver runs down his spine. The Black boys' faces harden.

"If it was that easy to rob us," says one of them, "there wouldn't be much left in our lockers by now."

The one who spoke laughs as if he didn't care. "What did I tell you? Those Latinos are born thieves!"

*

14

In the boys' washroom at École-Saint-Pascal-Baylon, there was a long wooden bench where we got changed before gym class. Some kids, already wearing their Phys. Ed. outfits under their street clothes, proudly dropped their pants; others discreetly went and put on their shorts and T-shirt in the stalls. We didn't talk much: Serge, the Phys. Ed. teacher, only gave the boys five minutes to get ready, and when time was up, the high-pitched sound of his whistle came through the half-open windows. All we heard was the rustling of clothes and, from time to time, the water washing through the urinals.

When the new boy came in, we all stopped for a moment, looked him over, then deliberately finished slipping on our socks or tying up our laces. Seeing that no one said a word to him, the boy went towards the urinals and stood there, looking awkward. He was Black, short, with a slim body. His delicate features and long eyelashes made him look like a girl. He was wearing a blue striped T-shirt. Remember, Marcelo: sitting there at the end of the bench, near the new boy, already in your PE clothes, you looked up at him. Since he kept standing there looking at the ceiling, you asked him, "Aren't you going to put on your shorts?"

The boy looked at you, then lowered his head.

"Nobody told me it was Phys. Ed . . ."

There were discreet coughs. One student, in the back, repeated the sentence softly, omitting the d's as he had. You all wagged your heads, trying to stifle your laughter. Just like with you the first time, Marcelo: they were making fun of his accent.

"What's your name?" you ventured.

Without giving him time to answer, Sylvain, who had got up to do his warm-up exercises, shouted, "Chocolate Bar!"

The whole class burst out laughing. Even the two Black boys at the other end of the bench guffawed. And, to everyone's surprise, the new boy joined the concert. He had a strange, joyful laugh, that unfurled in an uninterrupted series of i's. No, no, he explained. His name wasn't Chocolate Bar. How silly! His name was Cléo. Akira, next to you, asked him if he was Haitian. Yes, he was born in Port-au-Prince. Akira pointed his index finger towards the two Black boys at the end of the bench: they're Haitian, too.

"You good at sports?" Sylvain asked.

He shrugged his shoulders, as if to say he did all right, but that was about it. Sylvain kept his eyes on him, as he continued to warm up: touching the tip of his sneakers with his left hand, then with his right, going from one foot to the other more and more quickly.

"Have you ever slept with a girl?" Sylvain continued.

This time a chuckle arose, then greedy eyes settled on the new boy.

"Oh, sure!" he exclaimed, as if there was nothing more natural in the world. "That kind of thing happens all the time where I'm from."

First, there was some hesitation, as if you only half believed him, then there was a howl: *wowowowowo*! The class was amazed. We examined him from his head down to his feet, but differently this time, kind of like we looked at high-school boys. The new boy smiled broadly, displaying a mouth full of uneven teeth. Motionless now, Sylvain stared at him, breathing hard, his mouth open.

"Come on! Tell us how it happened!"

"What? We slept together, that's it."

"You want to keep it to yourself? I get it. I'm the same way."

"You never slept with anyone!" shouted Akira. "Don't even start!"

Woooow! On the bench, the members of the class sniggered, lifting their feet off the floor, covering their mouths with their hands: Akira, you're gonna get it. We glanced at Sylvain: there was no question the Jap was going to get a beating. Sylvain was furious. He pounced on Akira and grabbed him by the collar.

16

"Who was talking to you? Answer me!"

"Okay, okay, I didn't mean anything."

Cléo stepped closer to them, "Okay, I'll tell you. But I don't see what you think is so interesting about it."

Remember, Marcelo: all eyes were on Cléo. Again, you could hear water flowing through the urinals. Remember his childish face, his urgent desire to be accepted. Like you, on your first day. We'd all thought he was more mature than the rest of us. *¡Ay, Marcelito!*

"In Haiti," Cléo began, tugging on his T-shirt, "I used to go to see my grandmother a lot out in the country. My family and I would spend the night there. And since there was only one bed-room, I'd sleep in the same bed as my little cousins. That's all. I told you there wasn't anything interesting about it."

Laughter burst out around him. Some of the boys put their heads in their hands and shook back and forth, others hid their faces in a towel, still others pretended to beat their foreheads against the wall. Finally, everyone calmed down, and Sylvain came and stood, with his hands on his hips, puffing out his chest, a few centimetres from Cléo.

"I don't think you understood my question. I'll try to be more clear. Have you ever put your dick inside your cousin's pussy?"

After snapping out the words, Sylvain ran a proud gaze around the room. Now, impassive, he waited for the reply, while the others giggled, and squirmed. You saw Cléo frown, like he was trying to figure out the meaning of the new words he'd just heard. His pupils darted about and he clenched his hands as if he was squeezing lemons. His face tensed: he was going to cry.

Serge's whistle rang out.

"We're not done with you," Sylvain warned, leaning over him. "We still have one more test to give you."

Oh, yes, the famous test, Marcelo. Remember your first day: c'mon, new kid, pull down your shorts. Your underwear, too, what do you think? You felt a tingling in your cheeks, as if a fine

17

rain was falling on your face. You forced yourself to hold back your tears so they wouldn't laugh even more. At first, you didn't understand what they were asking you to do. How could you understand, since you couldn't grasp the words coming from their mouths like balls of fire. Then, it was like a revelation: you were supposed to pee from the bench to the urinals. Your stream reached the target. What luck! A salute of applause followed. What a baptism! Later, you witnessed what they did to anyone who didn't succeed on the first try: they pissed on them, can you imagine?

Swallowing their smiles, the boys formed a long line, began to trot in place and jogged out. As for Cléo, he didn't appear in the playground until a little while later, and Serge motioned for him to come closer: come on, hurry up! A new boy showing up with his hands in his pockets wasn't a good sign. He spoke to him for a moment, then the boy started jogging with the others. He performed the warm-up laps unenthusiastically. When Serge had his back turned, Sylvain and Evangelos, two boys who were inseparable, came up to Cléo from behind and hit him repeatedly on the neck: hey, Caramilk! Cléo would turn around and they'd shout at him, oh! you know your name! Each time the new boy started to laugh, leaving the other two speechless.

Remember the beginning of that school year, Marcelo: it was September and already the sun only appeared on rare occasions. Now and then a cold wind blew, you could feel it on your legs, and you ran faster to keep from shivering. Yes, the leaves of the spiral-barked maple tree in the playground, as tall as the school, had already turned yellow and purple. But the school . . . Was there a single other building in the neighbourhood that was any drabber? ¡Ay Marcelito! The warm-ups were done, the group moved towards Serge, who was standing on the stairs with his stopwatch in his hand. He always, always looked severe, military, but, they had to admit, passionate, too. That day his long speech

18

was about relay races, about how important it was for them to be the best so the school could improve its image. Despite it all, it's strange, isn't it, how his fanaticism was contagious? How they would play along with him! Immense hope swelled their hearts. Yes, Serge, we'll practise. No, we won't eat any more junk food. First, we have to beat the other schools in the neighbourhood, then it would be the Jeux de Montréal, then, if all went according to plan, the team would go to the Jeux du Québec. Today, they were going to choose the teams for the grade-five relay. It wasn't only about getting the four best times in the class, but the best times for the whole of grade five. Everyone understand? Okay, now let's get to work.

Serge inspired such admiration that the other teachers were jealous. Whenever the kids spotted him, they'd run towards him and hang from his neck – especially the girls. They'd throw themselves into his arms, give him kisses, tell him secrets. He was a sort of larger-than-life hero for the boys, and the first love of most of the girls. But only races and practice interested him: come on, come on, what did they think, that he was just some sort of entertainer? He'd extricate himself from their hugs and blow a lungful of air through his whistle. Even though there was no chance most of the students would participate in the competition, they would all run, impassioned, trying to outdo each other in the hope of winning his esteem. After a race, it was something to see the losers trying to swallow their sadness.

As the girls were qualifying, Cléo, standing off to the side with an intrigued expression, watched the boys imitating the way the girls ran. He laughed at the right times and went back to his warm-ups when there was nothing interesting to see. When it was the boys' turn, silence immediately fell over us. We watched each other furtively. We remembered the relay team from the year before, whispered the names of the team members: Marcelo, Akira, Sylvain and Yuri. Last year, the team hadn't made it to the Jeux du Québec because of a stupid disqualification. But this year we were going to get the revenge we deserved! Yep, the other schools were going to get theirs!

The whistle blew and Akira, the first to position himself on the starting line, took off as if hurtling into space. Since he was one of the fastest boys in the class, it was a good half hour before anyone pushed him out of first place. On the other hand, his time didn't beat the record held by Yuri, who was the fastest in all of the grade five classes. Sylvain took third place: without his knowing, his mother had put his running shoes in the washer the day before and they hadn't dried in time. So he'd had to settle for his brother's shoes, although they were two sizes too big for him. Look! He was swimming in them! Otherwise, there was no doubt, he would have beaten everyone no problem! he said when his race was over, snapping his fingers under Akira's nose.

On your marks! You knelt behind the starting line. On Thursday mornings, the day you had Phys. Ed., you had no trouble getting up as soon as the alarm went off. Get set! Your legs tensed. And, although for your Latino friends in the neighbourhood nothing was as good as playing soccer, you liked running the best, especially sprinting. Serge gave the Go! signal and you leapt like a spring, clenching your fists. You felt free when you ran: you moved forward, usually with your eyes closed, trying to express the person you knew you were but that no one else knew anything about. Your mouth always tasted like blood. At the finish line, a circle of students formed around Serge as he waited for you, his stopwatch in hand. We ran towards you, good job, Marcelo!, and we slapped you on the back, man, you run fast! You caught your breath, your hands on your hips, your head lowered. You'd run your best time, Marcelo, can you imagine! Serge came towards you: yes, your time was even better than Yuri's. He hugged you with a smile: nice performance, champ!

So, the team would be the same as the year before. So much the better, it was such a good team. We talked about the order they should run in, about each member's strengths and weaknesses. Most of the boys were quiet, hurt about being left off the team again. Just a second, Serge cut them off, there's still the new boy. They looked around for him, where had he gone? Alone, under the colourful maple leaves in the middle of the playground, he was observing you and biting his nails. Serge motioned for him to come over, and, since he wasn't wearing gym clothes, asked if he'd prefer to run another day. No, he'd rather do it right now and, without being asked twice, he went nonchalantly towards the starting line. They all looked at their watches: after this, it's recess, so hurry up, new kid!

Cléo's take-off was so clumsy and slow that you, Marcelo, thought he'd probably never sprinted. He had no technique, raised his head way too high, needlessly thrust out his chest. But, *Dios mío*, once he got going, once his legs warmed up, he sped up so much that, one after the other, each head turned towards him. He stubbornly kept his eyes fixed on the sky and smiled as wide as he could. Still, he was paying so little attention to where he was going that he changed lanes. After a little while, he was running like you'd never seen anyone your age run. Several students, who had already lined up on the stairs, came back down, open-mouthed. How could anyone explain it? It was unbelievable! He was so small and looked so harmless!

When he finished his run, he came back towards you, an apologetic smile on his lips, as if asking to be forgiven for his achievement. Your eyes ate him up, but you didn't dare come too close. Serge announced that he was, surprisingly, the fastest boy in grade five. Half-stifled ohs! and whoas! rose from the group. You made your way over to the new boy: there, he was right in front of you. How could you be jealous of a boy who'd only shown you who he really was? You put out your hand, the other boy shook it, his eyes laughing. The ice was broken: Cléo received an avalanche of pats on the back. Boys took him by the arms and raised them over his head. He laughed with excitement. We teased him: did he eat spinach like Popeye in order to run that

21

fast? No, he hated spinach, he shrugged his shoulders and again gave in to naïve mirth.

Suddenly, Sylvain got angry with Serge: why wasn't he saying anything? The new kid had left his lane! In a real competition, he would have been disqualified, obviously! Serge remained quiet another minute, then, remember his reprimanding tone: who did he think he was to talk to him like that, disrespectful brat! It was just that, the new boy wasn't disqualified because it wasn't a real competition! And he'd better not forget, Serge was the teacher! He gave a long blast on his whistle, class was over, it was time for recess. Serge was too fond of winning, he knew he'd be taking no chances with Cléo. In the middle of the playground, Sylvain, his arms crossed, stubbornly stared at you and Cléo. When you walked past him, with controlled anger, he shouted, "Go back to your own country, goddamnit . . ." At that moment, your eyes were fixed on Cléo. Remember, Marcelo, his smile had disappeared.

Four silhouettes advance along the Côte-des-Neiges sidewalk, occasionally lit up by the headlights of the cars speeding past them. They go along Avenue Appleton, the northern boundary of Parc Kent, pass by the pétanque pitches where ten or so old men are assembled, most wearing skullcaps. In the lead, Pato and Alfonso make their way, their heads lowered, their hands behind their backs, while, behind them, the two Haitians, taller and with broader shoulders, chat about a girl they saw on the bus. One of them describes her as he sculpts imaginary curves while the other smiles. It's already dark out and, strangely, the April air is as stagnant as a sweltering summer evening.

In front of the baseball diamond, Pato notices boys who are older than him, almost all Asians, playing a game he doesn't know the name of, a kind of volleyball you play with your feet. On the right, despite the falling darkness, three boys, with very dark skin, are tossing a football back and forth. As he advances towards a good beating, life goes on all around him. People's movements, their smiles, seem somehow unreal. He clenches his fists to boost his courage, but he realizes his hands are damp. He has to keep his cool, as his brother likes to say. When his brother finds out he got caught, he's going to be furious, no doubt about it. Pato closes his eyes: there's only one thing left to do: take it like a man. He realizes, *Dios mío*, his teeth are chattering! I'll never steal again, *Dios mío, ayúdame, que no me peguen*, never again! What if I just start running, right now? What if I yell? Suddenly he remembers: the condor. That's it, he's done for! With his usual bad luck, the chain will fall out later right in front of those niggers, and then, well, they'll kick his ass good! *¡Putamadre!*

The Haitians gesticulate a lot as they talk, but they don't take their eyes off them. Yet he and Alfonso are out of their league: they're in grade seven and the Haitians are in grade ten or eleven. To his great surprise, when they caught them red-handed they laughed at them more than they threatened or hit them. How long had they been spying on them, hiding behind the lockers? Probably from the very beginning. Afterwards, the Haitians decided to go eat some Kentucky Fried Chicken while they waited for CB to show up at Parc Kent. While they stuffed themselves in the parking lot, Pato'd had to cough a lot to cover up the rumbling in his stomach. Then they took them to Parc Vézina where they met some other Haitians and ordered the Latinos to get down on all fours so they could ride them like in a rodeo. Around seven o'clock, they headed towards Parc Kent to meet CB and the other Bad Boys.

They step over the imaginary line, set foot in Haitian territory. Pato is almost completely unfamiliar with this part of the park: he's always been forbidden set foot in it. They walk beneath the spray of the streetlights and, once they come out at the running track, they turn and, their backs hunched, make their way beneath the bleachers that seem to form a tunnel. It takes an

23

eternity. Then, at the end, Pato can see a group of Blacks chatting, gathered around a guy slumped in a patio chair. They're all wearing baggy pants and backward baseball caps. They cut off their discussion and, as they notice the Latinos, their eyes open wide. One of their escorts triumphantly tosses the cap and sunglasses on the ground. A heavy girl with short hair rushes towards the objects. She shows them to the guy sitting in the chair.

"CB, check it out!"

He sits up quickly. After a pause, as if he regretted his initial reaction, he sinks back down against the back of the chair, strokes his goatee at length, and then, one by one, cracks each of his knuckles. Finally, he motions to the girl with his chin and she immediately says to the two Haitians, "What are you doing with that stuff?"

For a moment, the two young Haitian boys look at each other. Come on, Ketcia, one of them stammers. Doesn't she get it? These two Latinos broke into CB's locker!

CB waves his hand at the two Latinos to call them forward. They walk towards him and Pato can finally make him out. He's always surprised to see how gentle his features look, and how unmuscular he is. The distrust he inspires comes from his slow, calculated movements. CB also motions for the two Hatians with them to approach: *sa k pase?* He speaks very little, listens to them, his face expressionless and, from time to time, with his hand, asks them to repeat or provide more details. Finally, he raises his thumb and says goodbye, and the two Haitians leave, visibly upset at being unable to stay.

Pato keeps telling himself he should have handed over the condor to the Haitians as soon as he got caught by the lockers. If he takes it out now, CB will want to know why he didn't give it back sooner and he'll get suspicious. He'll think he stole other things, too, and will get mad. His brother and Flaco have told him lots of stories about fights with CB. The guy fights like an animal. Yes, it's better to keep quiet. But . . . he can't feel the chain

24

anymore! Has it fallen? Casually, he looks at the ground: he doesn't see it. He spreads his legs: finally, he can feel it. Could it fall?

CB leans towards them, places his elbows on his thighs. He examines them from top to bottom, like police officers do.

"I have to admit, it wasn't such a bad idea to rob me during Barbeau's speech. Let's even say I think it was pretty clever. Especially for a couple of wusses like you."

Nonchalantly, he begins to applaud them. Ketcia and the other three Haitians standing behind CB burst out laughing. After a minute, CB slowly raises his hand and a lethal silence falls over them.

"Listen to me carefully, you guys," CB continues. "If you treat me right, I'll treat you right. But watch out, no bullshit."

He snaps his fingers and immediately one of the Haitians leans in towards him. There follows a short, whispered exchange in Creole. All Pato can make out is the name of the boy, Mixon, and he remembers a story his brother told about him. Once, in class, he fell asleep during an exam and the teacher had to wake him up. He picked up the kid's paper and held it up by the tips of his fingers: it was dripping with saliva. Mixon rummages around in a cooler, takes out two Popsicles and hands one each to him and Alfonso. Surprised, they remain motionless for a moment, their Popsicles in their hands, not daring to unwrap them. CB motions towards them with his chin, and they hurriedly rip open the paper and start to lick the red ice.

"Tell me one thing," CB asks, fixing his eyes on Pato. "Was it your brother's idea to rob me?"

"No. Lalo had nothing to do with it. I swear."

"Then it was Flaco's idea?"

"Not his either. I swear."

"Then it was your idea?"

Since Pato remains silent, CB slumps back down in his chair.

"I think I see what you're up to, you little wuss. You wanted Latino Power to accept you, right? You wanted to show them you

25

could pull off a robbery like a big boy. And what could be better than robbing the leader of the Bad Boys, right? I already said it once, but I'll tell you again, you're a pretty clever guy."

Behind CB, a wave of sniggering immediately dies out.

"What else did you take from me?"

What if they decide to search me? wonders Pato. What if they tie me to a tree? What if they beat me like a dog and then abandon me there?

"Nothing else," he hears himself say. "I swear."

"You swear a little too much for my taste, wuss. In my opinion, that means one of two things. Either you lie like the devil himself, or you're planning to become a priest."

Again, his remark sparks laughter.

"You like to run?"

The question surprises Pato, who then replies, yes, he likes to.

"Isn't it true nothing's more fun than jogging in a park?"

"It's true. Nothing's more fun."

"On a nice summer day, with your friends following along and all that?"

"That's true, CB."

"It would be too bad if something unfortunate happened to your legs, wouldn't it?"

Pato is silent.

"Answer!"

"Yes, that would be too bad."

"Okay, let's say it would be too bad. It would really be too bad if you lied to me."

CB directs an enquiring gaze at Alfonso. "What about you, wuss, what do you think? Is your little friend here lying to me or not?"

Pato sees the sweat pearling on the heavy boy's forehead, as he turns his head towards him, and to his great displeasure, he notices the frightened, hesitant shine in his eyes. Pointing a finger

26

at Alfonso, Ketcia declares, "Just look at him, CB. The guy's shitting his pants. I think it means they're hiding something."

"Yeah, I can feel it, too. These two are just politely shoving a cucumber up my ass."

CB's eyes turn back to Pato. His breathing becomes shorter and sharper.

"Deep down, I really don't care if you're lying to me. First of all, I made a peace agreement with Flaco not too long ago. Also, because tomorrow, one way or another, I'll know if you're telling me the truth or not now. And because you're nothing but morons, I really wouldn't enjoy giving you a beating. But there's just one thing . . ."

He jumps up and brings his face in close to Pato's.

"It's true I don't like liars, but there's one category of people I hate, who I never forgive for anything. Every time I've fought in my life, it was to beat one of them up. Now, we're going to see if you two fall into that category."

Pato hears CB's whistled breathing and smells a mix of cigarettes and mint candies. It occurs to him to take one step back, but he is unable to do it, as if his body is no longer following his orders.

"Why did so many Black men die during the Vietnam war?" CB asks them, dead serious.

The Latinos exchange a surprised glance, and, one after the other, reply that they don't know.

"Well, I'm going to tell you why. When they were getting bombed and the general would say 'Get down,' the Blacks would all start to dance instead of lying down on the ground."

The Haitians roar with laughter.

"Christ, that's a good one, CB!" Mixon comments, between two torrents of laughter. "I didn't know that one."

Pato repeats the last line of the joke in his head, then looks up at the Haitians and sees shadows swaying in the night, shadows with white teeth sparkling like diamonds. And suddenly, feeling like he could just as easily start to cry, he bursts out in strange laughter, too. Alfonso does likewise. Deep down, and Pato knows this, they aren't laughing, they're so worried the sound they're making is more like a moo. The Haitians laugh even harder, but CB settles for just an amused smile.

"So – did we have a good laugh?" he asks after a bit of time has passed.

"Yeah," Pato says, in an exhausted voice. "That joke of yours was really a good one."

"That's right, it was good, wasn't it? . . . But now, let's move on to more serious things. Why did you like it?"

"Well, I don't know, because it was good. What? I don't understand the question."

"Why was it good?"

Not really knowing what to answer, Pato says, "It's funny, when I saw you all laughing, I wanted to laugh, too."

Sinister-looking faces draw closer to him, exhaling noisily through their noses.

"What?" says CB. "You were laughing at us?"

Suddenly Pato feels like the ground is going to open up beneath his feet and swallow him up.

"No, that's not it. It's that . . . the way you opened your mouths, I don't know how to say it, but I thought it was funny."

"You thought our mouths were funny? Is that what you're trying to tell us?"

"Yeah, that's it. No . . . Wait . . . I mean . . . I'm all mixed up."

CB lets out a long, tired, unenthusiastic laugh, and then Pato is as surprised as the others to hear himself sobbing. Then, Alfonso begins to wail like a baby, too.

"You didn't pass the test!" CB articulates above the concert of whining. "You get an F-! You know what, you're a racist!"

He steps back, laughing quietly.

"Be glad you're nothing but a little wuss, or else I would have taken care of you myself."

And going back to sit down, "They're all yours!"

The other Haitians surround them, taking the Popsicles from their hands. Now, Pato closes his eyes, and forces himself to cry in silence. Like a man, he says to himself. He feels someone take him by the collar and lift him up. With the first punch, he feels a warm liquid running over his lips. The pain is so intense it makes him dizzy. But after the second punch, he doesn't feel anything else, it's like some other person's face is being pounded on.

Usually, after Phys. Ed., we'd push our way upstairs, sweating and shoving in the lineup, and then take over the classroom with rowdy conversations. Sister Cécile would pace back and forth, furtively observing the ruckus, and once they were all quietly seated at their desks, and this sometimes took a long time, she would look at her watch: in order to make up the lost time, class would end, let's see, ten minutes late. And she'd better not hear any complaining! Then, inevitably, she'd go into a long speech about proper behaviour at school: fists and jostling should be left to the animals, did they understand? Also, the young ladies had to pay special attention not to be taken as "easy." Did they understand what she meant?

On that day, however, the students filed in, surprisingly quietly, grouped around the new boy. And several of them told Sister Cécile about his exploit in Phys. Ed. And right away she said, that's wonderful, congratulations, but it would be even better if he were good in French, too. What country was he from? Haiti? That's what she thought, she'd recognized the accent. How long had he been in Canada? Lord, time was flying, she'd speak to him after class. The rest of you, that's enough, it's time to take your seats.

Remember the postcards she handed out that day: the Rockies asleep under a snowy blanket, the Laurentian lakes still as mirrors and stands of pine trees as wide as the sea. They had to choose one and use it to inspire memories of a family vacation, and then come to the board and tell the class about it. At the slightest stutter, memory lapse or nervous gesture, the whole class would start to laugh. Remember the madness when it was Cléo's turn. Four times, Marcelo, four times, he repeated the same sentence: Hello, my name is Cléo . . . unable to go any farther. That enigmatic smile on his lips the whole time. All the respect he'd managed to earn with his run evaporated. The laughing was so loud a head appeared in the doorway: could they, please, lower their voices? Mr. Daigneault had sent someone to ask. Sister Cécile: yes, yes, she'd take care of it. She stood up, placed one fist on her hip, pursed her lips: come now, children, what's got into you! This is how you welcome newcomers now? You have no manners!

When the day was over, you were walking alongside Akira on Rue Carlton, and you could still see the new boy's face. Despite his smile, you had read the despair in the glimmer of his eyes. Your school bag on your back, you were walking nonchalantly, as Akira described the images in Magic Sword, the new Super Nintendo game his cousin had got for his birthday. The guys were incredible, the drawings were even better than in King of Dragons, which had been his favourite game till then. But you weren't listening anymore: behind you, Cléo was walking alone kicking at the fallen leaves covering the sidewalk and pretending to daydream. How long had he been following you like that? Akira motioned for him to join you and he ran up, holding his school bag in one hand and his lunch box in the other.

Akira continued to describe the video game: now he was going on about how many points you got for stabbing someone with a sword, or tripping them or winning a fist fight. Then he turned towards Cléo, "Where do you live?"

Cléo thought a minute, then he shook his head. Crap, he'd forgotten the name of the street again. It was because they'd just moved. The day before yesterday in fact. But he knew how to get home, he'd recognize the street when he saw it.

"You just came to Canada?" Akira asked.

"No, I lived in Saint-Léonard for three months. But my mother didn't think there were enough Haitians."

"That's an Italian neighbourhood," Akira remarked. "My cousin says if you're not Italian over there, in no time, you've got the Mafia on your ass. They think they own the whole neighbourhood."

"Your cousin lives over there?"

"You kidding? His family barely lasted a month, not a day more! My father told them to move down here. Côte-des-Neiges ain't exactly full of Japanese, either, but at least around here he won't get beaten up when he gets out of school."

"One time," remembered Cléo, "I beat a guy at marbles. His name was Luigi. He said he was going to shut me up in a locker because I'd cheated. I thought it was crazy, because it really wasn't true what he was saying. It's lucky I was faster than him. After a few days he got tired of chasing me around. So he'd just shout insults at me. And I'd just laugh."

"Well," you said, "when it comes to running, you sure run fast. With you we've got a pretty good chance of making it to the Jeux du Québec."

"In my class in Haiti, I wasn't even one of the best. Now if I'm a pretty good runner, it's because my mother used to send me to buy bread in Port-au-Prince, and she'd say, 'C'mon, Cléo, hurry up.' It was good practice."

You'd turned left at Avenue Légaré and you saw cars, one behind the other, in something that looked like a traffic jam. In the very front, a man had his head stuck under the hood of a black Dodge with a seriously rusted body.

"In Haiti," Cléo continued, "all the guys play soccer. They don't know what hockey is."

31

"In Chile, it's the same way," you explained. "In my letters, when I told my cousins about the Montreal Canadiens, they thought I was talking about people who lived in Canada."

"What a bunch of jerks!" exclaimed Akira.

"Well, how were they supposed to know?"

"I'd like to play hockey," said Cléo. "I've never played."

"You can play with us," Akira offered. "We play all the time. In the summer, we play in the street with a tennis ball. In the winter, we play in the park, on the rink, with a real puck."

He stopped for a moment, then, in a solemn voice, said, "Hockey is my favourite sport."

"You any good?"

"I'm really good!"

At the red light on the corner of Van Horne you stopped on the cement median where the cars were racing by, then you walked as far as Avenue Linton.

"Here it is!" shouted Cléo. "This is it, this is my street."

You and Akira looked at each other and laughed.

"You live on the same street as us!" you said. "Wow, are you ever a space cadet!"

You burst out laughing. Cléo looked hurt.

"What does 'space cadet' mean?" he asked.

"Nothing," you answered. "It's not harsh. It just means you're a little . . . how can I explain . . . a little out of it."

Linton, Marcelo, the street you grew up on, that street of dreams and tragic disappointments. In all Montreal, was there a grimier, more dilapidated, more hopeless street? So how do you explain that every time a colour, a face, a noise brings you back there, the emotion that rises in you is both sweet and unsettling? ¡Ay, Marcelito! Lined with three-storey buildings, almost all made of faded orange brick, Avenue Linton was really like a dumping ground for the island. Garbage cans were always overflowing, and the grass, which had been dead for ages, was as yellow in spring as it was in summer. Do you remember the early days of July, when everyone was moving house? The City would clear out two or three buildings where the vermin had taken over, you all liked it when that happened, because then you would take them over next, and you'd play in them, or the older kids would take them over so they could smoke or make love. At night, from the beginning of spring till the end of fall, under the streetlights, teenagers would gather and sit or lie down on the parked cars. But you all were too young to be part of those groups, your parents wouldn't let you go out at night.

"You have any brothers or sisters?" you asked.

No, he was an only child. He lived alone with his mother.

"What about your father?"

His father? You saw the expression on his face change, like when Sylvain kept pushing to see if he'd ever slept with a girl. You'd felt like you'd put your foot in it when you'd asked that question.

"My father? He's usually away. He's in business."

"Does he come to see you sometimes?" asked Akira.

"Not a lot. But he calls me on the phone. When he finishes his business, he's coming home and he'll bring me lots of toys."

"My parents got divorced," Akira continued. "It doesn't really bother me much, it happened when I was little. My mother's the one who left, but she comes to see me every weekend."

"Well, my parents are still together," you said, "but they fight all the time. Sometimes I can't even get my homework done. Lots of times they yell at each other and then they start laughing: even they can't believe how much they fight over stupid stuff."

You stopped in front of a building that was just like the others, except that the front door was cracked all the way through as if someone had tried to break it down. Hesitating, with a shy laugh, Cléo started down the alley: I think I'd better go home. So you said, Okay, whatever, see you tomorrow. But he came back, scratching his forehead: you like marbles? You looked at each other: yeah, yeah, we like marbles. Why don't you come over

33

then? He was going to show you his collection. Okay, why not, and the three of you stepped into the building. You climbed the stairs leading to the second floor, and at apartment number three Cléo took out a key he wore around his neck.

"My mother will be asleep. So, don't make any noise," he ordered, with his finger on his lips.

He let you into the living room: sit down, I'll be right back, and he was lost in the darkness of a narrow hallway. You and Akira sat there for quite a while with your mouths gaping open, you'd never seen so many paintings. There were paintings on the floor, piled one on top of the other, on the sofa, on the desk and on all the walls. The canvases were crammed with very bright colours: black-skinned men and women were labouring in sugar cane fields, carrying baskets on their heads, or crafting straw hats. In one corner of the room dozens of masks were piled up, their oval faces seemed to wish to extract both laughter and tears from anyone who looked at them too long. Nonetheless, in the very middle of the living room, what attracted your attention most was an easel, which bore a painting that was just being sketched out. Cléo came back with two small bags in his hands.

"Is your mother a painter?" you asked in a low voice.

Circling his arms to encompass the whole room, Cléo answered, "She's the one who painted everything you see here."

You were especially fascinated by the masks: you examined them, touched them, weighed them in your hands, turned them all around. Akira put one of them on and pretended to roar. Cléo immediately rushed towards you: he'd told you – absolutely no noise!

"I know what we'll do," Cléo said softly. "You can each take a mask home. If your parents like them, tell them we'll sell them for forty dollars. If they don't like them, you can bring them back. But tell them they sell for double that in other places."

You and Akira each shoved a mask into your school bag: okay, you'd show your parents, you promised. Then, Cléo showed

34

off his porcelain marbles, decorated with spellbinding spirals and eccentric arabesques, in rare, exotic colours. They're fantastic, Akira said excitedly. Check out this one! To which you replied, "Wow!" Cléo gave you each a bag, he had lots more. Thanks, Cléo! Thanks a lot! Why don't we play a little now, on the rug? Now? No, no, you couldn't, he'd already told you why.

"Cléo!" boomed a gravely voice. "*Va ten dewò!*"

For an instant, you looked at each other intently. The voice sounded like it had a cold, it was changing, drunken.

"But, Mom. . . ."

A long exasperated sigh, then footsteps caused the wooden parquet flooring to creak. Then the sound of broken glass rang out, it sounded like a lamp had been thrown on the floor. A few seconds passed, then the voice continued, "*M ap bezwin dòmi! Yo pa fè com toujou ak done tout jwè la!*"

You tried to hand the bag of marbles back to him, but Cléo shook his head no, with his index fingers in front of his lips once again. Then he quietly asked you to get your school bags, you'd better leave. Outside, the three of you stood there looking at your shoes for quite a long time. It's no big deal, Cléo said, my mother was taking a nap, that's all. She works a lot at night and has to rest during the day. Akira looked at his watch: in any case, he should go, the Power Rangers show started at four-thirty. Yeah, you said, I'm gonna go, too. You and Akira began to move away but, after a little while, you turned around and saw that Cléo hadn't moved a centimetre, so you shouted: after dinner, you want to play hockey with us? The Haitian boy's face lit up: okay. But there was a problem, he didn't have a hockey stick. No problem, you'd lend him one. Seven o'clock, in front of his building? Okay, okay, and each of you went home.

II

"You're always out!" his mother shouts. "What's going on with you, Flaco? Can't even spend one night at home . . . *¡No sé para qué tuve un hijo!*"

Standing in the doorway to the living room, his hands in his pockets, Flaco rocks back and forth in his sneakers as she stares at him and shakes her head, as if she's trying to knock loose any sad thoughts. Opposite the TV with the sound way too loud, she's lying on the sofa cleaning her toenails. It's only eight in the evening and she's already in her beige pyjamas and her pink synthetic wool slippers, as always. Why does she resent me so much? thinks Flaco. Why won't she just let people live in peace? His mother's eyes make him uncomfortable. He runs a hand through his hair.

"You're so disrespectful," she goes on. "You know I don't like it when you look at me with that sarcastic smile. You think you're better than me, don't you?"

She turns her eyes away and fixes them on the TV screen, her lips pursed. *Les Héritiers du rêve* or something else along those lines. Sometimes, he feels like shaking her, but he ends up asking himself, what good would it do? He won't change her. At other times, he's overcome by a pressing desire to show her his world.

36

Why does he always postpone these urges until later? He's sure about just one thing, in the end: he only has one life to live and he's not going to miss out on it. No one is going to hold him back, not even his parents.

He turns around and walks back to his bedroom with careful steps. After he turns on the lights, he opens the top dresser drawer, takes out a black headband and leather gloves with the fingertips cut off, and he puts them on. He looks up to examine himself in the mirror. He wants only one thing: for people to respect him. He lets out a long breath that fogs up the mirror, but after a few seconds his face reappears. Why can't he ever talk to her when she's right there? For the first time in his life things are getting serious with a girl, and his mother doesn't even know it! But she would hardly even listen to him, she has enough problems of her own, she's not going to start getting mixed up in other people's business, no, really, what's Flaco thinking?

He shuts off the light and feels his way to the front door.

"I'll be back in an hour!" he shouts. "No later, okay?"

"Please, Flaco. The least you could do is not take me for a fool. I know perfectly well that last night you came in at two in the morning. And drunk, too . . ."

He opens the door a bit, makes his way out, grips the knob, then slams it loudly behind him: anyway, he can't do anything with her! He makes his way along the corridor, with its eternal stink of spices, and then he goes down the stairs: sometimes, he wonders if all parents are like that – forcing their children to feel guilty. The truth is, he can't stand them anymore. At the end of the school year, when he finishes high school, he'll find some two-room apartment or something, looking out on a park and, most of all, in some other neighbourhood, maybe Notre-Dame-de-Grâce. He sighs: it really is time to move on. Plus, his older friends have told him, since he'll only see his parents when he wants to, his relationship with them will certainly get better. And, for about a year or so, he's been telling Paulina, his love, and a few close friends, that he wants to become a writer, but he hasn't done much to make it happen. On his own, he'll have peace and quiet and then he'll see if he's got what it takes.

It's a cool night on Rue Linton. He sees them from a distance, about a dozen of them at least, under the usual streetlight, across from Lalo's building. They've been drinking, it's obvious: music rings out: *"We'll hang out in the clouds, then we'll come down, have a hangover. . . ."* And they double over laughing. He tries to pick her out: it's strange, he can't find her, but all her girlfriends are there. He crosses the median and whistles as he raises his arm: heads turn towards him, *hola*, Flaco, where were you?, we were waiting for you, *compadre*. He shakes hands with the guys, hi, everybody, and kisses the girls on each cheek, did anyone happen to see Paulina? They elbow each other, and cluck like chickens, *¡huy!* Flaco's looking worried!

After a minute, he feels someone squeeze his shoulders, stroke his chest, give him little kisses on the neck. He recognizes the delicate fingers and their manicured nails, the smell of her peach-scented soap and turns towards her. Without giving him a chance to say a word, she whispers in his ear not to get mad, she wanted to see if he really cared about her, and she gives him a wink, she's satisfied now, *corazón*. He studies her face for a moment, unsure if he should get angry or laugh. Finally, he takes her by the waist and kisses her right on the mouth. Around them, there's whistling and clapping, and Teta dances his way over: hey, you lovebirds, cut it out, you're making me wanna do it myself! The others laugh good naturedly, and Flaco and Paulina step back from each other, lowering their eyes, their arms around one another's waists. He smiles: this is his real family! Then he sees Lalo, with a beer in his hand, as he walks, unsteadily, to sit away from the group on the grass. He's completely out of it, he thinks.

All of a sudden, above the Nirvana guitar solo and the rapid, wet-sounding noise of the passing cars, people are murmuring around him. Flaco turns around: with lowered heads and hunched shoulders, Pato and Alfonso are making their way towards them. Something's not right, that much is obvious. As they come to a stop in the light of the streetlamp, Flaco notices Pato's nose is dripping blood and Alfonso has a black eye. Their arrival brings Lalo back to life: someone turns down the radio, and he rushes over to his brother. Despite his sniffling, Pato tells them what happened somewhat proudly, although Alfonso continues to whine. When Pato says they hit them, Lalo turns towards Flaco: did you hear that? A moment later, staggering like he just got off a ride in an amusement park, Lalo finally slumps down onto the grass.

Pato's news surprises them. Not even two weeks ago, Latino Power signed a peace treaty with the Bad Boys. It was getting so you couldn't be out in the neighbourhood without worrying about getting hit over the head with a baseball bat. The two sides had agreed there'd be no more stealing from each other, no more fighting, no more rivalry over girls or territory – they'd continue to share Parc Kent, as they had for the last year or so. Now Pato, in an astonishingly clear voice, tells them how he broke into CB's locker and robbed him. Ah, that makes things clearer. Alfonso, who still hasn't said a word, explains that the Bad Boys beat them up because they'd laughed at a joke about Blacks in Vietnam. Flaco finally gets it, he's well acquainted with CB's little games.

"And you say you gave him back his cap and his sunglasses?" he asks.

They answer yes. With the blood now partly coagulated under his nose, Pato stares at him again, looking strangely sure of himself. Without undoing his pants, he shoves his hand in like he's going to scratch his dick, making the others laugh. What the hell's he doing? The half-circle that had formed around the boy tightens. He pulls out a chain and waves it under Flaco's nose. Flaco takes it in his hand and contemplates its weight for a long time, like he's hypnotized.

39

"The condor was in his locker, too," Pato explains. "As soon as I saw it, I figured it was something that had been stolen from a Latino. I did the right thing when I kept it, didn't I?"

How many years has it been since the last time he saw that condor, Flaco wonders. He'd completely forgotten about it. He turns towards Alfonso. "See, what did I tell you? He can't believe that a couple of wusses like us pulled it off!"

Flaco examines the boy's face: his scratches, his bloody nose, and his smile, all make him look sinister. They really roughed them up! They sure didn't hold back!

"So, Flaco, it's good I brought it back, right?"

"Yes, you did the right thing."

Flaco stuffs the condor into his pocket. He runs his hand through Pato's hair and wipes the blood off his face with his shirt.

"So you wanted to impress us with this?"

The boy nods his head.

"I already told you that you had nothing to prove," Flaco continues. "This isn't the first time you've done this kind of thing. But I'll tell you something: we all know Pato is a real fighter. Right, everybody?"

Flaco turns towards the others: they nod their heads. Pato can't keep from smiling proudly.

"It really is true," Flaco goes on, "what you did was very brave. You, too, Alfonso. But I'm going to ask you both a favour. From now on, you check with us before you do something. Get it?"

Yes, they got it, Flaco.

"And I promise that from now on, we'll take you wherever we go. And first thing tomorrow, at school, we'll have a talk with the Bad Boys."

The boys look at each other and smile.

"You've got it, *compadre*, we'll have a real good talk with them!" shouts Lalo, raising his beer in the air. "We're gonna pound those Blacks! What the hell do they think?"

He tries to stand up, but he can't. He sits back down despite himself, and, punctuating it all with hiccups, he continues to grumble and complain.

"One last thing," Flaco adds. "Don't tell your parents a thing. You were both playing soccer. You fell and you got kicked in the face, by accident. That part is very important – ac-ci-dent-al-ly. We really don't want them getting mixed up in this, they might lose it and call the police. And we don't have anything to do with the cops. ¿Está claro?"

"Yes, it's clear." Flaco gets back up and looks at the two faces, one at a time, shifting his head now and then to get a different angle.

"You don't look too badly hurt. Nothing's broken, that's the main thing. In a week, you'll be good as new. And don't worry if every colour in the rainbow shows up on your face. It's normal."

Flaco smiles at them, slips away from the group, leans on a car fender and lights a match, a cigarette hanging from his lips. The music's stopped, the conversations are picking up again at a slightly lower volume. One by one, they examine Pato's and Alfonso's wounds. That CB is a mental case! someone shouts. Mixon? Nothing but the worst kind of lazy! And what about Ketcia? She acts like a boy! The girl with three balls! A few of them burst out laughing, but the sound melts into the stubborn buzzing of mosquitoes in the light of the streetlamp.

The music starts up again and Teta turns up the volume till it's blasting wildly. Let's change the tape, Nena suggests. She's tired of always listening to Nirvana. And Teta says Okay, but watch out, he's going to surprise them. Suddenly, with a squeal, the radio spits out a crazy *cumbia*. Oh, no! Nena complains, take that off right now! He should stop being such a pain in the ass! She's sick of *cumbias* and salsas, she can't take it anymore! That's all her parents listen to! Teta imitates the frenetic, syncopated movements of a Caribbean dancer, shaking an imaginary pair of

41

maracas in his hands, but no one laughs. He's so fat that his breasts jiggle back and forth, back and forth, beneath his sweater. There's a good reason we nicknamed him Teta, Flaco thinks, his eyes following his dance steps. The breast! Teta now grabs Nena's arm, she tries to get away, he pulls her towards the sidewalk, why so glum, Nena? and they dance cheek to cheek, as if it were a tango.

Paulina, who's remained off to the side, steps closer to Flaco. A black nylon suit hugs her body from her neck to her heels. The first time he met her, a day he still remembers like yesterday, even though it's been six years now, he was struck by the fact that she had an unusual look for a Latina. Her light brown hair was always pulled up in a ponytail, her face was delicate with slightly dark skin, and she always looked slender, athletic. With one hand on her hip, she's rocking back and forth on her Adidas, looking mischevious.

"So, the fighting's going to start up again?"

For an instant, he examines her. She surprises him.

"Don't worry about it. What I told you still stands: at the end of the school year, I'm done with the gang. Tomorrow, we'll straighten this whole thing out *rápido*. It has to be a mistake."

He's annoyed with himself for lying: tomorrow, he won't forgive them for anything. He has no choice, he must be respected, keep them from starting up again. Besides, he can't lose face among the members of his own gang. He knows very well they were shocked when they saw Pato and Alfonso's faces. To disguise his uneasiness, he takes a drag off his cigarette.

"I saw how you reacted when you saw the condor," she goes on.

He turns his head towards her and slowly lowers it a notch, to indicate she should talk in a lower voice.

"I'll tell you about it when we're alone. Not now."

She shakes her head, "It's always the same with you guys. It's always about honour and courage."

"I'll tell you about it when we're alone," he repeats in a low voice.

After a little while, as if she's agreed to change the subject, she takes him by the waist with a little smile, then, with a roaming hand, tousles his hair. He takes one last drag off his cigarette and then sends it flying onto the roadway, near the open space. He still isn't completely used to the idea that he can kiss her whenever he wants. Sometimes, when he's walking down the street, he stops suddenly: he can't believe he's going out with her. She puts her arms around his neck, then strokes his face. She, his childhood friend, the only girl he ever dared flirt with, the only girl he can't think about when he masturbates because he immediately feels like he has to piss. It's so new it feels like he's dreaming. It was like a revelation. He'd invited her to the park, and, just like that, point blank, he'd declared his love for her. Calmly sitting on a bench, she replied that she, too, had been trying to get him off her mind for a long time, afraid that he thought of her just as a friend. But she hadn't had any luck. A long kiss followed, it wasn't feverish like he'd imagined it. Yes, it was the first time he'd fallen in love. Today, compared to her, all the girls he'd known seemed unimportant. He looks into her sparkling eyes, and she licks her lips: "The other day you where asking me when. . . ."

For a moment, their eyes meet.

"I think it's time."

Now it's his turn to slip his arms around her: is she sure? With her high cheekbones, she offers him a radiant smile: she's never been so sure of anything in her life. Good, Flaco brings his face close to hers, whenever she wants. Nervously they laugh, then suddenly Paulina's face becomes serious, almost fearful: he knows it's the first time she's going to make love, right? He says yes, he knows. Does it make her nervous? No, not really, she feels so good when she's with him, Flaco. He presses his lips against hers and feels a warm tongue slip between his teeth.

*

43

Weekdays, before supper, you'd play hockey in the entrance to your building's garage, for an hour or two, never more: when October came, the darkness fell early in the evening and then the goalie couldn't see the tennis ball anymore. You were already wearing wool sweaters and mittens and sometimes a toque, but no coats or scarves yet. Then your mother would sweep out onto the balcony and lean against the rail: and when do you think you're going to do your homework, Marcelo? You turned a deaf ear, pretended to be absorbed in the game, and your mother would end up losing her patience: okay, then, no supper! And she'd slam the door. Regretting it, you'd stop playing, you had to go. Akira would stop, hesitating, then he'd pick up his equipment, too. All this time, Cléo was sweating buckets: crap, just when he was starting to get warmed up! Akira? Would he lend him the tennis ball? Marcelo? The hockey stick? Thanks, guys, and he'd go practise against the wall. Sometimes he'd stay there until the night swallowed him up.

On weekends, sometimes as early as the first uncertain light of dawn, you'd organize long hockey tournaments and you wouldn't go home till evening. You'd skip meals, you'd slip away to piss in the courtyard of some building under a balcony, so that the game wouldn't be interrupted too long. Alongside you were Alberto the Italian, check out my wrist action, man, Glenn the English Canadian, look at my goalie pads, my father bought them in Boston, Danny the Haitian, why do you always have to hit me in the butt with the ball! and still others, pupils of both Francophone and Anglophone schools. Some times there were so many of you that a group of onlookers would gather around you: they'd spot the good players and cheer when someone scored a goal.

In the afternoon, a few buildings away, groups of teenagers would appear, cleverly scattered around, boys and girls mixed together, passing the time having a smoke, chatting amongst themselves and getting high on rap, rock or heavy metal. They hardly seemed to notice the hockey game going on a few metres away, though you observed their world of flirting, cigarettes and alcohol attentively, knowing that when you got to high school it would be your turn to taste all these things. To all this would be added the comings and goings of Guylain, the acid-faced wino, who always wore his Montreal Canadiens jersey and who'd been deep in discussion with himself forever. He'd look up at you, like he was coming out of a dream, and, for no apparent reason, he'd threaten you with his fist and mutter racist insults. It had become such a custom, that you waited for his visits almost impatiently, they'd become something of an inoffensive, comical distraction.

After Randy moved away, you, Marcelo, started delivering the *Gazette* on Rue Linton, from Côte-des-Neiges to Avenue Victoria. On Saturdays, the papers were thicker and Cléo, always at the ready, helped you. Often, still bathed in the hostile darkness, you'd meet outside his building and walk side by side, yawning, famished, in the quiet, morning cold, and you'd each pull one of the carts your mother used for her shopping. Each one was responsible for one side of the street and you'd compete against each other: you'd fling the papers and climb the stairs four at a time, occasionally, corpse-like faces appeared at the window to gaze at you, and one of you would get scared. When the other heard the shout, he'd come running: what happened? He'd put an arm around his friend's shoulders: don't be afraid, it's just an old man who can't sleep. When the work was done, Cléo would refuse the seven or eight dollars you'd hold out to him, and you'd end up buying him breakfast at McDonald's. Deal? And Cléo said, with a huge smile, deal, and you'd shake hands.

At school, you were almost always on the same dodge ball team. Luck even had it that your desks in school were right next to each other. But remember how many times Cléo had to go stand in the corner, because he got caught in the middle of a conversation with his neighbour or hadn't done his homework right? With his hands behind his back, right next to the crank-handled pencil sharpener, he'd keep his eyes on the wall, fascinated, as if he had an unfathomable painting before his eyes. After a half hour the teacher would let him sit back down: she hoped he'd learned his lesson, this time. At the end of the day, they'd ask him why he'd only done half the problems on the math homework and he'd explain in a low voice that it wasn't his fault, he'd fallen asleep.

It's true that it was pretty easy to fall asleep at Cléo's, an oppressive silence always reigned there. Even though you'd gone back a few more times, you still hadn't met Cléo's mother: your curiosity about her absorbed you more and more, Marcelo. For a long time, you didn't know what was wrong with her. One thing was for sure, it always happened the same way: she'd call Cléo, always in that same gravelly voice, he'd go see and then you'd just hear their murmurs. Didn't she ever get up? Why was her voice so tired? Because she paints at night and needs to sleep during the day, Cléo invariably answered. And why wasn't his father ever there? How many times did he have to tell him! His father was on a business trip. What kind of business? His father had told him, but it was hard to remember, he'd forgotten. Come on, we're going to miss the Power Rangers.

One Sunday morning since it was raining and the hockey game outside had been postponed, you'd gone into the kitchen to see your parents and your Uncle Juan, who generally came over to have lunch with you on Sundays. Your father had made *sopaipillas* and your mother, whipped cream and bananas and some carrot juice squeezed in a sock. Since the conversation revolved around Cléo, you went to your room to get the mask sculpted by your friend's mother so your uncle could take a look at it. It was an oblong face, made from black-painted wood, and the lips were in the shape of an O. Your uncle looked at it for a long time, in an amused way, turning it this way and that.

"*Compadre*, can you believe it? I paid forty dollars for that damn mask!"

46

Your uncle bit his lip to keep from laughing.

"Don't be narrow-minded, Roberto," he said. "What would a Haitian think of a Temuco poncho, eh? He'd probably think it was ugly, or, at the very least, utterly useless."

"One thing's for sure," your mother said. "I wouldn't put it up in my room. It scares me. But I can recognize art when I see it."

"Anyway," Roberto clarified, "we didn't buy it because we thought it was pretty. Since it was made by the mother of a friend of Marcelo's, it was the right thing to do."

"But, Dad," you joined in, "I thought you liked the mask. That's what you said, isn't it?"

"Well," Roberto answered, "I don't hate it, but I can't say I really like it either. What do you want, I mostly bought it because Cléo is your friend. And because we felt bad for that woman – she really seems to be a hard worker."

"If immigrants don't help each other out," Carmen went on, "who's going to give them a hand? Eh? That's what I think."

"And would you please tell me what this woman does for a living?" Juan inquired. "Is she an artist?"

"Yes. She makes paintings and masks. She mostly works at night."

"Well, that's a well known fact," Juan commented, "inspiration comes at night. If I could have, I would have been a writer. I would have written the story of my life. People would turn around when they saw me in the street, they just wouldn't be able to get over all I'd have to tell . . . Artists have a good life. Those people have more fun – ."

"In any case," said Carmen, "Cléo's mother isn't the kind to spend her time in salons and at cocktail parties. According to what Marcelo tells us, she doesn't sell many paintings. She's just like us, she arrived in a completely new country and you know how that can slow you down, how it can knock the stuffing out of you."

"But Haitians have a big advantage over us, Carmen," Roberto said. "They already know French. I see them at Phillips, they get along with no problem. Plus, you have to admit, there's a difference between painting and packing computers all day long. I'll grant you that she probably doesn't make much money, just like us, but at least she's doing what she likes."

"What about the father?" Juan asked. "What does your friend's father do?"

You repeated what Cléo always said about his father's business trips and all the presents he promised him. Roberto let out an exasperated sigh and stiffened.

"Marcelo, listen to me carefully. Dads don't leave for months and months on business trips. You're big enough now not to believe everything people tell you. Don't you think?"

"Roberto, please!" Carmen cut in. "Leave him alone. He's just a boy!"

Roberto stared at the tablecloth for a minute, as if he was thinking deeply, then he turned towards his wife, "Why should Marcelo believe this guy's lies, too? Why doesn't he have the right to know the truth?"

Remember the discussion that followed, Marcelo: you felt like you'd been swallowed up by a black hole, you felt strangely dizzy. Then your father spoke to you again. "What's wrong? Listen, I thought it was better to start telling you the truth about things like that. Or would you rather we continue to hide them from you?"

"What are you trying to tell me, Dad?" you shouted. "Eh? Say it! You think I don't know he's gone off with another woman? You think I'm stupid? You think I don't know anything about it?"

Without really knowing why, despite your best efforts, you were unable to deflect the emotion swelling up in your throat like a ball. Why did your tears always appear at the worst time? Why did they bother you so much? When they saw you like that, they were silent, surprised, nervously watching you. And

Carmen said in a low voice, "God, that boy is sensitive! See? You see what you did, Roberto? Are you proud of yourself now? You're so cruel!"

She came over to console you: she held you against her stomach, rubbed your back. Then Juan remarked, "Those Haitians are awful! There are two of them at the restaurant. They're married and they both have children. Every Monday, I swear, they tell me about all the screwing they did all weekend. We laugh like crazy, because they're like us, they tell everything, with lots of details. . . ."

Then, getting hold of himself: "Yeah, but I also figure it must not be a lot of fun for their wives."

He immediately moved his head closer to Roberto, touched his arm, and whispered, "Those Haitians have quite an appetite for sex! Oof! They're worse than us, *compadre*!"

Roberto and Juan laughed without holding back and looked around for approval.

"And it's not racist to say that," Juan added, "it's a fact."

You'd stopped crying. Carmen had got up, picked up the plates and placed them in the sink.

"If I was in your shoes," she retorted as she ran the water, "I wouldn't laugh too hard. Neither one of you has any reason to make fun of anyone else. None at all, and you know it!"

The men's joking mood disappeared.

"Well now, that's just like you, Carmen," Roberto muttered. "Waking up old demons. And in front of the boy . . . How many times do I have to explain it to you: all men occasionally have 'little indiscretions.'"

Roberto and Juan exchanged an amused look and then shrugged their shoulders. Carmen turned her head and went back to scrubbing the glass she had in her hands.

"But don't go telling those things to your little friend," Roberto said, seeking out your eyes. "You might hurt his feelings."

You didn't answer him, you hated him, and your uncle and Cléo's father. You were angry at all men. You jumped up and ran to your room. Before you slammed your door, you heard your father's rushed, low voice: "You satisfied now? Look what you've done. And then you say I'm cruel!"

Along the cafeteria wall, Ketcia paces back and forth, eyes fixed on the ground, hands behind her back. From time to time she looks at the students flowing towards the entrance with carefree, smiling faces, carrying their lunch trays. She, though, is so nervous that she's not hungry. Her black corduroy pants and her Chicago Bulls cap, turned backwards, are giving her hot flashes, and her sneakers, which come up to her ankles, are like a ball and chain. As they go by, some of the students respectfully call out Hi, Ketcia, or even What's up, Ketcia? but she's happy just to reply with a nod of her head. What's that idiot up to? It's always the same old story! For the past few weeks, she's noticed that his newest technique for getting attention is arriving late on purpose. She's always said that guy became a member of the Bad Boys for the wrong reasons: to have fun and to avoid getting beat up at school. At the end of the hall, in the midst of a rainbow-coloured crowd, she thinks she recognizes Mixon's lazy gait. Yes, it's him: he's the only one with a black T-shirt that has a picture of the members of Public Enemy on it. With a sharp wave, she motions for him to hurry up. Oh my God, even when he runs he looks like he's asleep. He comes to a stop in front of her, a stupid smile on his lips.

"Do you have any idea how long I've been standing here waiting for you?" she says. "More than twenty minutes."

She looks him over.

"I told you to meet me right after your class. Why don't you ever listen to what people are saying to you? An order is an order, Mixon! How many times do I have to tell you!"

Mixon looks down and, when he looks back up, she notices he's still got that annoying smile.

"Chill," he defends himself. "I was catching some rays outside with the girls. A guy has the right to do some cruising, doesn't he?"

He shoves his hands into his pockets, looks around in amusement. She thinks, I ought to wipe that smile off your face with a good punch! Of course, she doesn't do anything of the sort and settles for snapping, "CB's going to get expelled!"

The statement takes immediate effect: the smile disappears. Mixon's forehead wrinkles, as if he wants to know more but is afraid to ask her.

"I bet you didn't even know," she goes on. "Everybody in the whole school knows, except you. Where were you this morning? How come you didn't get to school until eleven o'clock?"

Ketcia stares at him with disgust, as if she's trying to force a reply out of him. Mixon lets out a long sigh as if to relax a bit.

"Okay, all right, I'm sorry. It's just that I had a really bad headache this morning. I think I had too much to drink last night with my brother, and since my alarm goes off every fifteen minutes after it goes off the first time, well, I put it in a drawer and went back to sleep. . . ."

He cuts his story short when he realizes Ketcia couldn't care less about his morning difficulties. Then he tries, "Tell me what happened."

Okay, he's finally realizing how serious the situation is. Ketcia's face relaxes. She takes off her cap, furiously runs one hand through her hair and then puts it back on.

"It's completely ridiculous! Right this minute, CB is in the principal's office. But he should be here soon."

"How long's he expelled for?"

"That's what we're waiting to find out."

"What did he do?"

Ketcia glances around suspiciously, then brings her gaze back to Mixon.

"Everything started this morning, when we got to CB's locker. The lock had been forced, but we already knew about that. I knew there was something else bothering CB and I asked him what was wrong."

"Just think," CB said as he closed his locker, "I was feeling bad after that lesson we taught him. I thought maybe the wuss had been telling the truth after all. Just think, I felt bad about beating up that lying little shit!"

"What?" Ketcia had asked. "He stole something else from you?"

"The chain," CB answered, as if he were talking to himself. "I should have guessed it."

"A chain?" asks Mixon. "I never saw him wearing one. I didn't know he liked jewellery. Once, I think he even said jewellery was only for girls and fags."

"It's cause he never wears it," Ketcia explains, "but I'd already noticed that every time he opens his locker, he checks to make sure it's still there. I always wondered what that chain meant to him. But you know how CB is, he doesn't like people sticking their nose in his business."

"I'm sure it's something personal," says Mixon. "I know: it was a gift from a girl he was in love with, but she broke up with him. The memory of the chick still causes him pain today. Unbelievable! Our CB is a romantic!"

"It was a gift," CB had continued.

"No way, I got it right?" asks Mixon. "I was kidding! It's really about a girl?"

"A gift from your parents?" Ketcia ventured.

"No. From a friend I used to have."

"A guy?" says Mixon. "Oh, that's a disappointment! Did he at least tell you who it was?"

"He was my best friend," CB had explained. "But that's not the case anymore. We've both changed."

"Who was it?" asks Mixon.

"No," CB had said "I'd rather not tell you his name right now. You all know him. But I promise to tell you everything one of these days. But just you, no one else in the gang. Only a girl can understand this kind of thing."

"He said that?" asks Mixon. "He really said that? I can't believe it!"

Mixon falls silent, hurt, then he adds, "He's always treated you better than the rest of us, just because you're a girl. I'm starting to get sick of it . . . But, just so it's clear between us, I'm not mad at you, I'm mad at him."

For once, thinks Ketcia, raising her cap a bit and wiping her forearm across her damp brow, Mixon isn't wrong. It's true, CB's always a real gentleman with her: he takes her opinion into account and, often he even makes sure she agrees with him. Before she became a member of the Bad Boys, she watched him from a distance when he defended the Haitians in the schoolyard and she'd secretly admired him. Then, when she'd joined the gang, she didn't know what to expect with him. But the facts proved her right: under his hard exterior, he was a good guy. She loves him, she means, she's not in love with him, but as a friend. Of course, there are plenty of idiots around who think she joined the gang because she is in love with him. But she couldn't care less about that kind of rumour. Besides, she's not pretty and she knows it, and she doesn't try to fool herself. She understood that if you run as fast as the boys, if you drink as much beer as them and if you walk around with a knife like they do, they stop looking at your breasts when they're talking to you and start looking at your eyes. And CB's the one who seems to appreciate her the most for what she is. In fact, he's like the big brother she'd always wanted.

"So what happened?" asks Mixon. "I don't understand why he's still in the office."

"Wait a minute and I'll tell you."

As usual, at eight-thirty, the alarm sounds and a mob forms at the foot of the stairs. Without a word to Ketcia, CB hurtles forward after the other students, as they climb the steps in drowsy silence. He turns a few of them around to look at their faces. Ketcia catches up and tries to grab him by the arm: where's he going like that? They'll settle it later, outside, one on one with the Latinos. This is no time to act crazy, CB! But he evades her: let him go, he knows perfectly well what he's doing. When he gets to the third floor, he zigzags between the students and steps into each classroom. Sitting at their desks or on the radiators near the windows, the students stop chatting when they see him and focus their eyes on him: Hi, CB! Hey, man, how you doing? Is he looking for someone? Does he need some help? He doesn't respond, then he sees Pato at the end of the hallway, walking with another boy. They go into the classroom and CB quickens his step, jostling another group of students.

Inside the class, a few students stretch and yawn and take their notebooks from their school bags. In the back, the short, paunchy teacher, with baldness devouring the top of his head, writes on the board on his tiptoes. When he catches sight of Pato, CB motions for him to come over but, like a spring, the Latino jumps from his seat, no way, it's not possible! Now what? CB comes towards him, he shouldn't worry, nothing's going to happen to him, he just wants to ask him a few questions. And the other boy, with his purple, swollen face, steps backwards and hits a desk, ouch! CB holds him by the shoulders to immobilize him and tries to calm him down.

In the doorway, Ketcia is watching the scene and wondering what's got into him. Why is he acting like a jerk? Pato starts yelling as loud as he can to attract the teacher's attention and get him to turn around: now, now, what's going on here? No, really, what's this all about? CB seems not to have noticed that the teacher was there, focusing as he is on Pato: why didn't he tell him he'd taken the condor? The other boy struggles, moans,

54

refuses to answer. Was all this Flaco's idea? No, he won't say a word! He doesn't want to hurt him, insists CB, but he'd better answer! CB shakes him and Pato closes his eyes. Leave me alone!

With his hands on his hips, the teacher coughs: isn't he ashamed picking on a boy who's smaller than him? Coward! CB lets go of Pato and turns towards the teacher. The man's tongue turns again in his pasty mouth: savage! Where does he think he is? CB hesitates for a moment, then gives a weak laugh. He bites his bottom lip and hits his fist into his palm twice. He steps closer to the teacher who freezes, suddenly turns pale, his eyes popping out of his head. CB's hands land on his shirt collar like two fireballs as an unexpected tic forces the teacher to blink several times. CB holds him in the same position for a moment, then lets him go and bursts out laughing. Did you see what he said to me? he asks Ketcia beseechingly. Do you see how they think they can do anything to us? He looks at her with imploring eyes and Ketcia understands what he means. The whole time, the teacher has been leaning on a desk, catching his breath, while all around, frightened students keep silent. With his wits about him again, the teacher brushes past CB and heads towards the door: we'll see what the principal thinks of all this. Getting threatened like this – it's the last straw!

CB looks around him, displaying a strange, stunned smile, as if he's suddenly wondering what he's doing there. He places one hand on Pato's shoulder: tell Flaco he wants to talk to him at twelve o'clock, on the soccer field. Pato slips away from his hand and steps back with a shudder: Flaco wants to see him, too. Don't worry, he'll pass on the message.

"But just when CB and I were leaving," Ketcia explains, "the teacher came in, with the principal and two hall monitors."

"If I know CB, I bet he fought like a madman," says Mixon. "I've seen him get away from three monitors!"

"No," says Ketcia, "that's what surprised me. He didn't resist at all. He just said, I hardly touched him, I don't see what I did

55

wrong. And the principal said, that's enough, we'll talk about it in my office. Come on, let's go."

"With CB, you never know what to expect," Mixon points out. "You never know what's going on in his head. Sometimes, when he looks me in the eyes, it makes me feel weird. What about you?"

Thoughtful, Ketcia answers yes. It's true, sometimes, she's afraid of CB's unpredictable reactions too, especially when he gets mad. Luckily, it doesn't happen often.

They stand there for a moment without saying anything, noticing the commotion going on around them. Finally, they notice CB coming down the stairs in his usual casual way. He stops in front of them.

"So?" asks Mixon. "What did they say?"

"So, nothing," retorts CB, an enigmatic smile on his lips. "Since I didn't hit him, only threatened him, they gave me a week's suspension. It's not so bad."

Yeah! They're happy for him! Then CB claps his hands, "Let's hurry up and eat and get to the soccer field for noon. Latino Power will be there."

"We've only got five minutes left to eat," Ketcia clarifies, looking at her watch. "I don't want to be late. The Latinos'll think we're scared."

Remember how much hope and apprehension you packed into that one day, Marcelo: getting off the school bus that morning, a good number of you were yawning your heads off and had circles under your eyes from lack of sleep the night before. Woken by a chilly wind, you stood stock still in the middle of the schoolyard and glanced around in astonishment. Unlike your schoolyard, theirs stretched on and on with no uneven spots or holes in the asphalt. The painted lane-markers for the races and the two dodge ball squares were still immaculately white. The silver-coloured fence that bordered the yard had also been recently repainted and, beyond, on every side, the Outremont duplexes showed off their charming gardens and oak doors of various designs. Yes, it was a sunny autumn day and, though most of the leaves had already fallen from the trees, there weren't many of them to be seen in the schoolyard: with a rake, a groundskeeper was gathering them all into a pile.

The big school doors opened with a creak, a stream of students flowed out into the yard and the two teachers greeted each other with a firm handshake. The two clans looked at each other aslant. Unlike you, they were all dressed the same, in mauve shorts and T-shirts that said *École Lajoie*. As soon as the competitions began, your side started joking with each other and calling out the runners' nicknames to encourage them, and soon you began to shout. On the other side of the schoolyard, the students of the host school, leaning against the fence, chanted "la-la-la-Lajoie"! Is that when you noticed the police officers for the first time? They casually greeted the Lajoie students as if they'd known them forever. Remember the way the walked, their cautious scrutiny, their moustaches, Marcelo. They made light conversation with the other Phys. Ed. teacher.

But what a disappointment – Lajoie won most of the races easily. When Cléo won the grade five sprint, you exploded with joy that was as euphoric as it was liberating. You hugged him, congratulated him, carried him in triumph: he was the best, the fastest! And Serge said, put him down right now, you're going to hurt him! Yes, Marcelo, one day they made fun of him, the next he was a hero again. It seemed you only liked him when it was convenient. Then the police officers came to help Serge and backed you up against the fence: come on, now, children, that's no way to act! Let's go, everyone sit down now. And after his victory, Cléo started to act like the others: he clapped his hands, cracked jokes, laughed, pushed back when someone jostled him. Yes, every day, he was becoming more outgoing.

Then it was time for the grade five girls' hundred metres. Cléo stood so he could cheer them on better, and Sylvain followed suit, for once Caramilk had a good idea, and the rest of the school did the same. Sylvain couldn't contain himself since Serge had told him he was going to replace Yuri in the relay race, the Polish boy had a bad case of the flu and had had to stay home. They clapped their hands, stomped their feet, they made fun of the opposing team, "Loo-loo-loonies!" "Lo-lo-lo-Losers!" Obsessed by the races, Serge rarely came over to you, but when he did, he would order, Lower your voices, children; but you'd start up again a few seconds later. The groundskeeper, an old man with a tanned face, came over. You quieted down so you could hear what he had to say: settle down, children, the residents around here don't like that much noise. And, without missing a beat, Sylain replied, screw the residents! What do you say about that, gramps? Shouts acclaimed Sylvain's fearlessness, and the old man walked away grumbling.

Just then, the two police officers came towards you, toddling along, as if they were just taking a stroll to stretch their legs a bit. Smiling, they pretended to be supremely absorbed in their own conversation. They looked a lot alike in their navy blue uniforms, though one was shorter and visibly more nervous than the other. Stocky and bowlegged, the nervous one was tossing his nightstick in the air and catching it expertly. They stopped in front of you, whispered something in each other's ear and gave a hearty laugh. Finally, the officer put his nightstick back in its holder and noisily cleared his throat.

"Children?"

He had to call you like that several times before you paid him any attention.

"Children?" he repeated. "I have a riddle for you. Do you want to hear it?"

This surprised you. Some of you surveyed him with distrustful looks: what was he up to? Others kept talking, as if nothing was going on. Suddenly Sylvain's voice could be heard, let's hear it, you Smurf, tell us your riddle! This was followed by some laughter, but the officer said shhh! and asked again if you wanted to hear his riddle. In unison, several of you called out yeeeessss! in a childish tone, and then laughed even louder.

"That's enough!" ordered the police officer, raising his voice. "Or else, I won't tell you and that will be the end of that."

His ultimatum worked: with your heads tucked down into your shoulders, you studied him in silence now. He turned towards his colleague and winked with a big smile. Then he turned back to you, "Okay!" he said, clapping his hands together. "That's better. Let's start by sitting down."

You obeyed. He licked his lips and pronounced the following sentence, articulating carefully as if he were speaking to the hard-of-hearing, "What-is-the-most-beautiful-sound-on-earth, children?"

You looked questioningly at one another: what could it be? You repeated the question out loud, stroking your chins. Then you all shrugged your shoulders.

"Your farts!" shouted a desperate voice.

Contagious laughter lifted you up like a wave. As the commotion reached its climax, the officer lost his playful expression. He squinted as he searched for the guilty party.

"Is the disrespectful person who said that brave enough to stand up now? Or am I going to have to come looking for him myself?"

You all knew who it was, you'd recognized Sylvain's voice. Crouching in his corner, he was having a hard time not laughing.

"Oh, I see!" said the officer seeing that no one was going to stand, "we're dealing with a smart aleck. Well, I'm warning him, he's going to hear from me but good if he doesn't turn himself in."

The group was silent.

"I did it," said a voice.

You all looked up at the student who was on his feet. What? Cléo! What was he up to? What had got into him? He played with his fingers, embarrassed.

"So, you're the funny one," the officer went on. "The school clown. . . ."

Cléo didn't move.

"It was just a joke, off'cer. It was just for fun."

"Obviously," the police officer cut him off, "I know it was a joke. We all got that part, my friend. You think I'm angry? Come on, son, I've seen worse than that."

The officer gave a little laugh, then turned to his colleague and rolled his eyes.

"No," he said to Cléo, "it's just that I thought I was dealing with children with good manners. I can see now I couldn't have been more wrong . . . But, my boy, do you at least know the answer to my riddle?"

Cléo shook his head no.

"That's what I thought. Well, I'll tell you. It's silence. That's the most beautiful sound there is."

Now he was looking down on you smugly.

"So, children, learn to have a bit more respect for silence. You'll see how relaxing it is."

Then a meaningful smile spread across his face. And as he was walking away, he turned around one last time. "And you," he said, lowering a finger at Cléo, "I've got my eye on you."

The police officers moved away and you and Akira huddled around Cléo: why had he stood up for Sylvain? Had he fallen on his head? Sylvain gave everyone a hard time, even him. Cléo shrugged his shoulders and let his hand drop back down: Sylvain's okay, he just pretends he's tough. You wondered, Marcelo, just what does he want? for everyone to like him? Akira leaned towards him and tapped on his head with his index finger, you're sick, kid! There's no point in sticking up for jerks like that! At the far end of the crowd, Sylvain was watching Cléo, as if he was hesitating to come thank him. Finally, he turned away.

After lunch, you and Cléo went to buy some gum on Rue Bernard. As you walked back, chewing it, you saw the two police officers strolling down the other sidewalk. When the shorter one noticed you, he crossed the street, looking around with a feverish expression, and then he came and blocked your path, his arms crossed, his face sullen. His colleague hurried to catch up with him: what do you want with these boys, Gilles? He was staring into the whites of Cléo's eyes, a wily look crossing his face: did you mind, Maurice, he knew what he was doing. Remember Cléo's round eyes going from the pistol to the nightstick. After a moment, the boy pointed a finger towards the baton: could he see it a minute, sir, he'd never held one in his hands. Gilles was like a statue, then he looked around again, a little anxiously this time: he wanted to know one thing . . . how come he liked to make other people laugh so much, eh, Blackie? Surprised, Maurice almost choked as if he'd swallowed his own saliva wrong, what's got into you! What are you after? Slowly, his face still stoney, Gilles turned around: do you mind, I'm talking to someone. His lively, icy eyes locked on Cléo again, and his frightening smile reappeared. So, Blackie? He was waiting for an answer. Was it because it was cool to give cops a hard time? Was he trying to show off in front of his friends? Maurice placed one hand on his colleague's shoulder: it was time to go. That's when Cléo burst out sobbing. Yes, his shoulders shook convulsively. Christ, said Maurice, look what you did, as a clownish grimace spread across Gilles's face: what's wrong, my boy? Can't take a joke? You can dish it out though, eh? Then Maurice slipped between Gilles and Cléo and whispered in his colleague's ear through clenched teeth: okay, come on! Yeah, you're right, we may as well go. . . .

You put an arm around Cléo's shoulders, you led him into the schoolyard and the two of you sat down, your backs against the fence. You were telling him to forget about it, to concentrate on the upcoming relay race, but Cléo was shaking his head no. You were wrong, Marcelo: how could he forget? His crying escalated to a continuous, painful moan. So you kept quiet and quite a while went by as he sniffled, wiped his eyes and cried. The others came back, and Akira, noticing his swollen eyes, asked Cléo what happened. Nothing serious, you explained, he fell. Then Serge came over rubbing his hands together and made you all sit down: all that was left were the relay races, it was time for them to show what they could do, right?

Not a single team, from grade one to grade four had managed to outdo Lajoie's teams. A little before it was your turn, Serge ordered your team to go stretch and warm up near the school door, so you wouldn't be in the way of the races. When your turn came, you started shouting the runners' nicknames again and clapping your hands, while on Lajoie's side, they stuck with the same cheer, "La-La-la-Lajoie!" The starting gun went off, and from the first runner to the third, Lajoie kept increasing its lead. But when Cléo got the baton in his hand, the race became spirited. Yes, still out of breath, your hands on your hips, your eyes followed him without blinking: calmly, as if he had his whole life ahead of him, he caught up to his opponent and passed him right at the finish line. It looked like he'd had it planned from the beginning. However, this time, after the race, there was no smile. His face showed only a kind of rage, a calm despair.

The whole school came over to congratulate you, and Sylvain was the first to step up to Cléo to shake his hand. Then Evangelos, Sylvain's best friend, looked disgusted: what was he doing there? Why was he shaking Caramilk's hand? And Sylvain answered: be quiet! We won because of him. Cléo looked both delighted and astonished. But, let's be clear, Sylvain added just for him, that didn't mean he forgave him for stealing his spot on the team. And Cléo said, okay, I get it, and he slipped off towards where you and Akira were waiting for him. As Akira flung his arms around his neck, you gave him the usual pats on the back: anyways, if we can't win the Jeux du Québec with you on our team, I don't know what you have to do to win. And Akira said, you're right for sure! If we keep on like this, we'll end up in the Olympics! The three of you laughed like crazy and couldn't stop, without a second thought for the envious stares of the others. Your arms linked, you walked along as happy and free as brothers.

III

All wearing the same black headbands across their fore-heads, the members of Latino Power stand stiff as poles in the middle of the soccer field, their eyes fixed on the back door of the school. Flaco, Lalo, Teta, Pato, Alfonso, Lucho, Gonzalo, all of them are there. Once in a while someone taps his foot in impatience, crosses his arms with a sigh, or noisily swallows whatever was in his nose. All around, outside the line markings, where the grass is still hanging on, students are biting into their sandwiches and, with their mouths full, discussing the latest episode of *Friends*, or remembering an unforgettable party. Three girls, dressed in black, sit with their legs crossed around a crackling radio . . . "*Naked woman, naked man, where did you get that nice sun tan, naked woman, naked man. . . .*" With his hands behind his back, a monitor slowly walks around the perimeter of the field, absorbed in his thoughts. The sun is shining straight down, and three little white clouds have stopped directly above their heads. Okay, the Bad Boys are coming out one by one. Flaco glances at his watch: it's exactly twelve o'clock, at least they're on time. Perfect, there are fewer of them then there are of the Latinos: CB, Ketcia, Mixon, Richard, Max, and Étienne. The Bad Boys walk along like rappers, letting their right arms drop just as their left heels hit the ground. The music suddenly stops, several of the students in the area scatter.

As the two leaders draw closer to each other, in the distance, the monitor emerges from his thoughts, stops and points a finger at them, as a warning. They give him the thumbs up, the monitor thinks, he thinks, weighs the pros and cons, then goes back to his rounds. CB is slightly taller than Flaco, but they both have the same slim build. Silently, they look each other in the whites of the eyes, their faces expressionless. Their breathing is audible. All of a sudden, the noise of a motor distracts them. Heads turn towards the school parking lot: wearing a huge white helmet adorned with black fringe, stuffed into a leather coat too small for his girth, Mr. Dupaulin stomps on his motorcycle pedal with rage. The English teacher is known for his cynicism and never misses a chance to demonstrate to the students that the only reason he teaches is to earn a living, not for love of the profession. The motor finally catches. He pulls the zipper on his leather coat up to his chin and then he notices them.

"That's right!" he shouts. "Exterminate each other! . . . Good riddance!"

He straddles the motorcycle, turns the handgrips, then turns them again, and takes off. The engine backfires as if it was having a coughing fit. When Dupaulin drives past the soccer field, Teta gives him the finger. *¡Bien hecho!* the other Latinos remark. *Es todo lo que merece ese viejo estúpido*, Lalo states. Once he's out of sight, they each stare into their opponents' eyes again, and start to breathe loudly for a second time, as if they had to start all over again from the beginning. Flaco is focusing his gaze on CB's sharp irises: what a grotesque mask he's made! What an admirable actor!

"So?" CB says in his drawling voice. "Our peace treaty didn't last very long, did it?"

Yes, thinks Flaco, all this is nothing but a strange, painful, cruel game. Behind him he hears someone mutter *¡Qué huevón* *más grande!*, was it Lalo or Teta?, and he hurries to reply, "What can I say? Some people have a short memory. As soon as they get the chance, they start beating up people who are smaller than they are. It's easier and less dangerous than picking on somebody their own size. Right? In Spanish, we call them *los cobardes!* . . . Cowards!"

Sarcastic laughter bursts out behind Flaco. But when CB joins in, they immediately stop. They look at him with an unruffled gaze.

"What are you talking about, man?" CB says after a moment. "First, those wusses," he points at Pato and Alfonso, "rob me and lie to me. Then I get suspended for a week because of them. And you're trying to say we beat them up for nothing? If that's not a good reason, I wonder what the fuck would be a 'good reason'."

Behind CB, the others nod their agreement. Then the leader of the Bad Boys closes his eyes and flares his nostrils, taking in a deep breath.

"I can only see one way to reach an understanding," he says. "Those two wusses have to apologize to us on their knees. Right now."

Yeah, the group of Bad Boys chants. On their knees! On their knees!

"Just a minute," Flaco raises his hands to stop them. "It's not that simple. Look at them."

They turn towards Pato and Alfonso, scrupulously examining them from head to toe. Both their faces seem even more swollen and purple than yesterday. Pato pretends to be tough and proudly shows off his injuries, while Alfonso looks down and nervously bites his lip.

"When Pato's mother saw his face," Flaco says, "she almost passed out. He had to lie to his mother to keep her from calling the police. Did you really have to mess them up like that? I mean, that bad?"

66

Flaco's slightly condescending gaze encompasses all the Bad Boys.

"I think you guys have a screw loose," he continues, tapping his temple with one finger. "And now you expect them to apologize? It wasn't enough to beat them up like a bunch of goons?"

On the Bad Boys side, a variety of murmurs rumble, as CB, frowning, scratches his head.

"Sorry," he goes. "You said we beat them up like a bunch of what?"

"Goons! Goons! . . ."

Then a couple of seconds later, "Shit, everybody knows what that means!"

Behind CB, they repeat the word, they consult each other with a simple nod, they shrug their shoulders. Flaco can't really tell if they're pulling his leg or if they're sincere.

"You're kidding me, right?"

Then, when he sees no one's answering, "You really don't know what that means?" he says in a superior tone.

CB turns back to his group and there follows an animated exchange in low tones. *Yon moun ki konnèt signification nan mò 'goon', nan non Dye? Mon chè, pa gen ide. Non, pa gen sawè. Mwen pa gen sawè sa a. Bagay la sa sale.* They point at the Latinos again and again. Finally, CB turns back to Flaco and clears his throat.

"Is that some kind of insult?"

In turn, Flaco consults his group in Spanish. *Compadres*, he asks, what do you think? Should we tell them it's an insult? Teta leans his head in close and whispers to him, tell him it's worse than an insult, man. Tell him if somebody called me that, personally, I wouldn't take it. Tell them I'd strangle any guy who called me that . . . And, tell them . . . Oh, just tell them to go fuck off! They all burst out laughing together.

"Now you're making fun of us right to our faces?" CB stiffens.

"Listen," Flaco explains, "'goon' can be taken as an insult. But it all depends on the context."

67

"What are you talking about, man?" CB retorts indignantly. "Fuck the 'context'. What did you mean? That's what we want to hear! Use normal words!"

"I just meant that I think it's stupid for guys in grade eleven to beat up guys in grade seven. And if they have to apologize, then we want you to apologize for pounding them."

CB gives a feeble laugh, then makes a melodramatic face.

"Listen, I made those two wusses take a test and they both flunked. The results are clear: there are racists in your gang!"

"I know you, CB. It's not going to work with me. If they hadn't laughed at your joke, you would have pounded them anyway. So, who are the racists then? Them? Or you guys, who beat them up like a bunch of savages?"

"Racists, us?" CB asks in surprise. "Us? Are you really serious?"

He pivots towards his group and they each give a throaty, theatrical laugh.

"We," he continues, a smile on his lips, "in case you don't know it yet, are anti-racists. Every day we fight anybody who gives Blacks a hard time. How can you say that, man?"

And again CB turns towards his group, and like good actors, they hug their sides again, and this time they shake their heads, too.

"We," Flaco interrupts, "are against racism, too. What do you think? We even formed our group before you did!"

"That's not the question, buddy. You always mix everything up!"

CB suddenly drops his smile and squints his eyes.

"Another guy who should apologize on his knees and lick the soles of my shoes is the one who told them to rob us. Don't you think?"

The remark whisks Flaco off to another place. He doesn't really know why, but he can see himself on a balcony on a clear summer day, when suddenly the balcony gives way and falls, he drops, the descent is long and dizzying. . . .

"What are you insinuating?"

"I'm not insinuating anything, I just want to know who gave the order. That's all. Would you happen to have any ideas? I swear, I'm gonna make that guy pay!"

Flaco continues to tumble, like when he used to jump and touch the bottom of the pool with his toes. He shoves his hand into his pants pocket and takes out the condor. The bird swings at the end of the silver chain. CB freezes, then runs a hand through his hair.

"Listen," the leader of the Bad Boys says, "the condor is between you and me. We'll talk about it when we're alone."

On both sides, behind each leader, they question each other: what are they talking about? Where'd that condor come from? Lalo asks someone to explain what's going on to him, *putamadre*.

"If you say Pato and Alfonso are racist," Flaco retorts, "then as far as I'm concerned, you're saying my whole group is racist. Do you know what I mean . . . Cléo?"

CB freaks out.

"No one's called me that name for years. You'd better cut it out right now . . ."

"You ashamed of your name, Cléo Bastide?"

"I told you not to call me that anymore! You're playing with fire, man!"

What's got into you? What are you doing? ¡Ay *Marcelito!* A chain of words falls from his lips, unwinding like a snake, "You bunch of racist Black bastards! . . . Don't you get it, you're ashamed of being Black!"

CB leaps at Flaco, aiming for his throat, but he doesn't manage to push him down or even knock him off balance. On their feet, neither can land a punch. They grab each other's wrists, glare at each other as if their eyes were daggers. When they see the monitor taking long strides towards them, the others on each side hold them back. The monitor sighs, the back of his hand on his hip, and makes a bored face.

"I really don't care what you say to each other. But no fighting, or else you're expelled, boys."

He invites each group to go on its way. When the Bad Boys are already a good distance away, CB turns around and wipes a finger across his throat, then, with his hand next to his mouth, he shouts, "The treaty's off! It's war!"

All the members of Latino Power reply with a middle finger raised high in the air. Secretly, Flaco slips the condor back into his pocket. Then he notices Paulina coming towards him, between the tall rusty fence and the sluggish trees along the sidewalk. Did she see everything, he wonders in a low voice. Yes, Flaco, and then they're quiet for a moment as if they're trying to organise their thoughts. They're going to have to start carrying knives again. Paulina's forehead wrinkles, her lips relax. She shouldn't look at him like that, she has to be strong now. You get it?

Early in November, the first snow fell. It was a strange storm that people remembered for a long time: with no wind at all, the flakes fell down, bewilderingly straight. Traffic stopped, and, after school, dozens of children went out into Rue Linton. In many cases, they threw the first snowball of their lives, they slid for the first time along a driveway, usually on a piece of cardboard. From one end to the other, the street was transformed into a huge battlefield, the children didn't care at all if one of their snowballs hit a pedestrian. Quite the opposite, the courageous one who'd so boldly challenged adult authority was congratulated.

In class, Akira, Cléo and you sniffled nonstop and your noses had a hard time putting up with the painful irritation of all those tissues. In every subject, Cléo was falling farther and farther behind, and Sister Cécile would often catch him tracing his eyes along the ceiling cracks, or, since he sat near the windows, absorbed in contemplating the ice crystals on the maple branches. Still, when she asked him questions, she forbade the others from making fun of him, because it had become your favourite pretext for getting rowdy. But the restriction made you even more jittery and the whole class would turn scarlet from trying to hold in their laughter. You had a hard time figuring out why Cléo was so excited on the playground and so moody in class.

On November 15th, you and Akira had been the only students from Saint-Pascal-Baylon invited to Cléo's birthday. He was the one who opened the door when you arrived: he was wearing a navy blue suit and a silk tie that was much too long for him, so he'd tucked it into his pants, and he reeked of cologne. He rolled his eyes to let them know he wasn't responsible for what he was wearing. The two of you stepped inside and took off your coats, and you crossed your arms to hide your red woollen tie: your mother had made you wear a tie as well. Akira, his hair parted on one side, exposing his wide forehead, kept glancing at the floor, as if he was looking for something: he didn't feel very comfortable, guys, really, not at all. You went into the living room and a dozen smiles welcomed you. There were boys and girls your age, all Black, mostly with their parents. It was the first time you'd met them, and you found it strange that Cléo had never talked about all the friends he had. Suddenly, a woman in a wheelchair came towards you, with her arms stretched out, "There you are, Marcelo. Finally."

Two kisses smacked on your cheeks, and she looked at you for a long time, her face beaming. Remember, Marcelo: with her black, slightly almond shaped eyes, her graciously curved forehead, and her tiny mouth framed by fleshy lips, she was a beautiful woman, despite her look of exhaustion. Around her eyes and on her forehead, tiny wrinkles were appearing, and her expression, even when she smiled, looked somehow tragic. She took you by the neck, leaned close to your ear: thanks for being so good to Cléo. She hugged you against her for a long time. You knew how to open up to friendship, Marcelo. Yes, that was about the time that your friendship with Cléo turned into a mission. Taking care

71

of him, being responsible for him, became an obligation. She placed one hand on her chest, her name was Carole, but you could call her "Auntie" if you wanted to. She kissed Akira, and, frozen in disbelief, you were thinking, this is her? It can't be! You couldn't keep from staring at the wheels on her chair and her lifeless legs.

Chairs had been placed around the living room and, as soon as you and Akira were seated, you were served some orange juice in little blue tinted glasses, then the conversations started up again in Creole, that funny language you sometimes managed to catch a word of. You looked up at the brightly coloured paintings, you could still smell the fresh paint, and the adults intimidated you: they were talking loudly, moving their hands emphatically. Once in a while, someone, a woman usually, would turn towards you: how long had you been in Canada? What country were you from? Where did you live? What did your father do? And your mother? Your answers were never longer than one syllable, Marcelo.

A woman in her thirties, her hair pulled up in a bun, stood, with a glass in her hand: shouldn't the conversation be in French so our two friends can follow? That's when something strange occurred. Carole rolled to the centre of the room, ready to talk, but then was speechless, as if she'd had a memory lapse. All the daylight was reflected in her sad eyes. What was wrong with her? What was going on? Finally, she gathered her wits back around her: yes, of course they should speak French, please forgive her. It's just that everything was done in French in this country and it made her feel better to speak Creole. Another rather heavy woman seemed annoyed: she didn't mind doing her shopping in French, she really didn't mind at all. As if she hadn't heard, Carole now laughed and looked around, confused, amazed, delighted, as the others looked on, embarrassed: to think that sometimes in Haiti, she'd found the winters tough!

Finally, it seemed that Carole deliberately retreated to a corner. What exactly was wrong with her? It was as if she needed to withdraw from everyone, to regain her strength alone with her conscience. After a while, her unoiled wheels started to squeak and she came towards you. And she hugged you in her arms, and in a conspiratorial tone, she said, you and I understand each other, don't we, Marcelo. Like a little girl, she repeated: we don't need them! Then she fell silent, as if she'd had a marvellous idea, she said: *¿Cléo te dijo que yo hablaba español?* Yes, yes, in Haiti lots of people spoke Spanish, because they were so close to the Dominican Republic. *Dios mío*, she spoke your language! Then, feeling like you were opening some sort of secret interview, you asked her why she'd left Haiti. She sighed: it wasn't easy to explain. First of all, Haiti's not an easy country to live in, she didn't want to go into details, but the political situation wasn't very rosy. Nonetheless, you see, she said she sometimes thought she'd made a mistake by coming to Canada. Her love life really wasn't going well lately. Cléo's father was a difficult man. . . .

"He's not interested in that, Mom!"

Remember, Marcelo, Cléo's trembling voice brought everyone to a halt. The conversations stopped as Cléo stared at his mother, his face hard, his gaze piercing. Carole looked around as if searching for approval from the other guests, then her eyes came back to Cléo: what's got into you? He didn't answer, a thread of saliva ran from the corner of his mouth. Then, as if nothing had happened, she turned her back on him and started up a conversation with her neighbour.

Later on, the woman with the bun served you some more juice, insisting that everyone raise their glass in a toast to Cléo, who'd been sitting there the whole time, his arms crossed, pouting. "*Happy birthday!*" you all shouted together. Okay, that's better, smiled the woman. She leaned towards you to introduce herself: her name was Maryse. Then, delicately, as if to avoid

73

jostling him or making him even angrier, she went over to Cléo: come on now, my boy, this is no time to sulk. Since Cléo was pretending not to hear, Carole, who'd been watching the scene from a distance, interrupted, they should leave him alone, if he wanted to spoil his own birthday, that was his problem!

They went into the kitchen, a Black Forest birthday cake stood in the middle of the table. Small and round, it had been placed with care on a white tablecloth, and adorned with a huge bouquet of daffodils. Only the children could sit down, the adults stood all around with their plates in their hands. The cake was set in front of Cléo, the ten candles were lit and everyone sang *Happy Birthday*. Kneeling on his chair, with his hands flat on the table, Cléo blew them all out with one breath: he received a long round of applause. Carole cut the cake into slices and sent around the first plate, which quickly made its way into Cléo's hands. With no hesitation at all, he handed it to you, Marcelo. Then, without making a sound, Carole set down the knife and spoke in a voice she struggled to control: Cléo, please, you know we serve the girls first. Cléo, already holding a second plate in his hands, avoided her eyes: no, it's my birthday, I get to decide. You, Marcelo, would get the first plate, Akira the second and then the others. Cléo, stop being stubborn and give that plate to one of the girls, now. He replied, no, no, no! They're my real friends. You could see the fury in his eyes, and Carole lost her temper: if that's how you're going to act, you can go calm down in your bedroom! That's all you ever do, Cléo defended himself, send me to my room while you cry all day! He ran away and slammed a door noisily.

Silence passed through like a cold draught and Carole started sending plates around again. You'd barely tasted the cake, when she came over to you discreetly: could she talk to you? She took you over to the refrigerator, bent over, with her hands in her lap: would you please do her a favour and try to get Cléo to come back? I know he won't listen to me. As a last resort, you could just tell him it'll soon be time for presents and he'll have to come out to get them.

Remember the closed door to his room in the middle of the dark hallway. You knocked once, twice, you turned the knob and slowly pushed the door which seemed almost to open on its own. Surrounded by darkness, crying like a fountain, Cléo was stretched out on his bed, his face buried in a pillow. With tiny steps, you made your way over to the bed and Cléo's face appeared, as sad as a guitar without strings. Your mother wants you to come back out. He shook his head no. Come on, don't be like that, it's almost time to get your presents. I don't care. Okay, whatever you say. Can I at least give you my present? You didn't wait for him to answer and you took a little square box out of the pocket of your pants. He sat up, took it and shook it vigorously beside his ear. Go on, open it up. He ripped off the wrapping, opened the box and looked for a long time at his gift, his mouth slightly open. Thank you, and you replied, you're welcome, happy birthday. Now he was smiling weakly: you were his best friend, Marcelo. He was your best friend, too. Cléo's eyes looked panicky: it's just that sometimes he hated his mother. She corrected him all the time, and it tired him out. Then, as you remained silent, standing there in the midst of all the objects enveloped by the soft light filtering in through the blinds, he slipped on the chain. The condor shone against the blue of his tie.

Standing in front of the living room window, Ketcia follows the cars filing down Rue Linton in the twilight. From now on, she's well aware, she won't be able to walk around alone. She'll always have to have someone with her. In the last two days, each member of the Bad Boys has got a call where a voice, intentionally deepened and distorted, has repeated two or three times: you're dead, buddy! Or else: watch out, if you don't want to end up with two broken legs! The Bad Boys talked it over at CB's for a long time and agreed they had to act quickly, to take advantage of the element of surprise. The idea worked, and in his opinion, their scheme was more imaginative than the one Latino Power came up with: they slipped threats written on bits of paper into the Latinos' lockers. Seeing them read the insults was something else, they looked stunned.

Still, and he should have expected this, Latino Power didn't waste any time either. She's still wondering how they did it, the bastards. Every Saturday she slept late, then took her shower and went to the kitchen where her two younger brothers and her parents were already at the table. Today the door to the courtyard was half open and, as if moved by a premonition, she went out onto the balcony. It was cool out, but it wasn't unpleasant. It took a while for her to notice the cat, stretched out on its side, its eyes open. Since it sometimes gets hot in the spring and since Vaudou is usually incurably lazy, at first she thought the animal had lain down just to be more comfortable. She stroked his grey fur but immediately jerked back her hand. His mouth was half open, his canines exposed. Frightened, she screamed, and her father came running. He examined Vaudou: sweet Jesus, what does this mean? He's dead. Slowly, he drew one hand along his beard, then put his finger to his lips: her brothers mustn't see the cat, it would be too painful for them. She should go get a plastic bag. When Ketcia came back out onto the balcony, her father winked: Vaudou ran away, okay? Okay, she agreed. As they lifted the cat to place him in the bag, a thread of blood came from his mouth and then everything had to be cleaned up. Ketcia carried the bag downstairs to the trash. She felt funny leaving Vaudou there. When she went back up to the apartment, her father took her aside: did she have any idea who could have done such a thing? It wasn't normal, cats don't just die like that. He had been killed, that much was obvious. Already she was thinking it was the Latinos, but she held back her anger: no idea, Dad, I really don't get it.

Outside, there was still no sign of the Bad Boys, only three boys tossing a ball back and forth in front of the building across

76

the street. But yesterday CB had said that they'd get together at about seven, seven-thirty. Finally, she sees them coming up the sidewalk, one behind the other, she waves to them and, as usual, they reply by making faces at her and waving for her to come down. With light steps, to avoid attracting her parents' attention, she slips on her Bad Boys jacket and goes out, being careful to close the door behind her without making a sound. Sitting on the yellow grass, or leaning against her father's old red pickup truck, they're smoking with their legs crossed and surveying the neighbourhood as if a threat could arise any second.

She shakes everyone's hand, the way the Bad Boys do, in a complicated series of finger snaps and hand slaps. Every single one of them is wearing a black coat that comes half way down their thighs, with an artistic drawing of the Bad Boys' logo on the back. Several of them, thoughtful and impassioned, swear to avenge Vaudou's death. Eh? says Mixon, his eyebrows transformed into upside down v's. He hadn't heard about it! Shit, why is he always the last to know, eh? And, without losing a beat, Ketcia imitates Mixon's voice and intonation: why don't you ever listen when people talk to you, eh? No one speaks for a moment, and Mixon suggests a moment of silence. Ketcia, both surprised and touched, smiles weakly: Mixon, what's got into you? You had a good idea! You sick? For a few long seconds, they all lower their eyes, contemplative, like in church, but suddenly, on the balcony of the building on the other side of the street, a woman in her sixties, her hair a mess, puts out a garbage bag. They know her, she came from Hungary or Czechoslovakia, and she's always grumbling about everything and anything. Mixon steps towards the balcony, a mocking smile on his lips: hello, Mrs. Masaryk, how are you? What can we do for you today? She stares at him, purses her lips as if to control her anger and, before going back into her apartment shouts in a nasal voice: *Bunch of delinquents! Get a job!* There follows an explosion of laughter, then Mixon rejoins the group, shaking his head, amused, Christ, I love that old woman!

Then he starts blowing on his nails and polishing them on his long, black T-shirt. With affected manners, he coughs several times and tells them that last night he went to Flaco's building and, with a little help from a can of black spray paint, wrote *Death to the Latinos!* on the garage door. What do they say about that, guys? Euphoric acclamations and warm handshakes congratulate him. Only CB doesn't look cheerful, Ketcia notices, something's on his mind. The others also become aware of this and little by little they fall silent. CB looks up at the sky, stuffs his hands in his pockets and kicks at a cigarette pack lying on the ground. Yesterday, his father got a call from the principal telling him about his week's suspension and there followed an animated conversation between him and his old man, and, he swears to them, his old man doesn't think it's funny at all to see him mixed up in this.

"You wanted to hit a teacher?" asked his father in a voice that was almost more amused than worried. "What got into you? You should know you never win when you lose your cool."

"It's nothing," replied CB. "He's an old racist who was trying to get on my nerves. But what's it to you? Don't you always say you don't give a crap about what happens to me?"

"Don't twist what I say, please," his father said, lying back on the sofa, his hands behind his head. "What I kill myself trying to get you to understand is that you have to take responsibility for yourself. I won't always be here for you. But there's one thing that's sacred, and you know it: you have to finish high school."

"Don't complain," Mixon interrupts. "Your father's happy with high school. My parents want me to become an engineer, man. Can you imagine? Six more years of school! The only good thing about the Polytéchnique, if I can believe what my cousins say, is they have some kick-ass parties!"

"You've got two months left to finish high school," CB's father said. "One piece of advice for you, between now and then:

78

stop scaring the teachers," he added with a laugh. Then he turned serious again: "I mean it, after that, you can do what you want. Even move out if it makes you happy."

"Your father's like Québécois parents," Ketcia says. "Once their kids are eighteen, they give them a kick in the ass and say see you later!"

"No, no," said his father. "I don't want to get rid of you. I want you to assume some responsibility and stop thinking you're entitled to everything! If you'd rather stay with me after high school, that's great. I don't see any problem there."

"Nice speech!" CB shouted. "It's all well and good for you to talk about responsibility. You never took care of me."

"Anyway," Mixon states, "your father's a real ladies' man. Every time I see him get out of his car, he's with a different woman. And he doesn't pick up just anybody, either!"

"All you care about is women!" CB exclaimed. "You think I don't know where all your pay goes? So, when you talk about 're-sponsibilities,' you just make me laugh. What you really mean is, 'get the hell out so I can screw in peace!'"

"It's the same thing, every time," Mixon continues, now displaying a mischievous smile. "Your father gets out of the car and comes around to open their door. Then, whether they're black, white, yellow, or whatever, they are *built*, my friends! Every single one of them, I swear to you!"

"Just a second!" CB's father said, still smiling. "We're talking about you, not me! My life is my concern. And, by the way, I never said I was perfect."

"My father," says Ketcia, "is the exact opposite: he's afraid of women. If a sexy woman even comes near him, he starts stutter-ing and shaking. Once, he was serving a friend of my mother's, a tall, beautiful woman, and he spilled the whole bottle of wine on her dress. The twit!"

"Anyway," CB's father continued, "we're not going to get along any better by insulting each other. Listen, I've been thinking about something for a while. I wanted to talk to you about it. You know, I've been driving the taxi now for three years. Let's just say I'm starting to get tired of it."

"Since we came to Canada," CB explains, "my father has tried all kinds of businesses. The problem is, none of them have worked."

"What I mean is, if I'm going to live like a zombie," his father continued, "I'd rather do it in Haiti."

"In Haiti," says CB, "there's always family to help him out. Even if he won't admit it, I think that's what he misses most: his family."

"But it's a zoo down there!" Mixon says. "Everybody knows that. It's even fucking dangerous right now."

"What would you say about coming to Haiti with me?" his father suggested. "A few months, to try things out and see if we want to stay."

"What?" says Mixon. "You leaving us, CB?"

"Are you crazy!" replies CB. "He brings that one out two or three times a year, when he's depressed. I tell him if he pays the flight, I'd be happy to go on a little vacation. But I know perfectly well we'll never go."

"Going would do you a lot of good," his father said. "Maybe you think I don't know you get drunk every weekend? That you smoke and skip classes? This society is corrupting you and it hurts me to see you like this."

"My father says that all the time," Mixon remarks. "He says Haiti may be poor, but it's a healthier society."

"And let me tell you," CB's father went on, "all that you've got left of Haiti is your looks. You're becoming more and more Québecois. Like one of my friends would say, you're getting Westernized!"

"What are you talking about?" CB said. "All my friends are Haitian. I even formed a group to defend our rights, just like you taught me yourself. And you say I'm not Haitian anymore?"

"Look at what you're wearing," his father retorted. "You dress like a rapper, you run to McDonald's whenever I give you money. You speak Creole less and less. And, and this is the big one, what do you know about Haiti? Not much. . . ."

"Maybe not, compared to you," CB said. "But at school, I swear, I'm the most Haitian of all the Haitians. Ask any of my friends."

"I can only imagine what your kids will be like," his father laughed. "They'll hardly be able to find Haiti on a map!"

CB leans against the door of the pickup, still hurt by what his father said. They all seem to be lost in their thoughts as the streetlights come on. Mixon steps away from the group and, concentrating hard, stares at his shadow and starts to box.

"In any case," he says, throwing jabs, "it doesn't matter who's more Haitian than who. All our parents think they're better than us 'cause they know Haiti better and they even talk Creole. But I'm here to tell you that's a load of B.S. . . . What matters right now is that the Latinos killed Vaudou and we're not going to take it."

"Yeah," says CB. "The next step will be extorsion. I guarantee that'll settle them down."

"Excellent idea," says Mixon enthusiastically, feverishly jumping an imaginary rope, imitating a professional boxer. "I'm telling you, if I had a Latino in front of me right here, right now, I'd squash him like a bug."

"Right," adds Ketcia, "brag about it a little more. And when we're face to face with the Latinos, who's the first one to shit his pants?"

Mixon comes to a standstill, out of breath, and all together the others shout, "Mixooooooon!"

A week before, Sister Cécile had received an honour that had left her pensive: at an elaborate ceremony at a five-star, downtown hotel, she'd been given a commemorative plaque emphasizing her fifty years of service to the Catholic School Board of Montreal. There was a long reminder that, with her seventy-four summers, as the superintendent put it, she was the oldest teacher in the city, a fact that disconcerted her somewhat. So much in fact that, when she returned to the mother house that night she wasn't feeling happy as she had first thought, but rather defeated: had there been a rush to celebrate her, now that she was soon to leave this lowly world? During the following days, two other questions occurred to her, and these were even more stubborn. Was she still a woman of her time? Wasn't it time for her to hang up her skates, as one of her nephews teasingly said, and retire? God in heaven, what if everyone was right?

Since her earliest childhood, she'd known she'd be a teacher, admiring nothing more than the work of those who had taught her. Towards the end of her teenage years, this premonition was confirmed: children brought her the greatest gratification. When she joined the community of the Sisters of the Holy Cross, she was moved by two convictions: serving the Lord with all the impetuous devotion of her youth, and dedicating her life to children. And that was exactly what she had done. At the same time, she'd witnessed the transformation that Quebec, and Montreal in particular, had undergone, and this hadn't always occurred without her heart tightening just a little. Sometimes, kneeling in Église Saint Pascal, her thoughts would roam and, troubled, she would wonder what had happened. What had happened to the people, the landscapes, the scenes of her youth? Originally from Sainte-Agathe, she'd first come to Montreal as a teen, and had never again left. Often, jokingly, in front of the other nuns, she'd say it was the love of her life, and the others would giggle like young girls, covering their mouths with their hands.

Sometimes she got angry with the so-called progress that had so changed what she cherished: a peaceful, healthy life, where nature occupied a prime position. That's why she thought it was important to tell the children what Côte-des-Neiges had been like at the time: on Sundays, young ladies showed off their lace dresses with a parasol on their shoulders, the men, in brown suits with white shirts and fedoras, smoothed their moustaches admiringly, coachmen paraded black carriages, farmers drove carts overflowing with fruits and vegetables. Didn't they know, she would say facing the children, raising a finger as if to announce they were about to be astonished, people came great distances, sometimes even from the other side of Mount Royal, to buy inexpensive vegetables? It didn't matter what countries the children were from, their reaction was always the same: they'd rush to the window and follow the flow of cars: horses on the Côte-des-Neiges? No, it was impossible! Really, Sister Cécile?

It pained her to think those days were gone forever. Sometimes, it's true, a reminder of the Quebec of her childhood would appear to her, as when that grandfather came to get his granddaughter's report card and they'd chatted for more than an hour, laughing and joking, like old friends meeting again after a long separation. But that was an isolated incident, and that made those times even more solemn and sad. Other times, she thought it had to be her own fault and she'd tell herself she hadn't aged well. On still other occasions, she'd stiffen up and tell herself she shouldn't make excuses and close her eyes. Just as Sister Lacasse had commented one evening at dinner, culture, their culture, real culture, was dying. Sister Cécile didn't blame anyone for this, but had it really been the right decision to accept all these children who came from all over the world? Sometimes she wondered. She adored them, she dreamed about them, bored the other nuns telling so many stories of their successes and their blunders, but she always asked herself the same question.

Why did certain children integrate better than others? How was it that some of them, as early as grade five, rejected Québécois culture outright? Was it the parents' fault? Sometimes she wondered about the upbringing and discipline they received at home. Like that Cléo Bastide, his head always in the clouds, his

83

homework almost always incomplete, only interested in sports, what kind of parents did he have? She had no idea, since they hadn't come to the report card distribution. The parents of the worst students never showed their faces.

That morning, the bell rang when she was still in the school-yard, chatting with a co-worker. She hurried into the classroom: if she wanted to teach the students punctuality, she'd better practise it herself. They were all seated at their desks, except Cléo, of course, who was on his tiptoes, watching the pedestrians out the window. As she removed her boots, she simply said, "Cléo? I thought I heard the bell ring. Didn't you?"

Without answering, the boy hurried to his desk. He was smiling as usual. At first, she'd thought he was mocking her, then she'd understood, it was a nervous smile. Maybe this was the right time to find out more about him. As she slipped on her shoes, she asked, "Tell me, Cléo. You told me you wanted to be a sprinter when you grow up, right?"

"Yes, Sister Cécile."

"I was wondering: why do you want to be an athlete? Because you're already good at sports?"

"Yes, a little. But it's because I love to run, too . . . Oh, Sister Cécile, a friend of my mother's told me that if some day I can be one of the best runners in Canada, I could make a lot of money. Is that true?"

"I don't know, Cléo. What I can tell you, is that it's very diffi-cult to become the best in Canada. But why do you want to make money?"

"That way, my mother wouldn't have any more problems."

"You want to help your mother. That's good."

"Then she could paint in peace and her paintings would be better."

Ah-ha, the mother was an artist.

"Even if you want to be an athlete, you have to do well in French and in math."

84

The boy seemed frustrated.

"I don't see how knowing my multiplication tables can help me run faster."

"If you're a good student, you'll be able to use your head better to find out what weaknesses are keeping you from going faster."

"My mother says just the opposite. If I want to play sports, she says, I don't have to go to school."

"Well, then, you can tell your mother I don't share her opinion."

Sister Cécile went to her desk. Obviously, there was nothing she could do with this poor boy. She took out a notebook from the top drawer and opened it to the page where the bookmark was. Sweeping her gaze across the class, "Your lesson was to learn the twelve times table. So, who's going to volunteer?"

She knew for a fact that no one would raise their hand and that she'd have to pick someone, but she always asked the question. A religious silence settled upon the class. Then, she made a point of choosing Claudia, an excellent student, to get things started, then Humbertino, a student who produced mediocre work. Both had learned their times table. After each student's turn, she asked the others to give a round of applause. Then her eyes fell upon Cléo, who avoided looking at her.

"Your turn, Cléo."

When he got up, the others muttered and chuckled and, sweeping her gaze over the whole class, she demanded silence. With a slight nod, she motioned for Cléo to begin. The boy looked up at the ceiling.

"Twelve times one, twelve; twelve times two, twenty-four; twelve times three, thirty-six; twelve times four makes . . . um . . . makes . . . twelve times four makes. . . ."

He fell silent and now looked at her in a way that was both uncomfortable and sorry, as if he were asking for her help. For a long time, the only sound was the feverish coming and going of cars drifting in through the partly open windows. After a moment, he murmured, "Christ, I knew it last night. . . ."

"Pardon?"

Cléo looked surprised. He didn't seem to understand. He stammered, "I said I knew it, that I memorized it last night. . . ."

"Sit down immediately!"

"But, what did I do?"

The innocent tone in his voice confirmed it: he hadn't understood. Now, she was pacing back and forth, she didn't know where to start, words were rushing into her mouth. It was fine to be open-minded and all that, but there were limits that were not to be crossed in her classroom.

"No one is allowed to swear in here!" she finally said. "Understand?"

She came to a standstill, one hand lying flat on her desk.

"I have no control over what you do at home. But here, no one is to show Our Lord a lack of respect."

Then she went into a long speech about how important it is for young people to show respect for their elders, and, even more importantly, for God. She made an effort to make her message simple and clear. That helped calm her, then she looked back at Cléo.

"And as for you, for too long now you haven't been learning your lessons well enough. That confirms the decision the administration and I made."

Cléo's face became sombre. He glanced over to his friends, he could undoubtedly guess what she was going to tell him.

"We decided you should go to the *classe d'accueil*."

The entire class turned towards Cléo as if he'd just received the death penalty. He was imploring his friends with moist eyes. *Classe d'accueil* was the special class for those who couldn't keep up with the regular lessons. As its name suggested, it had been set up to welcome immigrants. In the students' opinion, and this was often heard at recess, it was nothing but a class for the "less intelligent," or, more harshly, for "the dummies."

"Don't be sad," Sister Cécile said, trying to make amends. "In the *classe d'accueil*, you'll be looked after better, the teacher will have more time to dedicate just to you. When you catch up to the same level as the others, you'll come back."

"Why?" Cléo said, "I want to stay here, my friends are here."

She asked him to come see her at three o'clock when classes were over. As she had other students recite their times tables, she would occasionally glance in Cléo's direction: he'd slumped down in his chair and was hiding his face in his arms. The bell for recess rang out, and he was the last to leave the room, she saw him begging her with his red eyes: she again said they'd talk about it at the end of the day, right now she had some things to take care of with the principal. Come on now, he should go play, she didn't want to hear another word about it.

When Cléo appeared in the schoolyard on the snowy stairs leading to the entrance, a circle formed around him. The students were rubbing their hands and hopping from foot to foot to keep the cold at bay: it was because Sister Cécile didn't like him, it was obvious. He really had lousy luck, man. He could see, now, it was important to do his homework or else they'd give him a hard time. Others, rubbing a hand along his back, tried telling him something more constructive: it's no big deal, Cléo, he just had to get as good in all his subjects as he was in sports and he'd be able to come back. Then Sylvain and Evangelos showed up, and Marcelo pulled on his coat sleeve: come on, there's no doubt they're going to give you a hard time. But Evangelos, stepping in front of Cléo, with his legs spread wide apart, was already sniggering: that's what happens when all you're good for is running. No two ways about it, Caramilk, you got what you deserved! Ah! Ah! Ah! Suddenly a deep voice thundered, "Buddy, don't you ever let anyone get away with anything like that."

87

They all spun around to see who it was. A Haitian in grade six, taller and sturdier than all of them, with his open mouth exhaling a light vapour, was standing there, looking stiff-shouldered. Cléo, too upset to notice the newcomer's arrival, repeated in a whining voice, "I don't wanna go to the *classe d'accueil.*"

"I'm in *accueil*," said the boy.

Cléo then looked up at him.

"I'll tell you one thing," said the stranger. "If your teacher's sending you to the *classe d'accueil* it's 'cause they're sick of you. They're trying to get rid of you. But there's no reason for you to be unhappy. It's not what everybody thinks, it's a lot better than regular class."

Now Cléo was listening with total attention.

"There are only eight of us in the class. Three from grade five and five from grade six. You don't get something, no problem: the teacher comes right over to explain to you how to do it. You learn more and the best part is when you get home, you've already finished most of your homework."

Cléo stared at him, fascinated.

"By the way," the other said, "I'm Carl."

Cléo told him his name and they shook hands.

"See you tomorrow in the *classe d'accueil*. And don't forget: never let anybody give you a hard time."

IV

Flaco leans on the front door and glances out through the peephole: their faces covered in mud, their hair so soaked it looks like they've gelled it, Lalo and Pato stand there, teeth chattering. *¿Qué les pasó?* He hurries to open the door: the two brothers shiver in their sock feet, their faces ashen, their windbreakers soaking wet. Flaco, one hand against the wall, can't keep from laughing.

"We just got robbed and all you can do is make fun of us," Lalo complains. "Just let us in."

They slip under Flaco's arm and into the foyer, where they continue to rub their hands together and squirm. Voices ring out from the other end of the hallway.

"You have company?" Lalo inquires in a hushed voice.

"Yeah. My Uncle Juan is in the kitchen with my parents."

"We bothering you?" Pato asks. "You look half-asleep."

Before Flaco can reply, Lalo cuts in, "*Compadre*, we have to talk to you. It's serious."

He runs a hand through his hair and drops of water fall to the floor.

"Come on. It'll be better in your room."

With Pato on his heels, he heads towards a closed door in the middle of the hallway, but Flaco immediately catches up and positions himself between them and the door.

"Wait. Just give me a second."

A meaningful look crosses Lalo's face.

"What? What are you hiding from us?"

"It's not what you think. It's just a little messy in there. It'll just take two seconds."

"Messy, my butt," Pato exclaims, as he wipes away snot with his arm.

Lalo exchanges a doubtful look with his brother.

"*¡Este huevón tiene una huevona metida allí!*"

They snigger and slap each other's hands, as Flaco opens the door a crack, slides in, then gently closes it behind him. He rushes to the bed, picks up the book and conceals it in a dresser drawer. Up to now, he's only talked to Paulina about his reading. The others know he likes to read, but he feels like they only let it pass because he's the boss. Several times already Lalo has insinuated that novels are only good for fags, and each time, stung, he's had to slap him down: he'd better stop talking like ignorant people, for Christ's sake! Since then, he's preferred to keep this part of his life secret, it's simpler that way and helps him avoid problems. He inspects his room one last time and his eyes settle on the condor, which, without really knowing why, he's kept on his nightstand. He hides it under the bedspread, the opens the door for the brothers. Their eyes scan every inch of the room: Pato glances into the closet and pushes back the clothes on their hangers, Lalo gets on his knees and inspects under the bed. He repeats that he's alone, that Paulina is at Nena's, if they want to know. After a moment, he goes to the bathroom and comes back with towels: they take off their drenched clothes, wipe their faces and dry their hair. Standing before him, they adopt an appropriately solemn air, and tell him what happened.

Every Sunday their mother makes them go to Rue de Courtrai to the apartment their Aunt Gloria and their grandmother share, to help them with the housework because they can't move the furniture by themselves. And that's exactly what they did this morning.

"You always have to go out in groups of four, minimum," Flaco reminds them. "It's more sensible. We agreed on that, didn't we?"

He should just wait a minute, Lalo says. When they went, they weren't alone, their mother was with them, and what bugs him isn't so much the threat of an attack by the Bad Boys, but having to adapt to his mother's slow pace. Besides, he thinks it's so annoying to waste part of his Sunday that way that, back in the second week, he asked his mother if they could be paid for their work. Don't be insolent! his mother replied, hitting him again and again. Did he fall on his skull? Demanding money from his own family! *¡Santísima Virgen!* She kicked them out for a whole day so they could think about the seriousness of what they'd said and to purify the apartment of their blasphemy.

"Just because you asked for money?" Flaco asks, surprised.

"You don't know my mother," Lalo replies. "The more time goes by, the less I understand her with all her junk about purification, and prayers that go on for ever."

"You know," Pato explains, "she never forgave us for not going to church with her anymore. She's always saying, see, Teta goes to church with his mother. But it's not the same with Teta, his mother is practically blind."

When the cleaning was done, they ask their mother contritely, their faces angelic, if they could leave. They make up homework they have to do. She hesitates, *bueno ya*, but she's going to stay a little longer. Free as birds, happy as kings, they leave the apartment, rush down the stairs and, when they arrive in the lobby, press their faces against the glass door: the coast looks clear. Outside, drizzle makes the sidewalk shine. They go past the

Hygrade sausage factory, and they head east rather than south as they normally would to get back to Rue Linton, because if they take Lavoie, they might run into some of the Haitians that live there. The whole way, they're constantly scanning their surroundings, and Lalo, especially, is worried: he swears to God he spotted Mixon this morning hiding behind a Buick. You're crazy, you're seeing things, buddy! Pato retorts. On top of that, according to Lalo, Rue Courtrai is one of the most dangerous streets in the area since it beat out Rue Barclay and Rue Plamondon for the drug trade four or five years ago. From time to time, they see heads checking for activity in the street: dealers. Whenever he hears steps behind him or a car door slam, through the fabric of his jeans, Lalo feels the handle of his knife in his pocket. Since they partied until the wee hours of the morning yesterday, he's feeling exhausted. On the corner of Légaré they come face to face with Guylain who, as usual, is wearing his Canadiens jersey and dragging along a cart he uses to pull his old cats down the street. The two brothers approach him: first he swears at them copiously, then, when he realizes they mean him no harm, he listens.

"Have you seen the Bad Boys around, by any chance?"

The Bad Boys? Don't even talk to him about those Black sons of bitches! He's sick and tired of having his stuff stolen by that bunch of thugs! They think they rule the world! His complaining goes on and on, they have no choice but to leave him there. They continue on their way, their hands stuffed into their pockets, their hoods over their heads. They go by the Multi-Caf, the neighbourhood soup kitchen they turn into a game room on weekends. Starting early in the spring, they keep the front door wide open to air things out, so, from the sidewalk, you can follow the activity going on around the Ping-Pong and foosball tables. Out of the corner of his eye, Lalo notices two Black guys he doesn't know who are taking turns smashing a Ping-Pong ball back and forth. The same instant, he thinks he recognizes Mixon coming out of the men's room at the back.

"Was it him or not?" asks Flaco.

"Wait," says Pato. "You'll see."

Deciding not to take any chances, they run flat out until they hit Côte-des-Neiges, where they turn around: an old woman wearing a pink raincoat and sheltering herself under an umbrella pulls on the leash of a reluctant German shepherd. That's all. But you can never be too careful and they slip into the Plaza Côte-des-Neiges where they spend at least forty-five minutes or an hour. *Compadre*, I swear to you, Lalo insists. Finally, they take the elevator and leave through the underground parking lot and go back up Rue Légaré, to be sure to lose the enemy in case they really were being followed. They cross Barclay and, right in the middle of the street, before they have time to react, they spot the Bad Boys, who've been hiding behind parked cars or mailboxes, coming from all directions. Suddenly, they're surrounded and backed up against a red Honda on the north side of the street.

"You should have pulled out your knives," Flaco states indignantly. "You always have to be on the lookout. *El que pestañea pierde* . . . The guy who blinks is screwed, as my father says."

"I swear to you, we barely had a chance to realize they were heading right for us," Lalo defends himself. Hi guys, he says, a smile plastered across his face like he was radiating happiness. Oh, how nice to see you! Out for a stroll?

From behind, nonchalantly, CB walks up and levels a neutral gaze on them.

"That's right, we're out for a walk," he answers. "We saw you go by and we said, let's go take a walk with those two idiots."

"Come on, guys," Lalo grumbles, as, casually, he tries to slip one hand into his pocket. "Be fair and attack us at least when there's as many of us as there are of you. Two against five isn't very democratic. Don't you think?"

Quick as lightning, CB grabs Lalo's arm and lifts it up: a little black knife appears where everyone can see it. CB weighs it in his palm for a moment, then hands it to Ketcia. Stupid, bloody, fucking Latino! Mixon welcomes them, then bites his fist as if to control his anger. CB looks over both sides of the street and, without looking back at them, as if they don't even deserve his attention, he orders, "Lay down on the ground. Right now."

"It's raining, man!" says Pato. "The ground's all wet."

"Shut the fuck up and do what you're told!" Mixon orders.

The brothers lie face down on the asphalt. A woman goes by, her face haggard, both her hands on her purse. Mixon puts his hands on his crotch and the woman shrieks and speeds up. On the ground, his cheek against the asphalt, Lalo notices a man in the window of an apartment building, then he feels a foot on his back.

"Well, well," CB says. "Those are some nice little sneakers you have there. Where'd you buy them?"

His foot presses down harder.

"At Zellers, I think," Lalo answers. "Listen to me, CB . . . *amigo haitiano* . . . I'm sure we can talk about this, we can make a deal."

"You keep your trap shut unless I ask you a question. Got it?"

Then, going back to his light-hearted banter: "At Zellers, eh? That's what I thought, I saw them there the other day on special. And, it's perfect, Nike is my favourite brand, too."

"Your Nikes?" exclaims Flaco. *¡Putamadre!*

CB snaps his fingers, Mixon and Ketcia bend down, pin Lalo's legs in place and take off his shoes. Ketcia hands the sneakers to CB, who takes them with his fingertips and sniffs them. A disgusted grimace contorts his face.

"Oof! Soap was invented a long time ago, you know. Smells like you still haven't heard of it."

"CB?" Mixon asks, holding Lalos's ankles. "Look."

His chin gestures towards Pato's watch, CB nods his head and Mixon undoes the band and removes it from his wrist. All this time, Lalo can feel his windbreaker and his T-shirt growing

94

cold. Then Mixon takes off Pato's shoes, slips the runners on and, like a child who's just got a new pair of shoes, paces back and forth to admire them.

"Mine were Nikes, too," Pato points out. "Can you imagine, Flaco? I saved for two months. Just so those Black assholes could steal them from me as soon as they got the chance."

They're getting ready to take off their jeans when Ketcia spots the flashing lights of a police car in the distance, heading straight for them, its siren silent. Immediately, the Bad Boys all take off in the same direction, jump a fence and disappear into the yard of the apartment building at the end of the street. The car brakes beside the Latinos, who are wiping themselves off and swearing as they get to their feet with difficulty. The two officers get out of the car, slam the doors shut and come towards them, slapping their nightsticks into the palms of their hands. The one with the moustache is the first to question them, "What's going on here?"

"Why are you barefoot?" the other echoes.

A strange reflex causes the two brothers to put their hands in the air, as if they'd just been told they were under arrest. The officers look at each other, taken aback.

"Why did you put your hands in the air?" asks Flaco. "You hadn't done anything wrong."

"Nerves," Pato explains.

"Put your hands down, guys," the one with the moustache says. "So? What happened?"

"A bunch of Haitians," Pato continues. "They robbed us . . ."

Instantly, Lalo cuts him off: *¡cállate, huevón!*

"You," the officer cuts in, pointing at him with his nightstick, "let him talk. What did they steal from you?"

For a long moment, the Latinos look thoughtful, suddenly absorbed by movements at the opposite end of the street.

"Listen," the one with the moustache continues, "we don't have time to fool around. We got a call from a resident saying

95

there was a fight. If you know who attacked you, give us a name, otherwise. . . ."

He leaves his sentence unfinished, attentive to their every move.

"If that's the way you want it, guys." Then, speaking to his colleague, he adds, "They come and complain that we don't pay attention to them, that we discriminate against them, that we persecute them. . . ."

The two officers get back into their car, start it up and drive away slowly. In the rear-view mirror, the driver glances at the two brothers then, at top speed, the car takes off. Without turning around even once, the brothers walk side by side in silence. At the corner of Linton, Lalo grabs Pato by the collar.

"What got into you, *estúpido*? You never answer the cops' questions! Get it? All they want is to find a reason to deport you."

"Your brother's right," Flaco confirms. "A cop is a cop."

For a moment, the three of them stand there in Flaco's room in silence, then Lalo asks, "Could you lend us some sneakers?"

Flaco goes to his closet and, after a few seconds, tosses them two old pairs of running shoes. They take the shoes and both of them automatically stick a finger into the gaping holes in the soles.

"They're pretty worn out," Pato comments. "Anyways, we'll tell Mom we traded with you or something. I hope it'll work so she doesn't have a fit."

All this time, Lalo is staring at the floor, lost in his thoughts.

"We have to strike back as soon as possible," he says, thinking out loud, "because I plan to get my sneakers back. But what can we do?"

After a moment, he's struck by sudden inspiration: "I've got it! That's it! It's simple and not too risky. We have to break CB's windows! . . . What do you think, Flaco?"

He doesn't answer immediately, then, in a low voice as if he were still weighing Lalo's idea, "Yeah, that's not such a crazy idea, not crazy at all."

In winter the white lines around the schoolyard would disappear under the snow, and you'd give up playing dodge ball in favour of soccer. The Québécois kids could grumble all they wanted, even though they preferred football, which was more familiar to them: the others were a majority and came from countries where soccer, often the national sport, was king. The girls, no longer able to skip rope, also turned into soccer players. Since recess was too short, teams were formed in class by sending a piece of paper from desk to desk, where everyone could write their name on a list. Boots, coats, toques, mittens, scarves were all put on in a rush, the children walked as quickly as possible since no running was allowed in the school hallways, you went down the stairs, pushing the student in front of you, and, once you got outside, slid on the ice, lost your balance and fell on top of one another. The monitor almost always caught one or two of you by the scarf and ordered them to stand in the corner for the whole recess.

A week earlier, a track-and-field meet had taken place at Notre-Dame-des-Neiges, which was in the same neighbourhood as Saint-Pascal-Baylon. Clearly better prepared, you'd won most of the races, and, delighted, Serge had pointed out in the locker room that you were getting better and better at passing the baton and handling the stress of the competitions. Once again, in the relay race and the fifty metres, Cléo had devoured his opponents singlehanded.

Since he'd been placed in the *classe d'accueil* last month, you saw Cléo hanging out in the street in the evening more often. According to him, he always finished his homework in class. And he didn't have to look after his mother as much, since his father had come back home. One afternoon, from Cléo's room, you heard Carole warn her husband: this was the last time she was going to get back together with him, was that clear? If he took off again, it was over. She wasn't joking. Jokingly he said: was it healthy for people in a relationship to threaten each other like that? How many times did he have to tell her, they were just business trips! Silence, then the father's voice, attempting to be sincere, solemn: you're getting worked up over nothing, Carole. All he wanted now was to live with her and his son. Why did she refuse to believe him? She said, I only hope you'll keep your word this time.

Since Cléo came to see you every day, you'd call him on days when he hadn't shown up yet, and Carole would be surprised: that's strange, where could he be? You knew where, Marcelo: at Carl's, just a stone's throw away, on Rue Victoria. On weekends, he'd give Cléo a call and invite him to the parties his big brother would throw, when their parents went out for the evening. At first, Cléo would refuse, saying there was a Canadiens game on TV or that he had the flu. Why do you lie to Carl like that, you'd ask him. He licked his lips: you couldn't tell anyone, but girls made him uncomfortable. Once, when he was starting to get fed up, Carl finally confronted him: why didn't he tell him the truth, eh? I really don't know what you're talking about. You get used to girls, Carl explained to him, there's no reason to feel uncomfortable, we've all been there. The next day, Carl went and picked him up and promised Carole her son would be home before midnight. Two days later, Cléo described his evening to you in great detail, emphasizing the couples who danced pressed up against each other and who sometimes gave each other long kisses on the mouth. You asked all kinds of questions, then, you ventured: could you come the next time? I don't know, I'll have to ask Carl. But I don't think there'll be a problem.

Indeed, Carl agreed and, the next Saturday, you were both at his place where, remember, it was awfully dark because, in the living room, the only light was a red bulb that made the apartment look like a brothel, a little like in the movies, Marcelo. The bass from the reggae music was making the walls vibrate, and it hadn't occurred to you that everyone would be Haitian. Almost the whole time, you and Cléo sat there laughing at the couples making out in the corners. Twice, girls bent down to you and asked you to dance, and suddenly your faces clouded over: no, thank you, you'd just finished track-and-field practice and you were too tired. Maybe later. Several boys paraded by you, hardly any older than you, squinting their eyes and taking long drags on cigarettes they rolled themselves. They gave off an astonishing odour, made you cough, and, apparently, made you dizzy, too. So why did they smoke it, Cléo asked, if it was so disgusting. With glassy eyes and pasty saliva clinging to the corners of his mouth, Carl's big brother replied that, in any case, he'd have to wait till he was in high school to try it. Got it? Then he turned towards you: the same goes for you, Latino.

During recess, instead of staying with the students from the *classe d'accueil*, Cléo preferred the company of Sister Cécile's class, but he insisted that Carl be allowed to join you, too. One day, Cléo accidently kicked a ball that went flying through the air and landed on a girl who had pulled her hood up. She spun around: crap, it's Manon, Sylvain's sister. She was a pretty red-head, used to receiving at least one anonymous love letter a week. Surprised, after a moment's hesitation, she let out a nervous laugh and rubbed her head. Cléo and Carl rushed towards her to get back the ball. Cléo got there first and when he went past Manon, he stopped in his tracks, as if it was the first time he'd seen her. White synthetic fur rimmed her hood and all that could be seen was her delicate face, with its high, red cheekbones. You're so beautiful, Manon! he blurted out. For a moment, Manon looked him in the face as if she was going to answer, but she ran off to join her friends. Carl reacted immediately: no doubt about it, you're starting to get more comfortable around girls, buddy!

The team made up of Cléo, Carl, Akira and you was so far ahead of Sylvain and Evangelos' team, that the two of them kept tripping you right up until the bell rang to end recess. Everyone lined up class by class. In the girls' lines, which for once were more boisterous than the boys', especially grade six B, Manon's class, each one turned to the girl behind her and whispered a few words in her ear. By the time the words reached the grade five boys and Sylvain's own ears, the sentence had nothing to do with its initial, "You're so beautiful, Manon!", but rather came out "You're no beauty, Manon!" In front, the monitor blew his whistle: one after the other, the lines advanced and climbed the stairs. But Sylvain turned on his heels and, when he spotted Cléo, rushed at him. A disorganized mob formed around them.

"What did you say to my sister?"

Cléo shrugged his shoulders: "Nothing. I didn't say anything."

"What? You're not man enough to repeat what you said?"

Cléo froze, he evidently had no idea what he was being accused of. For a moment he turned towards Carl and you. Sylvain didn't dare jump on him, he knew Carl would come to his rescue.

"Come on, just let me hear what you said!"

Manon made her way over to them.

"You think my sister'd want to go out with a guy like you?" Sylvain asked.

And he put an arm around his sister's shoulders: "That's right, isn't it Manon, you wouldn't go out with a dummy like him, would you?"

Manon looked him over from head to toe.

"I don't like guys who just show off when their friends are around."

Yes, Marcelo, in the end, Sylvain's not the one who finally finished him off, it was her. Still afterwards, there were no tears, no attempts to explain, nothing but unvoiced anger. Manon walked away and, to everyone's surprise, Cléo jumped on Sylvain and the two of them ended up on the ground in the snow. Cléo was hammering him with punches, and when the monitor saw the crowd, he didn't guess that it was a fight, and he ordered the students to get back into their lines. Remember his horrified expression when he saw Cléo: stop that right now! What's wrong with him? And Cléo, seeing red, let me hit you, hit you, hit you! The monitor grabbed him and slapped him violently. Cléo responded by struggling to swallow his anger. Sylvain got to his feet: his nose was bleeding and he was sniffling, tears in his eyes. Then the monitor took Cléo by the ear and led him to the principal's office. Come on, you too, Sylvain. Follow me.

In the schoolyard, after that fight, they changed the way they acted towards Cléo: we want you on our team. No, we chose him before you did! Yeah, Cléo we can't wait till you come back from *accueil*, we miss you, buddy. I don't miss you guys at all. It's a lot easier in the *classe d'acceuil*. Carl smiled, you see? What did I tell you?

Now that his math class is over, Flaco goes down the stairs, along the narrow corridor and comes out into the fresh air, a delicious relief filling him. He walks around the edge of the field, watches the match going on, and sits down with his back against the tree where his group usually gets together. The Latino wusses are humiliating the Asian wusses, and he enjoys the pleasure of watching them play: one pass this way, another that way, a tap with the back of a heel, a bounce off a chest, a long efficient pass, if you please . . . *¡Ay, ay, ay!* When he sees him, one of the Latinos waves at him, hi, Flaco, and he simply nods. Soon the ten other players do the same, hi, Flaco: he stands up casually, *hola compadres*. When did people start calling him that? He shakes his head thoughtfully: he doesn't remember anymore. Now, his mother is the only one who calls him Marcelo. When did that happen?

Soon Paulina appears in the distance and he watches her walk: her step is always hurried, as if she's being pushed along by something urgent. The exact opposite of him. She stops, looks vaguely bothered: you been waiting long? No, not at all, and he motions for her to come closer. They share a long kiss on the mouth, as if they were meeting for the first time after a long separation. Since Tuesday, when both of them pretended to be sick in order to miss a day of school, something has changed: the way she looks at him, touches him, behaves around him; she's more self-assured. That day, she arrived at his house early in the morning. They looked at each other shyly from a distance, in the semi-darkness of the hallway, hardly daring to touch each other. Although there was usually no situation that could intimidate her, now her eyes were lowered. Then he put his arms around her and to his great surprise, despite his greedy desire to discover her body, he felt a keen sensation of well-being just from holding her against him. Later, she'd taken off her clothes, then hurried to hide under the covers. Then, when he was naked, too, he pressed himself against her and held her face in his hands. Their mouths brushed up against each other, then they let themselves go, and he felt her relax. Paulina's smell enveloped him, carried him away. After they made love, he confided in her how much he needed her and how he felt funny being naked like that. She held him for a long time and revealed things about herself, too: she started to cry. It was one of the few times he'd seen her cry.

He contemplates her face: why does it always seem like sparks come from her eyes? She turns her back to him, sits down between his legs on the grass, and, in a slightly vague voice, he tells her about his plans: working, getting an apartment, writing. Next September, she asks, are you going to CEGEP? He signed up, but he's not too sure if he'll still feel like it then. They don't talk for a moment, watching the match, then she sighs: she doesn't think they spend enough time together. He thinks to himself that she's not really wrong. It's true, Lalo, Teta or one of the girls go with them everywhere they go. It's stupid, because he'd rather to be alone with her, too. He promises to take her to the movies on Saturday.

The noon bell interrupts their conversation. They stand up, pick the dead leaves off their sweaters, go to their lockers to get their lunch and then go to the cafeteria: Paulina branches off towards the table where the Latinas are sitting, he goes towards the Latino Power table. He shakes everyone's hand, takes a seat between Lalo and Pato, and takes out two sandwiches and a peach. Look, says Lalo, shoving a flyer under his nose. He reads: *Mega-Party, Friday April 26, put on by the Polyvalente Saint-Luc.* He shrugs his shoulders, picks up a sandwich and takes a big bite from it. Doesn't that sound fun? asks Lalo, it's tomorrow, and with his mouth full he answers yeah, maybe. Lalo tells him his mother ran across the old running shoes he lent him. As planned, he told her that they'd just exchanged shoes for a few days. Your shoes are in such bad shape, she was pretty pissed off, buddy. That's why, if she calls, he can't forget to explain to his own mother that it was just a trade. Just in case. Okay, Flaco? And he said, yeah, yeah, no problem.

They eat staring at the girls three tables away. Suddenly, Dupaulin, the English teacher, makes an entrance into the cafeteria and all heads turn towards him. He goes past the tables and then hugs the back wall with his nose in the air as if he can't bring himself to breathe the air they're breathing. Suddenly, out of nowhere, an egg sandwich falls on his grey vest. The teacher stops, his toothbrush moustache dancing, and squints his eyes. Not a single student budges. He gives them the finger and goes on his way as if nothing happened. Thunderous boos ring out, a dozen sandwiches are tossed at him. Two or three reach their mark as he continues to walk, barely taking cover, and then disappears into the teachers' cafeteria. Flaco saw that the first missile had come from the Bad Boys' table. The scene has been repeated every day since, at the beginning of the week, Dupaulin kicked Mixon out, because he'd raised his hand and asked, as seriously as possible, how to say "senile old man" in English.

Even though Dupaulin is no longer in the area, food continues to criss-cross the cafeteria. Little by little, the Bad Boys shift their target towards the Latino Power table. They retaliate, of course, throwing whatever is at hand. Soon the cafeteria is transformed into a huge battlefield where tomato juice, egg sandwiches, chocolate pudding, carrot and celery sticks sail through the air. The monitors come running, punish randomly, treat some students harshly. When the ammunitions run out, they settle down, consider the damage, wipe their faces and try to rub out the stains. With empty stomachs, they end up angry with themselves for having wasted their lunches. Several stand, beside themselves, search their pockets and stride towards the vending machines. But Eugène, one of the monitors, makes them sit back down. He still hasn't noticed he's walking around with a slice of ham on his receding hairline. Out of breath from running, he questions, "Who started all this? I demand that he stand up right now!"

Laughter rings out here and there. His fists on his hips, he spins around as if trying to catch the students behind him red-handed. It's obvious he's new at being a monitor, Flaco thinks. Then the more experienced monitor Gino enters the cafeteria with a determined stride. He walks over to the other man, relieves him of his slice of ham, which he throws on the ground, and whispers a few words into his ear. Then he addresses the students in a slow, almost affable voice, "I'm going to expel the next person who laughs or talks."

Now, they avoid his eyes.

"This is the last time we're going easy on you," he continues. "The next time there's a food fight, I don't care if I have to kick out fifteen of you morons, I'm going to do it."

He surveys them with a hostile look.

"If anyone knows something but is afraid to speak out, they can come see us in the principal's office."

For a moment, Gino speaks to Eugène in a low voice, then he leaves. Little by little the cafeteria empties out. The Bad Boys get to their feet, walk past the Latinos, whispering insults. The Latinos reply almost automatically, *¡huevones, maricones de mierda!* As soon as they're out of sight, Lalo says to Flaco, "Did you see? They really think we're afraid of them, that they terrify us. If we have to fight them bare-fisted, if we have to use knives, I'll be the first in line."

"Okay, okay," Flaco says, "I get it. It doesn't do any good to get worked up."

"We need a detailed plan," Teta suggests.

"I agree," Lalo seconds. "Breaking windows isn't enough. I still haven't got my sneakers back."

"Have you noticed that since we broke CB's living room windows and his father chased us around an entire block, they've been pretty quiet? I think those guys are up to something. Don't you think so?"

"Pato's right," Flaco says. "We have to do something to them before they do something to us. But what? That's the question."

Flaco takes the flyer from the table and hits it with the back of his hand.

"That's it! If I know them, they'll be at that party tomorrow, and they'll all be wearing their leather jackets for sure. Here's the plan. During the party, we'll steal their coats. It'll put us in a good position to negotiate: they'll have to give us back the shoes and the watch they stole."

"That's a good idea," Teta say, "because all you have to do is give those guys a little rap music and they'll dance for hours, they won't have anything else on their minds at all. World War Three could break out and they wouldn't notice."

"Exactly," Flaco agrees. "While they're dancing, we'll sneak into the coatroom and bang! we'll steal them!"

"Yeah!" Pato brightens up. "Christ, that's a good idea!"

"How are you going to do that?" asks Lalo. "We can't just walk into the coatroom and take whatever we want. They always have someone there watching it."

"That's true," Flaco answers. "But have you ever noticed who they usually put in there? It's always a girl. I'm telling you, it can't fail. One of us will distract her for a little while and in the meantime, the others will take the coats. It's as simple as that."

"I'll be the one to distract her," Teta says enthusiastically. "I'll cruise her like she's never been cruised before. I'll take her flowers and say things like, '*amorcito, te quiero, te amo, mi sol . . .*' She'll wet her panties!"

The others shake their heads and laugh.

"You can't just cruise her," Flaco specifies, "she has to leave the coatroom for a little while."

"No problem," Teta says. "I'll take care of it. I'll just have to take her outside and give her a good French kiss."

This time, the others look at him in disbelief.

"What? What's the matter?"

"The matter is that you're always thinking about having fun," Flaco explains, "and none of us trusts you. Right now, I think it would be better if someone else distracts the girl. You prove yourself and then we'll give you better jobs to do."

"I know the girl who's going to be in the coatroom pretty well," Pato says. "She's in my class. She's Vietnamese."

"I'll say he knows her pretty well!" Lalo says. "She's always calling him at home. So much so my mother's about to talk to her and tell her to leave her poor little Pato alone. Anyway, that girl's crazy about him."

"Super," Flaco says. "You sure she'll be the one?"

"I'm telling you, she's always asking me if I'm going to be at the party."

"Good. But listen to me good, Pato. You have to know one thing. The job you have to do is dangerous. You have to have nerves of steel. After the robbery, you'll have to meet back up with us, without getting caught."

"No problem. I'm in."

"It's cool then," Flaco says.

"What about me?" Teta asks. "What am I supposed to be do-ing all that time? Am I supposed to stand around with my fingers up my nose the whole night?"

"Calm down," Flaco stops him. "You watch Pato and you tell us when the coast is clear."

Like a ball leaking air, Teta lets out a long, exasperated sigh.

"You always manage to give me the stupidest jobs! Do you do it on purpose or what?"

The others turn away to hide their laughter. Then it's Flaco's turn to hiss at him, "That's what you're going to do. If you're not happy about it, don't come. That's it. I'm sick of your blubbering."

Teta chomps at the bit, chewing on an imaginary piece of gum. To the others, Flaco adds, "One last thing. Between now and tomorrow night, we're going to stay cool. If one of the Bad Boys starts bugging you, suck it up and take his insults without saying anything. They can't think anything's up tomorrow."

The only light in your room came from the little TV where mon-keys were jumping from tree to tree trying to grab coconuts hang-ing from palm trees. Sitting cross-legged, a few centimetres from the screen, Cléo twisted the joystick, as if hypnotized. "You have now reached step number two," a voice said, and a short tune be-gan and played through three times. He was wearing a grey vest, a white shirt and a black silk tie. Suddenly, the monkey slipped into a ditch, a dozen coconuts fell on his head and the words *Game Over* flashed on the screen. Cléo began a new game. When he came to your house, it was always the same thing: since he didn't have Super Nintendo at home, he hogged the game and you had no choice but to watch him play. "You have now reached step number one."

You walked over to the window and contemplated the big snowflakes falling in slow motion, the tires of a skidding Toyota whose driver never let up on the gas. As Sister Cécile said,

107

Christmas without snow wasn't Christmas. "You have now reached step number two." Because you'd left Chile when you were too young to have any concrete memories, you couldn't imagine a Christmas with thirty-degree temperatures, under palm trees, like the ones your cousins told you about in their letters. You went out of your room, you went to the end of the hallway and, since the bathroom door was wide open, you saw your father: Roberto was adjusting his tie in the mirror and looking at his profile, as if he was checking that he'd done a good job shaving. He looked you over from head to toe.

"Did you tie your tie all by yourself?"

"All by myself. Mom taught me how last week when we went out to celebrate Uncle Juan's birthday."

"Is your friend okay?"

Without waiting for you to reply, Roberto added, "Tell him we won't be much longer. We're leaving in five minutes."

When you got back to your room, Cléo had stopped playing and the room was in darkness. After a few seconds, you were able to make out the edges of the furniture and distinguish Cléo's shape contrasted against the bluish background of the window. You turned on the lights.

"You thinking about your mother?"

Cléo turned to face you, "Did you see the guy outside whose car's stuck? I think it's Akira's father."

You came closer, "Oh, yeah! I hadn't noticed it was his car."

"Akira told me that for Christmas, his father, him and some friends eat out at a restaurant. That's how they celebrate Christmas."

"That's because they're not Catholic. Akira wanted to have his confirmation so he could be with us, but Sister Cécile said he couldn't. He isn't baptized."

You sat down on the bed.

"You think your mother will get over it?"

"Don't worry about it, Marcelo."

"You sure?"

"Yeah. Yesterday when I told her I wanted to spend Christmas with you, we had a long talk and she kept telling me over and over: what do you think, it's the first Christmas I ever spent alone? Of course everything's going to be fine, what do you think? And she said, anyways, holidays never meant anything to her. She even said it would do her good to be alone for a while. That she was going to read."

"She's pretending she doesn't have any feelings. But deep down, she's sad. I even think she would have liked for things to work out with your dad."

"I already told you not to mention your father to me," Carole had said. "That bastard will never set foot in this house again. And you can be sure of that!"

"You see," you said, "if she doesn't want you to mention him, it's because she's still mad. Tell me something, Cléo. One minute your father came back home and it looked like everything was going fine. The next minute, your mother kicked him out. What happened?"

"It's because of another woman," Cléo answered. "A friend of my parents'. The only one who ever came to see my mother sometimes. Do you remember Mrs. Toussaint, from my birthday? Maryse Toussaint?"

"If that woman dares to call," Carole had said, "you hang up on her. I don't want to hear her excuses or have her feeling sorry for me."

"Yes, I remember," you said. "She seemed really nice. She played with us and everything. And she seemed to get along so well with your mother."

"Hypocrite!" Carole had said. "Now I understand why she was doing me all those favours. I'll help you with this, I'll help you with that . . . It was just a façade, a game."

"And your mother really isn't going to give your father any more chances?" you asked.

109

"Never," Carole had said. "She can keep that man if she wants to. Too bad for her. She doesn't know who she's teaming up with, the poor thing."

"I think it's that my father doesn't want to come back to my mother," Cléo explained. "He told me he couldn't take her anymore, that she'd become too bitter. You know, when someone is in a bad mood all the time."

"I should have acted sooner," Carole had said, "I could see it coming. Since my car accident in Port-au-Prince, he's become more and more distant. My God, what am I going to do . . ."

"How did she find out about the other woman? Did he tell her?"

"No," Cléo answered, "no way. One night, he came home drunk. My mother was already asleep and he slipped into bed as quietly as he could so he wouldn't wake her up. He didn't know my mother wasn't sleeping. After five minutes, he started snoring. My mother shook him cause she wanted to talk to him, and that's when he said, 'Maryse, please, let me sleep. . . .'"

"Ah!" you said in a low voice.

Finally, Carmen appeared in the doorway, wearing an evening dress and some discreet jewellery.

"Ready to go?"

You'd put on your coats in the entryway and you'd pulled up your hoods as you went out, to protect yourselves from the dry wind that was lifting up snow like gusts of sand.

When you'd asked your parents if Cléo could celebrate Christmas with you, Roberto had let out an annoyed sigh. He alleged that, since Cléo didn't know Spanish, he wouldn't be able to follow the conversations and therefore he'd be bored. Carmen began to pace around the kitchen with restless strides, waving her hands: was there anything sadder than a child spending Christmas alone? Think a little about what that boy is going through right now. Don't just think about yourself, you selfish so-and-so. Okay, here's what I recommend, sighed Roberto, his gaze

110

contorting. It's okay for him to come, but in the middle of the evening, don't ask me to take him home cause he's bored. *¿Está claro?*

The car skidded a couple of times as it climbed Côte-des-Neiges, almost did a 360 when it turned onto Queen Mary and rattled into the parking lot of the Auberge. The Latin American Club of Quebec had got into the habit of celebrating holidays there, at the foot of St. Joseph's Oratory, where the priests charged a reasonable rent. When you'd arrived, mass had already begun and Carmen hid behind your father so she wouldn't be recognized. You found seats at the back, and Roberto pointed out to you the local celebrities in the front rows, most of them community businessmen who'd set up establishments on Rue Bélanger or Boulevard Saint-Laurent. That was Don Salazar, owner of the travel agency El condor pasa, Don Balmaceda, owner of the chic restaurant Bolívar and Doctors Ponce and Gutiérrez, both tall fellows with long moustaches and greying temples.

During his sermon, Father Louis Cardinal, rector of Saint-Pascal, ex-missionary in South America, a thin sixty-year-old with pink skin and bright eyes, came down from the platform, leaning on the altar. Remember how the community loved him, especially for his tireless efforts to help refugees. He was the antithesis of Father Daoust, who refused to say mass in Spanish. Addressing us in Spanish with a slight Québécois accent, he asked the "more affluent" to create a climate of solidarity in the heart of the community and to reach out a hand to the "new arrivals and those who were more destitute." *¿Entienden?* The front rows nodded their heads and solemnly closed their eyes.

When mass was over, the altar was removed, tables were set up, and people hurried to cover them with tablecloths and place four chairs around each one. Then the buffet was laid out, and the women sucked in their breath, *¡ay qué rico!* The food was spread over four long tables: there was a huge *parillada*, Chilean and Bolivian *empanadas*, *humitas*, avocados served with raw

111

vegetables and shrimp, and all kinds of salads. The "more afflu-ent," grouped around the tables near the organizers, where Father Cardinal also stood, raised their glasses of red wine for toasts that would start sententiously, but invariably concluded with humorous remarks about their weaknesses for women and wine. A *¡salud!* in unison came next, then a burst of applause would shake the room.

Remember the meal, so long, copious and exhausting, Marcelo. You boys couldn't keep still any longer: in a burst of energy too long contained you started a furious race. At eleven-fifteen the tables were taken down and the room was transformed into an immense dance floor with subdued light-ing. The musicians set up their equipment, did a sound check and then played *cumbia* after *cumbia*, *merengue* after *merengue*, *cueca* after *cueca*. Zigzagging between the couples wiggling their hips, you were playing tag and Cléo was so fast no one could catch him. An older boy, visibly offended, persisted in chasing him and Cléo, spinning around, came nose-to-nose with a woman who was carrying the leftovers from the buffet and was unable to avoid him. They both collapsed to the floor amidst the clatter of dishes. The dress the woman, Aunt Glo-ria, was wearing was stained. She got up brusquely, ready to yell at the boy, but when she saw it was Cléo, she held back her scolding. Juan, her husband, already pretty drunk, stared at the dress dripping with sauce: *¿qué pasa? ¿qué pasa? Rien, querido*, just an accident, Carmen explained, as she hurried to pick up the spilled food. What did she mean, nothing? And Carmen stood up suddenly: it's just an accident, don't make a big deal out of it, okay?

After that, since you weren't allowed to run anymore, you went to hang out, as if by chance, near where the girls were. A mocking light crossed the eyes of Carolina, Juan's daughter, who asked you to play spin the bottle. What? You both said in unison, your hearts thudding. No, thank you, not here, not in front of the parents. Was she crazy? But Carolina, standing sideways, with her arms crossed, smiled suggestively: you chicken or what? Us, chicken? You're nuts! You huddled like football players planning the game before setting foot on the field, and Cléo stepped forward, suave and cool as a cat: Okay, we'll play, and we'll see who's afraid of who. When the bottle stopped spinning, the boy and the girl it was pointing at got up and kissed on the mouth for at least ten seconds. From time to time, an adult went by, looked at you out of the corner of their eye for a moment, then moved on smiling. All this time, the women's dresses were sweeping across the dance floor, one more lively than the next, while around the edges, people were gossiping non-stop.

The bottom and the neck of the bottle pointed towards Cléo and Carolina. She was first on her feet, her cheeks on fire, her eyes gleaming with momentary boldness: I never tried with a Black guy. All around the circle, children coughed, they giggled, they watched Cléo closely. Well, said one of the boys, the time's come. Cléo then got up, they took a step towards each other and delicately brought their lips together. After a moment, they were rubbing each other's backs as they kissed. Whistles burst out, jokes shot back and forth, prompting laughter that caused heads to turn. Juan staggered over and watched them for a second, his eyelids half-closed. The breath coming from his mouth as it hung loosely open smelled of alcohol. What are you doing? he asked his daughter, momentarily losing his balance. Don't you respect yourself anymore, *niñita*? Not hearing him, the two hugged each other harder, and Juan tried with difficulty to separate them. Then he grabbed Carolina's arm, pulled her towards him and insulted her, but she immediately pushed him away and pinched her nostrils. Not fazed in the least, Juan squinted at Cléo who, without blinking, met his gaze. It was as if Cléo was whispering: you don't scare me, sir. Who invited you? Juan questioned him in

113

his lazy voice. And, Marcelo, you were the one who answered: I invited him. What's the problem? Tell him to take it easy or he'd better watch out. What did he do? You kidding me or what? Juan said, as he gave a little laugh. You saw what he did. Remember the blood beating in your temples and the strength that came from who knows where and gradually took you over. Spilling out all your bile, you showered thinly veiled insults on your Uncle Juan: he was nothing but a *borracho*, a drunk! All he ever thought about was drinking! Be quiet, Marcelo, or else you're gonna get it, *caramba*! Then the shoving, then the music suddenly stopped, the dancers came to a standstill: what's going on, *por el amor de Dios?* There was no stopping your Uncle Juan: didn't everyone see that these kids were just a gang of degenerates! Roberto held him back while Father Cardinal raised his arms as if begging the heavens: come, come, *amigos*, it was the most important day of the year, they weren't going to spoil it over such a little thing, were they? In the disorder and confusion, Cléo got away from him and went to sit out of the way, hidden behind a speaker. He avoided everyone's eyes. Finally, the crowd broke up. Juan left without saying goodbye, and his wife, with a great many smiles and low bows, apologized profusely: my husband isn't feeling well, he doesn't believe what he said, I promise you.

The rest of the evening Cléo stayed in his corner and whenever someone came over to offer him juice or a dessert he'd reply by shaking his head. At about two o'clock, Roberto rushed in holding the four coats at the end of his arm: it was time to go. In the car, with the heater on high, he abruptly turned towards Carmen: you see, I told you it was a mistake! At the first traffic light, he hit the steering wheel several times and turned his head towards the frosty car window: but no, you always have to have things your way! Without replying, looking straight ahead of her as the snowflakes, as bristly as stars, flattened against the windshield, Carmen shook her head as if to say no, no, no. In

114

the back seat, you and Cléo remained silent as well. The car stopped in front of his building and, as he pulled the handle to open the door, you put a hand on his shoulder, but he shook it off: shut up, I don't want to hear anything from you. Yes, remember: from that moment, something – what exactly? – broke forever.

V

His head is spinning, pain drills his temples, and his eyes follow the cars sweeping their headlights along Côte-des-Neiges. On the other side of the street, his primary school, surrounded by a metal fence, hidden by leafless trees. Flaco thinks: at night it looks like a prison. Sister Cécile comes to his mind, with her slightly wavy grey hair, her sky blue smock and her thin-framed glasses. Is she still alive? She really used to bore them to death with her religious obsessions. And what about Akira, how was he doing in New York? And that disrespectful Sylvain? A number of families, more clear-headed than his own, had moved out of the neighbourhood. That was the solution. Someone tugs on the sleeve of his sweater, the bottle of wine has come around to him again. A few members of Latino Power are sitting comfortably on the bench, while others like him are standing and from time to time they shift the weight of their bodies from one foot to the other. Flaco considers them: does he look as disillusioned as they do? He tilts the bottle up over his mouth and takes a long gulp. On a bench to the left, a dozen metres away, some East Indians or Pakistanis have been watching them, as if they were trying to follow their conversation. They're the latest arrivals in the neighbourhood: they don't know what lies ahead, poor guys.

Lalo steps forward to speak, but for a moment he remains unable to string words together, wipes his red-wine-stained mouth with his palm. He stammers: he can't wait for the robbery. Yesterday and today, he'd had to let some Haitians make fun of him about Sunday's extortion, and he wasn't able to fight back. Teta suddenly straightens up and adds: he can't wait to see their faces after the robbery. My leather jacket! he wails, my leather jacket!

The others laugh half-heartedly, stiffly. Lalo upends the empty bottle and reddish foam trickles from its mouth. He pretends to take aim and throws the bottle hard. It hits the metal rim of the trash can, smashing into a thousand pieces. The East Indians mutter some guttural sounds. Right away Lalo gives them the finger. The East Indians hesitate, then give him one back. The two groups insult each other for a little while, everything's fair game, their mothers, their countries, their race, the Latinos in French, the East Indians in English. And Flaco gestures to his group: that's enough, guys, it's time to go.

They step off the grass and onto the sidewalk, skirt around Parc Kent. How many bottles did they drink? Three, four? In the darkness, they advance side by side, some keep their heads down, others puff out their chests and inhale the cold air. Despite the wine, their aggressive manners and pitiless words, Flaco knows their guts are squirming with fear. He starts to cross the road and, when he reaches the yellow line down the middle, bravado pushes him to take long strides towards the cars, whose horns start to howl on the spot. Yes, these are the times when he feels alive, when his existence is transformed into an unpredictable adventure. Outside the entrance to the Église-Saint-Pascal, dozens of students are already gathering. Some are smoking in groups, others wait in the lineup. Muted pounding, coming from inside, keeps the beat. Flaco steps into the lineup, the others follow suit. Carefree, it seems to them their happiness could last. Around him, rockers, rappers, straight kids, alternative kids, punks, skins, no sign of the Bad Boys.

Suddenly, from behind the church, Paulina and Nena appear. The latter is smoking a cigarette, but not Paulina. They wave at a group of Vietnamese girls, chat with them for a moment and, noticing the others, walk over with slow, deliberate steps. Flaco studies Paulina and, suddenly, he thinks her delicate features seem identical to a little girl's. He kisses her and leans heavily on her. You've been drinking! She wipes her mouth and he smiles, shrugging his shoulders. She shakes her head as if she's about to get angry, but finally she smiles, too. Doesn't he have a coat, she worries. It's chilly out, no? No, it's right in the middle of spring, can't she see? She gives him a funny look: you're really drunk, Flaco. As the line advances, he turns his back to her, stares at the cross on the church façade, and feels a burn of reproach on the back of his neck.

When he turns around again, she and Nena have disappeared. Did she leave or has she gone into the basement? Harassed by remorse, he forces himself to get it out of his mind by thinking of something else. They wait a while and, just before they go in, to mask their breath, Teta hands out gum. At the till, Gino sniffs them, is he dreaming or does he smell alcohol? He looks like a bulldog, Flaco thinks, taking care to keep his distance and pretending to be annoyed: of course you're dreaming, man. Gino looks them over and points his finger at them: no trouble today, get it? Flaco pays, don't worry, takes his change, we'll be good as gold, and extends the back of his hand to be stamped. The others snigger and Gino bristles: at the first sign of anything, I'm throwing you out, *capito*? Lalo goes in first and turns away to hide his irresistible desire to laugh: no need to get hysterical yet, at least wait until we do something wrong. Gino meets his eyes for a moment and in one voice Latino Power erupts in *iay ay ay!* Gino ain't in a good mood today! You're tough, you're tough! No kidding, you look like a killer, Gino!

It's dark and dry ice floats above the dance floor. Flaco can just make out the faces of a few shadows moving like bats between the cones of red, green and blue lights. They walk past the coatroom, and behind the counter, a little Vietnamese girl with smooth hair waves her hand when she notices Pato. He waves back, walks on with the others towards the dance floor and makes his way through the crowd. Two huge speakers, reigning over each side of the entrance, are making the floor vibrate. Latino Power forms a circle and begins to dance discreetly, then Teta shakes his head, pretending to hold an electric guitar in his hands. Then they get rowdy, just for fun. Paulina, with three other girls on her heels, enters the room, but doesn't join them: the girls dance together near the speaker in the back. Where had she gone? Is she mad at him, or what?

Half an hour passes and Flaco feels his headache getting worse. I'm starting to get sick of dancing. Suddenly, Lalo puts one arm around his shoulders: *compadre*, look who's going up to the coatroom. Through a haze of smoke tinted by the different lights, Flaco can make out CB and his associates taking off their leather jackets. See, Flaco says, I was sure they'd be wearing them. One by one, the Bad Boys start towards the dance floor, notice the members of Latino Power and turn back to confer with each other. What can they be saying to each other? B.S., probably, but he'd still give anything to be able to listen in. Finally, all of them, including Ketcia, head towards the men's washroom. They're going to smoke a joint. Okay, it's the perfect moment.

Flaco gives Pato a discreet signal and he heads off to the coatroom, climbing the stairs two by two, then he orders Teta to get into position opposite the washroom door, so he can warn them when the Bad Boys come out. The plan's in motion, there's no going back now. Flaco sees Pato lean over the counter and whisper sweet things in the Vietnamese girl's ear. She can't stop smiling. He hadn't lied, she really looks like she's in love with him. But is he going to be able to get her away from there? He takes her by the shoulders and tries to kiss her on the neck, but she shakes her head no three, four times and pushes him away with a laugh. Pato laughs, too, the way he doubles over is a bad sign: he's too drunk to be a great ladies' man. He whispers something in her ear, points to the exit and, a few seconds later, comes towards Flaco: I told her I had something important to tell her, but I could only say it outside, alone. As soon as the coatroom clears out, she promised to come. Flaco gives the thumbs up: Okay, hurry up.

Five, six interminable minutes go by, and the Vietnamese girl still hasn't left her post. To think that from one second to the next the Haitians could come out of the washroom and screw everything up. *Dios mío*, really, wanting to steal their coats is crazy! What a stupid idea! What got into him? But now the Asian girl is climbing the stairs leading to the entrance. She's running to meet her sweet little Pato in seventh heaven, Flaco thinks. Over by Teta, everything's looking great. Perfect! The members of Latino Power quickly join up, then walk to the coatroom, hugging the wall. They jump the counter and Flaco shuts off the lights to avoid attracting attention. On all fours, they look for the coats, but it's so dark they can hardly make out their own feet. Flaco is angry with himself for not foreseeing this inconvenience, a flashlight would have been a good idea. This slows them down terribly: in order to see them, they have to bring the coats over to the light one by one. Finally, Lalo whispers, almost choking: *¡aqui están!* He takes a garbage bag out of his pocket and slides the coats in. There's no one else around except Teta, who's still standing guard outside the washroom, his arms crossed.

At the very back of the coatroom, Lalo and Flaco pull up the blinds. Each one of them tries to open one of the big wooden windows. With all his might, Flaco tries to turn the latch. It doesn't budge. The two of them have to work on one window together. There, the latch is giving way! When they motion for Teta to come closer, Mixon comes out of the washroom, looking like a surprised bird. He eyes Teta, insults him, and the Latino, keeping cool, motions with his hands for the other boy to stay calm. Still,

Mixon keeps insulting him heartily, as if he suspected something was going on behind his back. He glances again at the coatroom, ventures over to the counter, places his hands on it, stretches his neck, but he can't make them out: on all fours on the ground, they force themselves not to move, holding their breath in the darkness. Mixon turns back towards Teta, bellows in his face, sends him flying with a push, but, surprisingly, Teta keeps his cool. Again, his eyes are drawn towards the coatroom and, again, he steps over to the counter. Flaco looks up: *¡putamadre!* one of the blinds keeps banging in the wind.

Teta tries to hold him back, but Mixon eludes him like a cat and jumps the counter. Desperate, Teta shouts in his direction, waving his arms as if he's directing traffic, but the other feels his way forward, drawn on by the moving blind. Despite the frantic rhythm of the music in the background, despite the intense buzzing in his ears, Flaco distinctly hears the blind beating against the window above his head ever more loudly. Mixon is searching through the coats, knocking more and more of them to the floor. He stumbles over someone's leg – is it Lalo's? – but he doesn't fall. That's it, he looks down and Lalo grabs his hand and pulls him towards them on the floor. Teta comes over and they jump on Mixon like piranhas: they put a hand over his mouth, and pin his arms and his feet. He struggles, he tries to bite, but Flaco notices he's having a hard time keeping his eyes open. Yeah, he was right, they were smoking up. He keeps fighting to free his hands and, exasperated, Flaco puts a hand on his throat and squeezes: calm down for Christ's sake! If he does what they say, nothing will happen to him!

Mixon frees one of his arms and, in a lucky break, punches Lalo right in the face. The Latino goes still for a moment, tears come to his eyes, pain contorts his features, blood spurts from his nose. On edge, Flaco slaps Mixon: calm down right now, will you! He climbs onto his stomach, face to face with him, while, behind him, Lalo holds his arms as best he can. Suddenly, Mixon writhes in pain, as if he were shaken by a sharp, tenacious, devastating spasm. *Dios mío*, what happened to him? For an instant, Flaco thinks he's having an attack, that he can't breathe. Dammit, he's stopped moving! He places one hand flat on his chest: his heart is still beating. That's when he sees Lalo putting his knife back in his pocket: that'll teach you, you Black bastard, that'll teach you. No way! It's not true, right? Teta steps back, as if terrified: you crazy or what? And Lalo tries to explain: he kicked my ass, he made me bleed, the bastard! Flaco is paralyzed, dizzying images are flying through his mind. Moron! he finally roars in a low voice. You didn't have to do that, *¡huevón!* Lalo suddenly loses his heroic look. Flaco shakes Mixon to wake him up, but he's probably fainted. Now what are they going to do, *putamadre*? What can they do? He takes a deep breath, blots his forehead with his sweater. Lalo looks sorry: I made sure just to shank him in the arm. Flaco starts to insult him, but he gets hold of himself. One thing's for sure, they have no time to lose. He jumps up: come on, hurry up, we're outa here, we have no choice. He picks up the garbage bag, looks back at Mixon one last time, the Black boy is lying on the floor, his mouth half open, his legs spread apart, as a puddle of blood grows around him. One after the other, they climb up on the radiator and slip outside. Flaco hides the bag in the bushes next to the church. No, he shouldn't think about it, but he keeps seeing Mixon's broken body. He looks at Lalo, as he staggers, pale, strangely hugging his chest with his arms. They walk around the church, looking for Pato, but they bump into a group of Paulina's friends. But neither she nor Nena are there, they must have gone home. There, sitting on the church steps, Pato's chatting naturally as anything with the Vietnamese girl. They climb the stairs, lean towards him and whisper that it's time to go, but he's so drunk he doesn't seem to understand what they're telling him. Off to one side, the Vietnamese girl suggests to Flaco that he take Pato home. They take him by the shoulders and they go down the stairs one at a time. They go back around the church in the opposite direction, retrieve the bag, and take off as fast as they can. On the way, Flaco realizes he's shivering, that his sweater is soaked with sweat. After they've covered a good distance, made it to Rue Barclay and the church is far behind them, Lalo asks them to take a break for a minute: he doesn't feel right, guys. He leans against a car and, after a few dry heaves, pressing his arms against his stomach, he pukes his guts out.

On Saturday the lanes at Barclay Bowling and its recently opened arcade were crawling with people. Retired people, mostly Jewish, played games of ten-pin that would stretch for whole afternoons, while the teens, whether they were Latinos or Arabs or Haitians or Asians, huddled around the video games. Since you were able to practise at home with your Super Nintendo, you were one notch better than Akira at Mortal Kombat. You won another game and when Akira saw his warrior's remains catch fire, he gave the machine a violent kick. Afraid he'd been seen, he looked worriedly around: with his back to them, the owner was chewing out one of his employees as he made a long serious of hand gestures. Akira asked you what time it was and, having slipped another two quarters into the machine, you quickly glanced at your watch before you started the next game: it was four in the afternoon. Can you believe it, Akira sighed, the guy was an hour and a half late.

You answered simply with a nod: it was by no means the first time Cléo had done this to you. Let's see, twice last week, one other time this week, yeah, that was right, this was the fourth time he'd left you hanging like this. Since January, although you called each other every two or three days, you saw him less often. According to what he said, Cléo didn't have a second to himself anymore: either he had to help his mother with the housework or go with her to do the shopping, or finish his homework, or go visit his father, and on and on. One night, he went so far as to say he

123

had to walk his neighbour Mrs. Masaryk's dog. That was the last straw. You knew for a fact that Cléo and his mother hated the woman since, as soon as they put on a little music, she'd start relentlessly beating on the wall with her broom. Who knows, he may even have told you another lie this morning: at his teacher's request, he had to go to makeup classes . . . on weekends. As soon as he was done, he'd come meet you at Barclay Bowling, cross his heart and hope to die. It was hard to sort things out, because, after all, there had to be a little truth in what he said, didn't there? Since his mother had found a job in a factory on the Main that made baby clothes, it's true, she demanded his help more frequently, so she'd have time to paint at night.

Carole had realized she couldn't earn a living by simply selling her paintings. She was also sick of being closed up all the time within the four walls of the living room which, at night, was transformed into her studio. It was becoming suffocating, she said. Cléo told you that, when Tony, the owner of the factory saw her come off the elevator, he told her from the doorway that he had no work for her and she could get out of here. But Carole refused to be intimidated: it was always the same old story, because she was in a wheelchair nobody wanted her. Well, she wasn't going to take it! No, sir! She'd heard there was work and if he didn't give her a chance, she'd make a complaint. Everyone would know. Tony hesitated, then approached with a smile that exposed every single one of his ruined teeth: ah, she was a fighter, that was a quality he didn't mind. Okay, he'd give her a try. But he was warning her, if she couldn't keep up with the others she'd be shown the door *rápido*: he wasn't the kind to feel sorry for people. After a week, coming up from behind, Tony surprised the other employees, hunched over their sewing machines, and grasped their shoulders: you should be ashamed, girls! Carole is faster than all of you! It was strange, Cléo said, as if he was talking to himself, since she'd started working, it was like Carole was enjoying life again. Sometimes, really early in the morning, he could hear her whistling. I swear, man! But he'd better not kid himself, Carole pointed out to her son, it wasn't that she liked her job. It was just that after all life had handed her lately, the job gave her something else to think about.

The only visits Carole ever received were from some old Haitian friends, a couple named Sarrazin. She should see her work as a temporary job, Mrs. Sarrazin insisted, all immigrants had to do the same thing, they themselves had gone through hard times in the beginning. Luck would eventually smile upon her, Carole, she shouldn't worry. Once she was in a stable financial situation, she'd be able to find a job in visual arts. Then she'd even be able to leave this neighbourhood, Mr. Sarrazin ventured. What did she think? Yes, Carole answered, she was tired of dealing with the cockroaches. Still, she also knew the Sarrazins visited her husband and his mistress, so she always managed to get some information about them out of the old couple. By the way, had they seen any of their other old friends lately? The Sarrazins would look at each other in embarrassment, then Mrs. Sarrazin would come and sit near Carole: I'd rather not talk about your husband, it makes me feel like a spy. No, no, go ahead, I'm telling you, it doesn't bother me at all anymore. Then, seeing that Mrs. Sarrazin still wasn't talking, she'd lay a hand across hers: she shouldn't be silly! She wasn't even mad at her husband anymore! Mrs. Sarrazin sighed, okay, but I warned you! Listen, Carole, he wants a divorce, but he's afraid to ask you. Then Carole smiled like she'd just been given a death sentence: what an idiot, I'll give it to him right away! Did you bring the papers? Give them to me right away and we'll be done with all this! And Mr. Sarrazin stiffened, ah, no, we're just playing messenger, not lawyers. It was a hard enough role as it was! You can take care of the paperwork with each other. Suddenly, Carole's face went dark, and quietly she kept repeating to no one in particular: I'll give him a divorce right now if that's what he wants.

As for Cléo, he'd found a new way to pass the time. Since he'd stopped helping you deliver the Saturday papers, the *Gazette* had given him Avenue Lavoie. With his digital watch, he'd time himself. One day, he'd burst into the entrance of one of the apartment buildings and he'd run into Guylain, the incorrigible neighbourhood wino, who was snoring, curled up, under some newspaper. Cléo had wanted to get away, but Guylain woke up suddenly, stretched his arms over his head and, rubbing one eye with the back of his hand: hey, I wanna talk to you! Don't be scared, son. He got up with some difficulty. He squinted his eyes and showed him his thumb: I see you go by every morning, you're fast as hell. His eyes examined him for a long time, in a way he meant to be penetrating: I'm telling you, one day, you'll be in the Olympics. I never saw anybody fly like you. Cléo smiled at the compliment and prepared to leave, but the man held him back by his coattail: why is it in the hundred metres, there are only Blacks, eh? Guylain bent over conspiratorially, his face shaken by strange tics. Cléo shrugged his shoulders, no idea, sir. I have to go now. As he was going up the stairs he again heard Guylain's nasal voice: you don't know anything, punk, you think you know everything, but you don't know a thing.

Since he liked running too much to turn it into an obligation, he only trained when he felt like it. He understood that with that attitude he'd never be a great athlete and it really didn't bother him much. What are you talking about, you said angrily one day on the phone, in every competition, you're the best, I'm telling you, you've got a chance. Maybe, but he wanted to do something else with his life, he didn't know what yet. In the meantime, the Jeux de Montréal were fast approaching, and he couldn't wait. For the time being, what interested him was having fun! Things had been going pretty well for him since he'd started hanging out with Carl: nobody teased him at school anymore. He finally had some respect.

You and Akira sat down on a long wooden bench, facing the bowling alley to watch the games. Half an hour later, you saw Cléo nonchalantly coming down the entryway stairs, Carl and another Haitian from the *classe d'accueil* close behind. He made his way forward, his head bobbing, the outline of a mocking smile on his lips: "Hey, guys."

"Where you been?" you asked as you got up.

"Sorry. The makeup class did end quite a while ago. But afterwards, we went to eat at McDonald's. The teacher took us out. The time went by really fast. That teacher's really cool. Isn't he, guys?"

The Haitians nodded their agreement.

"Sorry again. Let's forget about it."

You and Akira hadn't budged.

"I'll pay for a game of Mortal Kombat for each of you, okay?"

"We're sick of playing," you grumbled. "We've been waiting for you for two hours."

Then, unable to hide a smile, Carl ran a hand over his mouth, "Man, I hear you've got some pretty cousins?"

You lowered your head.

"The next time you have a party," Carl continued, "I want to be on the guest list. Don't forget, okay?"

You weren't too sure if he was making fun of you or not.

"You owe it to me. I already invited you to parties at our house."

You thought to yourself, he invited me once, and that was it.

"I'd like to meet your cousins," he insisted. "Cute little girls, it seems. Especially, what's her name again . . . Carolina?"

You turned your gaze on Cléo, whose bottom lip was quivering: he was having a hard time holding in his laughter, too.

"Anyway, your parties sound pretty cool," Carl said. "I heard you get good and drunk."

"It's not as much fun as all that," you replied. "A lot of the time, I'm bored. And some of the people there get on my nerves."

"Yeah, Latinos don't always know how to behave."

"What do you mean by that?"

"At Saint-Luc, where I'm going to school next year, somebody told me you have to watch out for them. They'll pull a knife on you for anything."

"Oh yeah?" you said. It was the first time you'd ever heard anything like that.

"Oh yeah. You turn your back on them and bang! out it comes. I also heard they're the biggest thieves around. They're real pros!"

"But they're not all like that," Cléo insisted. "Some of them are cool."

"Well, sure, there's nothing that says that every once in a while you can't come across a couple who are cool. But I'm talking about the majority. And not just the kids. The adults, too. Isn't that right, Cléo?"

"What are you talking about?" Cléo said.

"You know, that story you told me," Carl explained, lowering his head as if he was embarrassed. "About that fat Latino who insulted you. . . ."

"What?" Cléo asked. "What are you talking about? I don't remember that."

"Come on, you know, the one who. . . ."

"Just say it, Cléo!" you shouted, beside yourself. "Just say my uncle's a racist! Why don't you just say it?"

He turned towards you, his brow furrowed, his mouth part open.

"What are you talking about, buddy?" Carl asked. "It's something that happened to Cléo in the Métro. A fat Latino didn't want to move his feet so he could sit down. Cléo asked him to get up, and the guy started calling him all the names in the book."

"What's got into you?" Akira asked you in a murmur. "Why are you acting like that?"

128

Now you were appraising them, going feverishly back and forth. And Carl nudged Cléo, "What's this kid talking about? You know what he's talking about? Did his uncle do something to you?"

Remember Marcelo: you suddenly took off and rushed for the staircase. Just as you were climbing the steps, you noticed Cléo was right on your heels: come back, Marcelo, don't be stupid. With a disgusted movement, you shook your arm free: what's got into you? I don't understand you. Without zipping up your coat or putting on your toque, you ran two blocks, almost without realizing it. Then you suddenly stopped: what was getting you into such a state? What had got into you, since he hadn't said anything? You wanted to go back, but you couldn't.

The doors of the elevator open and Ketcia spots CB and Mixon's parents sitting in the waiting room at the end of the corridor on plastic chairs. On one side, stretched out almost to his full length, his legs apart, CB's leafing through a *Sports Illustrated*, on the other, Mixon's father is staring off into the distance and, when Ketcia passes by, his mother follows her with pitiless eyes. Ketcia sits and insolently returns her gaze: it's her moustache that makes her look mean. She hands CB a ham sandwich and a Coke. He sets them on his knees and rubs his hands, smiling with satisfaction. Starving, they eat noisily, as Mixon's mother looks at them aslant. Earlier, before she went to the cafeteria, Ketcia offered to bring her something to eat, but she turned her head away: when I want something, little girl, I'll go down myself. She's mad at them, Ketcia thinks, she's convinced that nothing would have happened to her son if he hadn't been hanging around with them. As soon as the doctor, a young redhead with effeminate manners, mentioned the joint, her whole approach to them changed: she turned a deaf ear to all their comforting words, examining them with a suspicious gaze. It must have confirmed what she already believed: supposedly Mixon was under CB's influence, and hers,

129

too. If you listened to her, and this was the funniest part, you'd think Mixon was some sort of model son, an angel. Didn't she know her son better than that? She feels more compassion towards the father: he has gentle eyes and gabs non-stop.

Ketcia bites into her sandwich and looks up at the clock: it's ten to three in the morning, and they still haven't visited Mixon. Since the ambulance arrived at Hôpital Sainte-Justine, they've been constantly carting him around on the gurney, in the elevator, from one floor to another. First, he was taken to Emergency, then to radiology, then to the operating room. Ketcia couldn't sit still and she paced up and down in the waiting room, but that got on CB's nerves and he asked her to sit back down. To tell the truth, they don't know if the wounds are serious. The bone may have been hit, there may be a risk of infection, that's what the doctor had revealed to them. Then at around two o'clock, they brought Mixon up to the second floor and his parents could see the damage with their own eyes. He's not in such bad shape, the father told them, but he looks awfully tired. He was only stabbed in the arm, but he lost a lot of blood. Then a police officer showed up: he's still in Mixon's room, and they're hoping he doesn't talk.

One thing's for sure, CB pulled off a good one earlier when he wormed permission to see him out of his parents. At first, the mother, predictably, had been against it: I don't want Mixon hanging around with these good-for-nothings anymore, she grumbled at her husband. Mixon's father took their side: don't forget that it's because of them that Mixon was brought to the hospital so quickly. You're forgetting that your son is on drugs because of them. The father gave a disheartened sigh: you simplify things so much you distort them. You have to hold Mixon responsible, not his friends. She didn't blink, just turned on her heel and sat down. He shrugged his shoulders, smiled at them and went to sit back down with her.

Ketcia isn't clear on what happened in the church basement. She sees a blinding whirl of lights swimming in dizzying smoke, hurried crowds of students, she hears the hammering of the music. One thing is certain, there's before and after the joint: in the beginning, movements are orderly and seem logical, afterwards, the scene becomes cloudy, unreal, threatening. She remembers they were in a stall in the men's washroom, around the bowl passing the joint around. After a few drags, Mixon was choking with laughter, and CB's features turned hard: either you calm down or you're out! What did I do, CB? Anyways, somebody has to keep their eye on the Latinos. Let's go! Mixon slammed the stall door: it's not fair! From then on things get hazy, even though she clearly remembers the growing anxiety that gripped her. Then the rest of them hobbled out of the washroom and, though they looked everywhere, couldn't find Mixon. At one point they even thought he'd got mad and gone home.

Leaning against the wall, she let herself slide down onto her heels, harassed by macabre thoughts and furtive images of her childhood. The smoke took on the shapes of phantasmagorical animals and, since her ears were blocked, the rhythm of the music was literally beating in her head. Suddenly, the little Vietnamese girl in the coatroom started to scream, then let out sharp little sobs, as if she was going to choke, and Gino came running. The group fell into step behind the monitor and that's when Ketcia noticed Mixon lying motionless on the ground as if he was dead. CB ran to the body: somebody call an ambulance, dammit! And Gino went to call. CB didn't seem to care about his bloodstained hands, but she barely had the courage to approach the body, something she's angry with herself about now. In the meantime, it was like a cold shower on the party: the music stopped and most of the revellers left. When the paramedics arrived with the stretcher, CB insisted on going with Mixon in the ambulance. It's okay, one of the paramedics said, that way you can call the injured boy's parents from the hospital. CB asked the other members of the gang to meet them at the hospital, but they all took off

131

saying they had a headache or were tired. Later, in the waiting room, CB punched his fist into his palm: I'm sick of them! Not even capable of coming to visit their friend who just got shanked, for Christ's sake!

CB finishes his sandwich and picks up the magazine again, stroking his goatee as he scans it. Ketcia sucks up her Coke through the straw and a deep gurgling sound comes from the bottom of the can, which again attracts Mixon's mother's icy little eyes. Now the police officer, a six-foot-tall gorilla, is leaving Mixon's room and coming towards the parents. In slow motion, he takes out a little pad and leafs through it after wetting his finger, he questions them and writes down the mother's words especially. Ketcia can only catch bits of her sentences. Twice he turns his head towards them and CB, his face contorted by a grimace, waves bye-bye at him. After a little while, the officer comes slowly towards them, his arms swinging, constantly glancing around as if to inform the nurses and the parents he's got his eye on them. That's all we needed, thinks Ketcia, a first-class moron. He comes to a stop in front of them, and, mechanically, clears his throat: he's not going to waste their time, he's going to get right to the point. Do they have any idea who could have stabbed their friend? CB sighs in frustration and avoids looking at him, while Ketcia feels obliged to answer, if only to get him to leave her alone, and simply tells him, they really have no idea. Do they have any enemies? No, Ketcia replies dryly. Everyone has some enemies, don't they? the officer insists, a vague smiling floating across his puffy face. This time, wondering if maybe she made a mistake by answering the first time, she doesn't even bother to look at him. The officer steps towards CB: and you? CB looks up, I don't know anything, then looks away. The officer mutters under his breath, scribbles in his pad and walks away without saying goodbye.

The elevator doors slide shut behind the officer and, without wasting any time, they head for Mixon's room, under his mother's

132

watchful eye. When they walk past the first bed, a pale child of six or seven years old, opens his violet-ringed eyes. In the two opposite beds, patients are sleeping. Farther in, near the window, Mixon is awake, his arms crossed over his stomach, his head turned to the side. Again, at that instant, Ketcia has the feeling he's dead. He slowly turns his head towards them and gives them a painful smile. CB stands close to him, while Ketcia positions herself at the foot of the bed.

"You see that?" Mixon asks. "A cop came to see me."

His voice sounds surprisingly clear. Ketcia examines his downcast face with some degree of relief: she doesn't really know why, but she was expecting worse. His arm, on the other hand, covered in bandages, swollen and purplish all the way down to his hand, doesn't look very promising.

"Yeah," CB nods, "he came and asked us a few questions, too. How did it go? He wasn't too annoying?"

"I told him a story that didn't make much sense," Mixon says with a forced smile, his eyelids half shut. "He didn't really look like he believed me, but since I pretended to be in pain sometimes, like this, 'ooowwww!' he didn't push too hard."

The three of them laugh. Mixon can't help but close his eyes.

"That's how you have to treat them," CB says.

"What about the joint?" wonders Ketcia. "Did he ask you anything?"

"Only if I sold it, too. Obviously, I said no. I said to him: I swear, sir, it was the first puff I ever took in my life. I wanted to know what it was like. That's all. He looked annoyed and he said: all right, all right . . . And he didn't ask any more questions about it."

"How do you feel?" Ketcia asks.

"Okay, I guess."

Mixon glances at his arm and Ketcia has the feeling he's going to burst out crying. It's as if he's using all his strength to control himself.

133

"I got five stitches. For sure, it hurts when I move. The doctor said I could leave the hospital tomorrow morning unless it's really serious. Any way, I'm keeping my fingers crossed. I don't feel like staying here for a week."

"You look really good," CB said, "I'm sure they'll let you go tomorrow. You'll see, in a few days, you won't feel anything anymore. You're going to beat me at arm wrestling."

CB smiles, looks at him warmly.

"And your parents?" he asks, "they came to see you before, didn't they? Did they ask you questions about the pot?"

"With them, it's a little more complicated. I think the doctor told them we'd been smoking. My mother had a freakin' fit. She said to me: why, Mixon? For the love of God, why are you on drugs? Haven't we told you enough about how dangerous it is? A bunch of stuff like that."

"We'll talk about the drugs at home, if you don't mind," his father had cut in. "It's embarrassing enough as it is, I don't want to talk about it here. Besides, Mixon has to get better, he has to rest."

"Okay," his mother had agreed. "But at least let him tell us who did this to him. Are you in danger, Mixon? Do you owe money? Because of the drugs, right?"

"Wow!" exclaims CB. "Your mother's really starting to lose it!"

"No, no, Mom," Mixon had replied. "The guys who did it were thieves. They weren't even from our school. They were a lot older than us. I think they were professional pickpockets."

"That's what you told her?" CB says, "That's great!"

"But if they wanted to rob you," his mother said, "why did they do this to you? It doesn't make sense . . ."

"They stabbed me," Mixon explained, "because I didn't want to give them my wallet. First, I fought with one of them, and since I was winning, another came up from behind and shanked me. That's all."

"You'll really never change," Ketcia comments with a laugh. "You're the best liar I know."

"Shanked?" asked his mother. "What do you mean? What does that word mean?"

"Oh, you don't know anything!" Mixon exclaimed. "It means when someone takes out a pocketknife and stabs you."

"One thing's for sure, you've learned your lesson," his father remarked. "Next time just give them your wallet right away. No more playing the hero, get it?"

"Yeah, I get it," Mixon had answered. "And after that, my father said they shouldn't tire me out and they left."

"Your father's okay," Ketcia offers. "He's cooler than your mother, anyway. I'm just afraid once you get home she's really going to get on your case with all this drug business."

"Yeah," sighs Mixon, "she might. But between now and then, she'll have time to settle down a bit. Well, I hope she will anyway."

For a while, they don't say anything.

"Now," CB says, leaning towards him, "you're going to tell us what really happened."

Mixon opens his eyes wide, as if stunned, then, punctuating his sentences with long silences, he describes in detail the events that took place in the coatroom. When he finishes his story, CB places his hands on his cheeks and stays in that position for a long time. Then, in a low, conspiratorial voice: "Latino Power's main objective was to steal our coats. That much is clear. The fact they shanked you looks like an accident, like it wasn't part of the plan. You have to understand me, Mixon. I'm not trying to excuse them, I just want to understand what they were up to."

From one of the beds next to Mixon's, short syllables filled with o's reach their eyes, as if someone was talking in their sleep.

"I want to ask you one question," CB continues. "But I really want you to think hard before you answer me . . . Who shanked you?"

135

For an instant, Mixon furrows his brow, grimacing as if he can hardly stand the pain anymore.

"I don't know," he answers. "It was too confused."

"Was it Flaco?" CB presses him.

"I don't think so. Maybe."

"We have to act now," Ketcia suggests. "It's urgent, if we want to get our coats back. And you know, if we don't do anything, they'll think we're just a bunch of chickenshits."

"I already have an idea," CB says rubbing his hands. "Every Sunday, I've noticed something about the fat one in their gang. What do they call him again?"

"You mean Teta?" Ketcia asks.

"Yeah, that's it. Teta."

Did the Centre Pierre-Marquette really host the Jeux de Montréal that year or was your memory failing you, Marcelo? What's for sure is that the stadiums looked alike and that children don't pay much attention to place names, and even less to architecture or decor. Early in the morning, amazed and excited, you'd paraded in and greeted the crowd, which was principally composed of students who'd come to support their schools. In the bleachers, they stood, they shouted, they did the wave. But the procession went on forever, tempers flared and right in the middle of track, a fight broke out. The music was interrupted and you stopped moving. A feverish crowd formed around two students trying to see who could punch the other's face the hardest. There was so much confusion the monitors couldn't get their hands on them. The crowd was fired up: with insults and provocations, they encouraged the brawl. Finally, the monitors got their hands on them. They appeared in front of everyone: not embarrassed at all, they were laughing to themselves, proud of having screwed everything up. The organisers had the players leave the field. They'd wasted enough time already. Come on, let's go!

You and Akira climbed up to the top of the bleachers, where your school's supporters were. The only topic of conversation was the fight. To avoid any other similar incidents, half the monitors took positions in the stairways, and the other half spread out along the track. With booming messages from the loudspeakers, you were constantly reminded to settle down. Finally, the qualifying races started, and as a result the crowd was re-energized and started shouting even louder. From one school to another, students threw confetti and balled up paper at each other, and then the monitors would rush over right away. The Phys. Ed. teachers sometimes got involved and when they lost patience, they'd order the rowdiest students to do push-ups.

You and Akira picked out Cléo at the other end of the red benches, making his way through the confusion on the stairway. When he went by École-Saint-Antonin, someone chucked a water balloon and it burst against his chest. The whole school was laughing and pointing at him. He wiped his T-shirt at length, looked at them for a moment, then shouted: screw you, morons! The students were momentarily stunned then they rained balled-up paper down on him. But Cléo casually went on his way down the stairs, stopped in front of a vending machine, bought himself a Coke, and, in an effort to avoid his attackers, climbed back up the other side, where you and Akira were sitting. In passing, Akira offered him a T-shirt to change into, Cléo accepted. He changed right there and sat down with you for a little while. So, you asked, what have you been up to? We hardly ever see each other anymore. Oh, nothing special. His parents were getting a divorce, but he didn't really care, it had been coming for such a long time now. Other than that, his mother was working a lot, and giving him more freedom. Remember, Marcelo, it was like he was telling you about someone else's life.

What about you, how were you doing? Okay, I guess. The other night, Akira and I went to a hockey game with his father. Yeah, Akira said excitedly, you should have been there, Cléo!

The Canadiens trounced the Flyers, five to nothing! Then you noticed the condor was hanging from his neck. I see you're still wearing it. He touched it, held it between his fingers: yeah, it brings me luck. Then the rest of the conversation unfolded like when two old friends meet again and promise to keep in touch although they both know it's no longer possible. Yes, you were sitting there with him, he was talking to you over the shouting and excitement bubbling around you both, and you kept asking yourself, obsessively, what could have happened between you. *Dios mío*, where did this dark, sneaky force separating you come from? You had the feeling, yes, he was looking down on you and Akira, that he didn't think much of you, that he though he was more mature than you. He climbed the stairs and went to sit back down with Carl and the rest of the *classe d'accueil*.

A little before noon, Cléo won the fifty-metre final, which made him the fastest grade five boy in Montreal. Serge hugged him and kept running his hand through his hair. Throughout the afternoon, he lavished him with all sorts of advice and tricks to get him ready for the relay race. One by one, the boys came to shake his hand, you're the next Carl Lewis, Cléo, while the girls elbowed each other and cooed, hi, Cléo, you cutie. Saint-Pascal-Baylon picked up three other medals in the individual competitions, but no other golds, which left Serge dumbfounded for a good part of the day. A teacher-friend of his, who'd come to watch the competition, consoled him with an arm around his shoulders, his voice gentle: the relay races are this afternoon, and that's where they had the best chance of picking up medals, wasn't it?

Around four o'clock, after some exhausting qualifying races, there were only eight teams left in the finals, including Saint-Pascal-Baylon, for the 4 x 50 metre grade five relay. You had a great start, Marcelo. That day, carried by the crowd, you felt light as a bird. Coming out of the turn, you had a good lead and you were first to pass the baton to the second runner, who happened

138

to be Akira and, despite his disorderly way of running, he managed to further increase the distance between you and the other team. Then, completely unexpectedly, Akira fell. Shit! For a long moment, he writhed in pain on the track. Two runners jumped over him so they wouldn't trample him. Remember: he'd sprained his ankle. All the runners passed him, he got up and limped to Yuri, who, by increasingly lengthening his strides, managed to get back into sixth position. Then Cléo got the baton and was off like a shot: he astonished the crowd and cheered Serge, who was stubbornly chewing his fingernails. At the first turn, he passed the fifth runner; ten metres farther, the fourth; he had a hard time getting ahead of the third runner, in slow motion. There were only twenty metres left and the second runner was maintaining a surprising rhythm. Just as Cléo was about to pass his rival, the finish line caught him. The opposing team began to jump and raise their arms in the air, confident that they'd won the silver medal. Serge rushed over to Cléo, they talked a bit then headed over to the officials, comparing their stopwatches. You didn't care about winning, all you were interested in was second place because it would allow you to move on the Jeux du Québec. After a few minutes, it was Cléo and Serge's turn to jump up and down, and the reaction of Saint-Pascal-Baylon wasn't far behind: beneath an avalanche of liberating shouts, confetti and streamers dotted the stadium.

You four runners were hugging each other, shaking hands firmly, and Akira, his ankle soaking in a bucket filled with ice, was consoled. Happy, but wound tight as a spring, Serge was checking his own heart rate, two fingers pressed against the angle of his chin, as he spoke: the important thing, my friends, is that we qualified for the Jeux du Québec, for the first time ever for their school. So they were going to show all of Quebec what they were made of! And, all of you added in unison, you got it! After the medal ceremony, when Carl and Cléo left by the back door of the gym, Carl's brother honked his horn, his elbow out the window of a sky blue Dodge: come on, move your ass, he had other things to do! They got into the back seat, put down the windows and, as the car accelerated, stuck out their heads: we won! At the apartment, Carl's mother heard about Cléo's victories and, as she set the table, she looked at him, her eyes sparkling with admiration: achievements like that would get the Haitian community accepted once and for all. She stepped closer to where he was already seated at the table, bent her knees and smiled generously: if you keep it up, you could go far, you know. But Cléo simply shrugged his shoulders: yeah, I don't know. They ate roast beef with Haitian rice, discussed all the details of the competition and imagined the upcoming ones. That night, since Carl's parents were going out to the movies, the brothers sweetly asked their mother if they could have a party. Okay, but please, boys, don't break my glasses this time, and she followed her husband to the door. We'll be good, Mom, we promise. As soon as they were gone, Carl's big brother turned towards them curtly: see, I told you she'd notice the broken glasses. They went into the living room: the brothers stretched out to their full length on the sofa, while Cléo sat in the chair, with his arms folded. Your mother's cool, she lets you do what you want. And Carl began to blow on his nails and polish them on his T-shirt: it's just that my parents are modern!

Carl's big brother went to the kitchen and came back a few moments later with glasses and some beer. Frightened, Cléo glanced nervously at Carl: all right, okay, just a little, I don't feel like getting a headache. Carl took the caps off two Molson Drys, poured them into the glasses, and took a long drink, as if it were a habit with him and, with a dreamy look, examined the ceiling. Then, as he handed Cléo a glass, he asked: where are the most beautiful girls in the world? The most beautiful beaches, eh? Cléo dipped his lips into the beer, the foam gave him a moustache, and his eyes stirred restlessly: wait, let me think. Idiot, Carl shouted, in your own country! And Cléo replied, is that true? You sure?

That's when Carl's big brother rushed at him and, half kidding, half joking pointed his finger in Cléo's face: don't ever question anything like that in my house again! The next time you do, I'll kick your ass, then I'll throw you out, head first! Understand? Carl's brother went towards the portable radio, shoved in a tape and, with his back turned, asked, tell me one thing, do you think of yourself as Haitian or Canadian? I don't know. Some of both. The brothers lowered their heads and shook them theatrically. The older one came and sat near Cléo, put an arm around his shoulders and spoke to him solemnly: there's nothing sadder in the world than someone who doesn't know where he comes from. You have to know your country well, little boy, get it? Cléo slowly shook his head yes, his eyes worried. Another thing, you have to be proud of your origins. Repeat after me: I'm-proud-to-be-Haitian. . . .

As the evening drew on, the living room filled up with more and more young people. Carl's big brother was the deejay, and most of the others were wriggling as they danced, casually holding their beers. Around ten o'clock, a few joints were lit. When a hand held one out to him, Cléo sharply shook his head no. Carl sat down near him on the arm of his chair, and Cléo swallowed another sip of beer: buddy, it's like there's a merry-go-round spinning in my head. Soon he was laughing about anything and everything, clinking glasses with Carl before they both downed their glasses in one swallow. Should I dance or not, he asked Carl. You should, there's nothing to be embarrassed about, you're just with us and we're like family. They ogled the girls, and imitating the older boys, commented on their bodies. From time to time, Carl's brother would come up behind them and stand between them: some of them aren't bad, eh, guys? Which one do you like, little brother? Carl had spotted a girl with long legs, moving languorously on the opposite side of the room. The big brother laughed in both satisfaction and surprise: I see you like older women. If you want her, I mean, if you really want her, you can have her. What

141

about you, Cléo? Me, uh, I don't know. What am I hearing there? You're trying to get me to believe there's not a single one you like?! It can't be! Either you're sick in the head or . . . and Cléo quickly pointed out a girl who was seated alone, not particularly pretty, but who kept turning her head towards him: her. Carl's big brother's hand squeezed his shoulder: well then, you shall have her, buddy, I promise! He went to talk with the two girls in question and, after a few minutes, they came over to them: so, looks like you're shy, eh, boys? They exchanged a surprised look, and the girls each took them by the hand and pulled them to the dance floor: come on, come on, now's no time to be sitting down.

In the middle of the living room, Carl was doing all he could to look natural to a Bob Marley song, while keeping an eye on his friend the whole time. Barely a month ago, Cléo never would have agreed to dance like that, as a couple with a girl. No matter what they said, alcohol had its good sides. It looked like he was in seventh heaven, freed from something that had been weighing on him for too long. Cléo, who at the beginning of their friendship had suffered from such shyness, was unrecognizable today. From time to time, the girl would turn her back to him, bend her knees and swing her rear end, and Cléo would follow the movements of her hips, his eyes popping out of his head. Later the couples sat back down and Carl's brother came by to give them more beer. Carl, who had already watched how his brother acted with girls, imitated him: he told joke after joke, eliciting cascades of laughter from his partner. In Cléo's corner, as things were going rather silently and he wouldn't stop scratching his neck and his arms like he had the hives, the girl who was with him turned towards Carl: was it true Cléo was in grade nine? And Carl, sensing his friend had been acting, understood: yes, yes, he goes to the Polyvalente Saint-Luc. A half hour later, Cléo was still chatting with the girl as if they'd known each other for ever. He was drinking his beer in such gulps that Carl had to confiscate the bottle. With his hands now free, he got it into his head that he should kiss the girl. Noticing he was drunk, she pushed him away nicely. Instead, she asked him to dance and, enthusiastically, he clapped his hands: whatever you say! But he had an awfully hard time standing up, and he leaned on the other dancers' arms and shoulders. Soon, they had to sit back down, and Carl heard him telling the girl he loved her, that he'd do anything, that he'd kill for her. She was laughing heartily, giving him little slaps on the cheeks: you're a real lady-killer. Okay, all right, she said, and she deposited a kiss upon his cheek, then a short one on his lips, like this, mouah. Soon, nobody could get them apart.

VI

One by one, the Latino Powers emerge from a building with peeling green paint and, grouped around an old woman Teta has given his arm to, look up and down the street in both directions. The air is warm and on this last Sunday in April, the bright blue of the sky makes them flutter their eyelids like Barbie dolls. Flaco notices the Bad Boys at a window on the other side of the open space: they laugh and wave at him. When Teta and the old woman step forward, leading the group, he points his finger at the window for the rest of Latino Powers to see and, when they do, they give them the finger and carry on with their escort.

Since the party in the church basement, things have gone way downhill. Mixon's stabbing confirmed Flaco's decision to leave the gang for good. At the movies last night with Paulina, he just couldn't get interested in Schwarzenegger's mission, no matter how action-packed and sexy it was. It was as if in the darkness he'd found the courage to confess and had only one desire: to tell Paulina everything. It soothed him to share his fears, it made him more clear-headed. Several times, she insisted that he put an end to the war, but he shook his head: I'm not in the habit of doing things halfway. Since the beating Pato and Alfonso had been given, he'd promised them no one would show them a lack of respect again, and he wasn't going to renege on that promise. Hadn't she been there that day? She turned her head away and pretended to be absorbed in the movie, her arms crossed, her lips pursed. Other parts of this business preyed on his mind, too. Even Lalo, since the incident in the church basement, had admitted he'd been having bloody dreams. Flaco is angry with him for acting like an animal, especially since he was always bragging about it to the others. What could he possibly have in common with a guy who's capable of such a thing? At least, he thinks to himself in consolation, the police don't seem to suspect them and the Haitians, rather surprisingly, seem to have upheld the tacit agreement to solve their problems on their own.

On the other hand, the Bad Boys are harassing them wherever they go. Early one evening, Teta had gone out on the balcony to get some air and Ketcia, who was passing by, shouted to him: if you all think you're going to get away with just a couple scratches, you're in for a big surprise. A piece of advice, keep your eyes peeled, we're going to strike when you least expect it, whether there's anybody else around or not. Since Teta was the youngest of a family of eight, and his brothers had left the house a while ago, all married or out on their own, he'd inherited the responsibility of looking after his mother, Señora Eugenia – a widow whose face was crisscrossed by wrinkles, who always wore a silk scarf on her head, and aviator-style smoked classes to hide a corneal oedema. Since one of Teta's sacred obligations was to escort her to church, Ketcia's threats had scared him to death and he'd phoned Flaco: could the gang escort his mother and him on Sunday? The prospect of not sleeping in and losing part of his day didn't exactly delight Flaco, but he knew only too well that Ketcia hadn't been joking, he'd even been warned himself in an incredibly terse letter: *watch out for your sheep, if you don't want us to bleed them.* Before he'd gone to bed yesterday, he'd called all the other members of the gang and wound his alarm clock so he'd get up on time.

Señora Eugenia, with a toothless smile, leans towards her son. "For once your friends are being nice."

Then extending her chin towards the others in a circular motion, "But they didn't all have to come."

With his eyes, Flaco runs the street through a fine-toothed comb and smiles back.

"No, really, Señora Eugenia, it's a pleasure for us to do it."

"*Muchas gracias, niño.*"

Flaco's smile turns into a clownish grimace: he hates being treated like a child. When they reach Côte-des-Neiges, they pass by McDonald's, Lebanese, Vietnamese, Chinese restaurants, then they go by the swings in Parc Kent that are already being attacked by a crowd of brats. When they turn onto the path leading to the Église-Saint-Pascal, to his dismay Flaco recognizes the Bad Boys, dressed all in black, hiding behind some bushes around the rectory. If they're already here, they must have taken a short cut, probably via Lavoie and Plamondon. They can't be planning on attacking them in the church! The other Latinos notice them, too, and Flaco signals to them to keep cool. He assists Teta in helping Señora Eugenia as she climbs the stairs and, as they go in, they lower their heads and make the sign of the cross, some even go so far as to genuflect. Men and women, mostly in their fifties, in their Sunday clothes, are chatting casually in the pews or in the centre aisle. Flaco knows them, he's been around them since he was a child, and, as is his duty, he greets several of them with excessive politeness. A short Guatemalan man with a puffy face, a friend of his father's, comes towards him with a big smile, *hola niño*, offers his hand, say hello to your parents, and then he gets lost in the crowd gathering in the front rows. Then Lalo comes towards him and, in a worried voice, whispers in his ear, "Don't tell me we're going to have to stay for the whole Mass?"

"It looks that way, man."

They exchange a defeated look. The priest climbs the sanctuary stairs, takes his place behind the altar, and, Señora Eugenia insists in her whining voice, attracting everyone's attention, that they all come sit with her in front, in the very first pew. To be as close to God as possible, she adds. Feeling the weight of dozens of reproachful eyes on him, Flaco coughs, informs her they'd rather stay in the back, and that they'll see her after the Mass. She shakes her head to show her disapproval, and Teta makes a face as he realizes he'll have to accompany his mother up to the front alone. Latino Power squeezes into the last pew in the back of the church, after welcoming everyone, Father Cardinal, his eyebrows raised, immediately motions his hand towards them: why don't these young people in the back come closer? There are some excellent seats here in front. Furiously rubbing the back of their necks, the gang gets up as one and comes to sit with Señora Eugenia, as joy flashes across her face. They'll see, they'll feel much better up here. When the sermon is good, you feel the thrill!

The Mass goes on forever. For Flaco, it's an irritating succession of unexpected moments where you have to sit, stand, sit back down and kneel. It's said in Spanish and twice when Father Cardinal can't find his words, the parishioners whisper to him. When it's time for communion, at Señora Eugenia's request, the members of Latino Power get in line. One by one, they murmur, "Amen," open their mouths and, when the host is placed on their tongues, even though they know it's forbidden, they chew. When Mass is over, the short Guatemalan hurries to speak in front of the altar: *amigos y amigas*, if they'd be so kind as to sit down again, please. He just wants to remind them that the soccer tournament, the Coupe Allende, is taking place in Parc Kent all day today. The best teams in the community will be facing off, it's a must-see. If they're busy, they should at least come to the finals tonight. *Es imperativo* . . . Latino Power heads towards the door, but Señora Eugenia stops them in the middle of the aisle, like a stubborn mule.

"Now what?" Teta asks through clenched teeth.

"Before, at home, you promised you'd go to confession. And now you've changed your mind. *¿Cómo es eso?*"

"I just said that so you'd leave me alone," he pouts. "Anyways, I went to confession less than a month ago. I swear, I haven't done anything bad since."

With her fists on her hips, she breathes through her nose and slowly shakes her head, as if she were trying to convince herself of something evident.

"You know what," she proposes, "you should all go to confession."

"Why do you say that?" Flaco asks. "Anyway, what would we tell the Father?"

"Son, I may be old, but I'm not stupid. You think I don't know you're up to no good?"

She turns her head and levels her sightless eyes on Lalo.

"Señora," he says, "I really don't know what you're talking about. I really don't!"

Secretively, the members of Latino Power exchange worried looks.

"Children, I will not leave here until you've all gone to confession."

A collective, "Oh no!" greets her warning.

"Or else," she continues, "I'll make a scene and I'll tell everything I know."

Her words chill them. All around, people are leaving the church, saying goodbye. Just what does she know? Is she bluffing? Flaco has to know for sure.

"I think you're making things up just to get us to go to confession," he states, almost mockingly. "I'm telling you, we have nothing to be sorry for. And, with all the respect I owe you, Señora Eugenia, I really don't like your trying to blackmail us like this."

Her composure unruffled, the old woman felt her way

148

forward, stopping a few centimetres in front of him, and breathed her bad breath into his face.

"Listen to me, my boy. In one way, I can forgive you for not telling me the truth. But not telling the Lord the truth is serious. I won't stand for it . . ."

"What are you going to do?" asks Flaco. "Turn us in to God the Almighty?"

He gives a little laugh.

"What about the leather coats my son has hidden in his closet? I suppose you bought them? No," she answers her own question. "You stole them!"

Flaco's heart skips a beat. The old woman isn't bluffing. *¡Putamadre!* And now what? Admit everything? Do what she wants? Almost against his own will, he says in astonishment, "Leather coats?"

"Stop fooling around, my boy. I'm old, I know when I'm being lied to."

Flaco glances at the others: their fists in their pockets, they turn their heads. Lalo and Pato whistle a tuneless song. It's always the same old story! They always wait for him, the leader to pull them out of the fire. He turns back to the old woman, "What else do you know?"

"It doesn't matter. I promise not to tell anyone as long as you go to confession."

"And if we go to confession, you'll leave us alone, is that it?"

She nods yes. Flaco hesitates, takes a deep breath.

"All right, okay."

Delighted, Señora Eugenia asks Teta to tell Father Cardinal, and indicates to the others, swearing under their breath, to go one at a time to the confessional. It's almost unbelievable! Flaco thinks. They come with the best intentions in the world, and now they're being told what to do by this old woman, while the Bad Boys are waiting outside, hiding, ready to jump on them like wild beasts. That takes the cake! As soon as the priest finishes putting things away in the sacristy, he comes down the middle aisle and, without looking at them, is swallowed up by the confessional. At his mother's request, Teta goes first and it takes an eternity, which worries Flaco: what if that idiot was really telling the priest everything, eh? What will I do? Twice he hears Teta's hysterical laughter and it gives him goosebumps. When Teta comes out, he and Lalo give him a furious look, and Teta reassures them, I made up a story, what did you think? So when Lalo's turn comes, he takes forever, too. He opens the door and brushes against Flaco whispering: I got three Hail Marys. Then Alfonso goes, and then Pato. When he comes out, Pato whispers in Flaco's ear that he didn't say anything, not a thing, boss, I swear. Flaco gives himself a good shake as he goes towards the confessional, closes the creaking door and places his bum on the austere little pew, as comfortable as a stone. Father Cardinal opens the screen, murmurs some words in Latin and crosses himself.

"Which language would you like to use for your confession? French or Spanish?"

"I don't care. We can do it in French if it's easier for you."

"*Le Seigneur est prêt à entendre vos péchés*," the priest says.

"Before I begin, I'd like to be sure of one thing. I want to be certain that everything is confidential."

"Absolutely, my boy. Just consider me a simple intermediary between the Lord and you."

"Okay. But I have another question, then. How can I explain this . . . What good does it do me to tell all this stuff to God? I mean, what's the advantage?"

For a moment, the priest doesn't answer.

"My boy, what's your first name?"

"Marcelo. But everyone calls me Flaco."

"Listen to me carefully, Marcelo. Two things. First, when you go to confession, it's so that the Lord forgives you for your sins. That's the 'advantage,' as you call it. The Lord listens to you

150

then He gives you absolution. But if you're unsure about what you're doing, if you're hesitating, I'd suggest you go and reflect on your own and say a prayer."

"Okay, okay. But one last question. Let's say I play the game and everything. Can you give me advice . . . sorry, I mean, can God give me advice if I ask him to help me?"

"Of course," says Père Cardinal, enthusiastically. "That's what he's there for, for you to talk to him. You can think of him as a friend."

Flaco coughs and looks through the screen: the priest's head is lowered and his eyes are closed.

"Did you hear about Mixon, the boy whose arm was hurt last Friday?"

"Of course, it happened in the basement of our church. . . ."

"Well, Father, I think I'm partly responsible for what happened."

"What are you saying, my boy?"

Feeling himself abandon his uneasiness little by little, Flaco starts to tell him everything in detail. Along the way, he even finds the exercise somehow soothing, a little like when he confides in Paulina. But after a few minutes, Father Cardinal interrupts him with a cough and straightens up in his chair.

"Listen to me carefully. If you want to tell me things that would compromise you with the justice of men, my boy, that's something else."

"But I thought I could ask his advice."

"You can do that by simply praying. Gather your thoughts alone, in the quiet of your room, for example."

"In my room? What good does that do, if I'm all alone?"

"You don't understand what I'm trying to tell you, my boy. Try to understand my position. I've had quarrels with the police before, because someone's told me things I'd rather not hear. Do you get my drift now?"

"But, Father, who can help me then?"

151

"As I just said, if you talk to him, God can help you. But you can find yourself another kind of help, too, the help of the authorities. Sincerely, my boy, I think a police officer could help you better than I could."

Without protesting, Flaco leaves the confessional and, before rejoining the others, he turns around a moment: what do you think of that? When she sees him, Señora Eugenia approaches, thanks him, taking his hands in hers. Flaco pulls them away suddenly and says it's time to go. Outside, there's not a single Bad Boy in sight, they probably got bored. Maybe going to confession wasn't a waste of time, after all, he says to himself bitterly. They advance in silence and, claiming her knees are burning, Señora Eugenia asks them to stop to rest from time to time.

They stop in front of Teta's building: everything looks calm. Still, Flaco orders Pato, just for safety, to go with Teta and his mother upstairs to their door. We'll wait for you, he adds. Before he leaves them, Teta asks if this afternoon, after lunch, they want to go to Parc Kent to watch the soccer tournament. Good idea! the others shout. Lalo suggests they meet in front of his house at about one-thirty. *Chao*, Señora Eugenia. *Hasta luego, niñitos. ¡Un millón de gracias!* Again, Teta gives his arm to his mother, as Pato runs ahead to open the doors for them. Señora Eugenia climbs up one stair at a time and stops for long breaks. It's dark, the landlord doesn't replace the fluorescent tubes anymore since people started stealing them. When they make it to the third floor, Señora Eugenia, breathing hard, searches her purse, pulls out a set of keys and feels around for the lock. Okay, you can go now, says Teta, see you later. Pato says goodbye to Señora Eugenia and climbs down the stairs two by two. When his mother opens the door, Teta feels someone grab his arm and pin him from behind. He tries to get free, but immediately feels a sharp object prick his back. He wants to shout, but a hand is clamped down on his mouth.

152

"Are you coming?" his mother asks, already inside the apartment.

Teta recognizes CB's slow speech urging him, in a low tone, to remain calm. Then the hand comes off his mouth. For a long moment, his frightened eyes follow his mother's wavering profile and he finally says, "I'll be right back."

Señora Eugenia takes off her dark glasses, puts her head out the door and rubs her eyes.

"Where are you going?"

"I forgot to give something to Flaco."

"It can certainly wait till later, can't it?"

"No, Mom. I'm afraid it can't."

She raises her arms towards the heavens, "Oh, Lord! The street's the only thing they're interested in! . . . Don't forget to come home for lunch, *niñito*! I'll wait for you."

He sees his mother close the door and hears her mutter words he can't quite grasp.

When Cléo woke up with a start, Carl, his hands behind his head, was replaying the film of the previous night's party in his head. Cléo was lying on the floor under a woollen blanket, parallel to the bed, from which Carl was now languidly observing him. Cléo sniffed his white T-shirt and closed his eyes in delight, a smile swelling his cheeks: it smelled like the girl's perfume, man. Carl laughed heartily, while the other sat up, his back against the wall: do you remember the party at your place after the Jeux de Montréal? Carl rubbed his eyes with the back of his hands, nodded yes, and Cléo livened up: do you remember the girl I was kissing all night? Why didn't they see her anymore, eh? At the next two parties he hadn't seen her, and she wasn't there yesterday either. Carl sat up on his bed, the box spring creaked, and he shivered from his toes to the roots of his hair: it's because she's going out with someone now. A guy in grade nine, I think. What do you care? Anyway, last night, you didn't seem to

153

miss her much, you spent the whole night feeling Marjorie's breasts. It wasn't that he missed her, Cléo responded, as he ran a finger along the skin of his arm, it was just that he wondered where she was, that's all. Carl looked him in the eye: what, you just want them all to yourself, or what? Cléo shrugged his shoulders and let out an embarrassed laugh, and Carl shook his head, amused: you Don Juan!

Cléo slipped on his pants, went to the window and pulled back the curtains as Carl picked up the notebook and pen that were on his nightstand. Cléo was absorbed in contemplating what the window had to offer him, then in passing, vaguely running one hand through his hair, he murmured: I had a strange dream. It can't be possible, Carl thought, he imitates everything I do. It's true that Carl often told him about his dreams, at least the ones that grabbed his attention, and he was in the habit of writing them down in the morning, so he wouldn't forget them. His big brother had taught him how to interpret them. You want to tell it to me? he asked nonetheless, putting down the notebook and the pen. It was the second time he'd had the same dream. Then Carl interrupted him: it's not possible, you never have the same dream twice. How many times did he have to tell him? What I meant, Cléo corrected himself, is that about three or four days ago, I had a similar dream.

Roughly, this is how it went. He and his father looked out his bedroom window. Low, thick fog slowly travelled down Rue Linton. It's time to go, his father said. They put on their coats, went outside and got into a black Cadillac. The driver, who Cléo couldn't make out because of the smoked glass between the front and back seats, pulled out fast into the traffic. Dad, where are we going like this? But his father frowned, as if he'd just spoken to him in a foreign language. He took out a cigarette and tapped it on his thigh several times. Cléo pushed a button and the window went down. Kneeling on the seat, he put his head out. All the streets were covered in the same creamy fog.

After a little while, the fog lifted and the Cadillac came to a stop. They went into a very long house that had a green roof. A rotten smell infiltrated every pore of his body. Standing at attention, men he didn't know were posted all along an endless hallway. Evidently, a room at the back had been prepared for them. They went towards it, but stopped in the doorway. An open casket was in the middle of the room, a fire crackled in one corner, and the reflection of its flames on the wall looked like a spider's legs. Cléo drew near to the coffin: his mother was wearing so much makeup he had a hard time recognizing her. She wasn't dead: beneath her closed lids, her eyes were moving. Slowly, he bent forward, kissed her on the mouth and tasted a brief, bitter smack of her lipstick. As for his father, he was observing them, his expression emotionless. Finally, a group of guests invaded the room and clapped to bring the roof down.

Woooow, man, Carl shouted, that's wild. Geez, you have heavy dreams! He absolutely had to tell his brother, there's no doubt he'd be interested. Cléo looked happy then, strangely he lowered his eyes and his face darkened: he wanted to tell him about his mother. Carl had got used to listening when Cléo felt the need to confide in someone. Last week, he'd explained, his parents had got a divorce and even if the legal paper didn't change anything concrete in his mother's life, it had had a deep effect on her: she stopped combing her hair, worked overtime at the factory, and, at night in the apartment, though she hated TV, she sat there, slumped down in her chair in the living room, channel surfing for hours. Cléo didn't see her much and, on the one hand, he liked it that way. Also, she rarely spoke to him. Could he imagine, Carl?

One night when he was getting ready to go out, she'd called him into the living room: where was he going? You know, Mom, over to Carl's, I told you this morning. She stared at the TV with hard eyes: you're getting more and more like your father. And he said, what did she mean by that? Wasn't she exaggerating just a little? As if she hadn't heard him, she continued: you even look more and more like him physically. No, no, Mom! It's just your imagination! Tell me, are you sick of living with a crazy woman, too? Mom, why are you talking like that? Cléo, I asked you a question. Cléo observed her twisting hands: don't talk like that, Mom, please. Come on, he should tell her straight out, did he think she was crazy, yes or no? Stop it, Mom. Without turning towards him, with a dark look, she murmured: he'd see, one day he'd do just what his father had done, he'd abandon her, too.

Cléo gave Carl a beseeching look: how come his mother wasn't like that, eh? And Carl pretended to get mad: I already told you not to compare, it's not right. Okay, it's time to go. Each of them took a quick turn in the bathroom, and then put on their coats and boots as if they were competing. As they crossed the hallway, Cléo asked: don't you think we should eat a bowl of cereal or something? No way, we don't have time, we're already late. Going down the stairs in the apartment building, Carl zipped up his leather coat and added, we'll have some hotdogs at the stadium. Outside, a thin layer of snow made the car windshields sparkle, and the cold air burned their lungs. Taking huge steps, they pulled up the collars on their coats. They turned right on Rue Lavoie, then went down Van Horne, and there, on the other side of the street, Marcelo was coming out of a bakery. Suddenly, Cléo ducked down behind a car. What got into him? Carl asked in surprise, still standing up. Shh! said Cléo with a finger against his lips, and he pulled him down by his coat sleeve. They waited until Marcelo had turned the corner. What's your problem? Carl then asked. I'm telling you, you have some pretty strange ideas some times! Didn't he want to say hello to his friend? No, no, Cléo answered standing back up. It's just that sometimes Marcelo would call him and he'd say he'd call back, but he'd forget. Anyways, I'm telling you, you're weird, Carl said, giving him a worried look.

At Plamondon Métro station, their two friends, Haitians in grade six, were stretched out flat on the escalator handrail. When they saw Cléo and his friend, they immediately got up and came over to shake hands: hey, guys. One of them, displaying a joking smile, said to Carl: listen, man, listen, I heard a good one. He took a deep breath, then with a vain grimace on his face, he recited: "Astros, Astros, ra, ra, ra, flush them down the toilet, ah, ah, ah . . . Max and me are going to shout that at the stadium. It's a good one, eh, Carl?" What did he think? That they were jackasses, sighed Carl. Everybody already knew that joke! Okay, that's enough fooling around. They were going to miss the first inning.

They slid down the handrail, fell on top of each other, and, huddled on the cement floor, let rip with a laugh that echoed around all them. They ran to the counter and since the ticket collector wasn't there, they jumped over the turnstiles. On the platform, Richard and Max put on their Walkman headphones and, simultaneously, went into the same syncopated steps and the moves rappers make. An old woman wearing a beige checkered raincoat knotted at the waist stared at them as she went by, and Richard abruptly stopped dancing: why don't you take a picture? The subway train pulled into the station, the doors slid open noisily, and each one stretched out on a two-person seat. Cléo couldn't keep his eyes off Richard and Max's brown caps, with the Chicago Bulls insignia on them, and their baggy jeans. Interrupting their conversation, he asked them where they'd got them. You want to redo your wardrobe? Max asked. It's about time! It just so happens that at the party yesterday, the girl you were necking with said she liked you and everything and she thought you were cute, but she'd rather not look at your flannel pants. Max and Richard hugged their ribs, for a long time, they couldn't stop laughing. Once in a while, Richard caught his breath and repeated: she'd rather not look at them. Yeah, why did he wear those pants?

Carl asked in a whisper. It's not my fault, Cléo defended himself, my mother bought them.

At the Lionel-Groulx station, since the connecting train was
slow to arrive, they amused themselves by climbing up the escala-
tors backwards, but they soon tired of this and took up a position
near a railing where they could stare at the people below. Just as
Richard was suggesting they spit on a man in his fifties who was as
bald as a billiard ball, the train pulled in. In the car, they ended up
opposite a group of young Italians in overalls, who, with orange
fingertips, were stuffing themselves full of barbecue-flavoured
Cheetos. Richard was trying to snip their straps with nothing but
his eyes and his lips barely moved: they think they're so cool, so,
so cool. . . . At Peel station, the Italians got out of the car single
file and, once the doors had shut again, they hit the window and
spit on it. Richard jumped up like a spring, hammered on the
glass himself and gave them the finger: I knew they'd do that,
bunch of cowards! Cléo watched the scene, his mouth open, his
eyes big as quarters. He nudged Carl's boot with his foot and, with
a discreet nod, he enquired: what, did they know those guys?
Richard and Max laughed scornfully. No, you idiot, answered
Richard, who'd jumped to his feet. Didn't he see? They were Italians! He didn't want to know them!

Grasping Teta's arms, they cross the yard whistling and bustle
into a building whose orange brick is incredibly faded. Ketcia is at
the head of the group, she climbs the stairs quickly and inserts the
key in the lock. They slip into the apartment, go into CB's room,
and, after listening to be sure they're alone, they lock the door.
Shadow warms the room, while the walls, the unmade bed and
the pile of clothes in the dark corner all stink of perspiration and
rank air. CB pulls the chair from his desk into the middle of the
room and orders Richard and Max to tie Teta to it, which they
accomplish with absolutely no trouble. The four Bad Boys, sit on
the bed, knee to knee, and observe the hostage for a little while.

158

Two minuscule black eyes, prisoners in a moon-shaped face, stare back at them. Richard and Max laugh nervously, then Richard steps towards Teta and levels his finger in his face: "Just what do you think you look like now, eh?"

He waits for the Latino's reply, then decides to answer himself, "Like a real idiot! It's too bad Mixon isn't here to settle the score with you himself."

Richard walks around Teta, puts an arm around his neck and, biting his bottom lip, squeezes Teta's throat. Teta moans and the other draws his mouth close to his ear like he was going to bite it: you fat, smelly Latino! Then, loud enough for the others to hear, he says, "That'll teach you, you moron!"

"And now, what do we do?" Ketcia asks in a worried voice.

CB stops her with a motion and changes languages.

"*Minit la*! . . . When we talk strategy, we do it in Creole. Everyone got that?"

He orders them to form a circle. In a low, monotone voice, he explains that the basic idea is to be respected. He doesn't hide the fact that he wants revenge. What they did to Mixon can't be forgiven, they agree on that, but, for the time being, the important thing is to get back their coats. With Teta as a hostage, he has no doubt Latino Power will have to give in. Afterwards, they'll see, it all depends. One thing has to be clear, though: vengeance is treacherous, it's to be wielded with the utmost precaution, they have to know exactly when to strike. Do they understand what he's telling them? One by one they nod their heads, then direct their eyes back towards Teta.

"We need you, Teta," says CB. "If you cooperate, everything should take place in a calm, friendly manner."

"You better talk, asshole," Richard bursts out, "or else I'm going to smash your face in!"

CB grabs Richard's arm and twists it until, with a contorted face, he lets out a heartbreaking cry.

"*A p rekòumanse sa a, m ap jete l dewò!*" CB rebuffs him.

Rubbing his arm, Richard straightens up again. CB turns towards the hostage.

"Tell me, Teta, where did you hide the coats?"

The Latino's face remains as lifeless as a mummy's.

"You answer, we get our coats back and you're a free man, Teta. I give you my word of honour."

Teta grumbles, leans forward and spits greenish saliva onto the floor.

"You're wasting your time, CB. I'm not talking."

As if he's just got third-degree burns on his hand, Richard suddenly starts to shake it as he hops up and down.

"*A p tou mèm pa lèsse l fè sa nan yon tàpì!*" Richard explodes. "*M ap pini l idio! S'il te plè! A p lès mwen vange onè nan Mixon!*"

CB gives Richard a ferocious look. Richard stuffs his hands into his pockets and is suddenly still. CB gets up, goes over to the window, and spends a long time observing what's going on outside: two boys decked out in Canadiens jerseys that are much too big for them are lazily playing hockey in the driveway in front of the building, one is the goalie, the other playing offence.

"You're not leaving me much choice," he says to Teta, without looking at him. "Richard is dying to punch your face in. If you don't want to help, I'm going to have to give him the green light."

He comes back over to Teta, kneels down in front of him, and makes an effort to speak to him in a persuasive voice, closing his eyes when he pauses: "You understand what I mean, Teta? Personally, I'm on your side. They're the ones that want to hurt you. I just want you to answer my question. Where are the coats, Teta?"

A grimace of disgust has settled onto Teta's lips, and, he's so full of boiling rage that his ears are twitching. CB goes back to the window and, without a trace of hesitation in his voice, he shouts to Richard: *va zi!* Now, he's examining his fingernails, humming a popular song and, from time to time, glancing furtively at Teta.

Delighted, Richard positions himself opposite Teta, he spits in his hands and rubs them together jubilantly. With a criminal look on his face, he makes a fist, bites it, then gets some momentum. But just at the second he's about to hit Teta, he stops his arm, his breath is short. He looks around, showing off a wide smile, as if he's overexcited. Stupefied, Max is watching his movements, while Ketcia, her head turned away, is staring at the rug. As for Teta's he's got his eyes shut; countless wrinkles appear all around his long lashes. Richard gets back into position, rocks his arm back and forth a few times, and building up momentum like girls do, he punches Teta in the ear. *¡Ayyyyy!* CB continues to clean under his fingernails, keeps whistling the same song. And as if he's conquered his fear, Richard deals the hostage two more punches in quick succession: one in the cheek, the other in the nose. In tears, his face scarlet, Teta has a long coughing attack, as if he's ready to cough up his lungs. A thread of blood dribbles from his nose and, in a reflex action, he cranes his neck forward to avoid staining his T-shirt.

"Check it out, CB." Richard points. "He's getting your rug dirty."

CB comes back over to Teta and, with the tips of his fingers, repositions Teta's head so his blood falls on his own T-shirt.

"You going to talk now?"

Although tears are running down his cheeks, Teta grits his teeth and shakes his head no.

"I think you broke his nose," CB says, as though commenting on the weather.

The Latino is shaken by pitiful sobs.

"Okay, that's enough playing around," CB continues. "If you're not going to open your trap, it doesn't really matter in the end."

CB goes over to his desk, dominated by a tangled mass of dirty clothes, loose-leaf paper and books. He opens the bottom drawer.

"This guy's not going to talk, I can feel it," CB says in Creole. "He's stubborn as a mule. We have no choice. I'm going to call Flaco and tell him his little friend's face is all bloody. We'll see how happy that makes him."

He takes out a small black pad, leafs through it quickly and turns over the corner of one page. Then, with long strides, he goes out of the room and, after a few seconds, he comes back with a phone in his hand. He plugs it in and dials a number.

"Hello. May I please speak with Flaco? . . . This is CB, I'm a friend of your son's . . . Okay, I'll call back tonight. Just a moment, please, can I leave a message? . . . Ask him to call CB . . . Yes, he has my number . . . Tell him it's urgent. Goodbye."

He hangs up.

He asks Ketcia to be the lookout by the window and Max to bring him some toilet paper. Ketcia doesn't understand what she's supposed to be looking out for, but doesn't dare ask. She sits on CB's desk in order to have the best possible view.

"You afraid your father will come home, CB?" she asks.

"On weekends, he stays at his girlfriend's. There's no danger of that."

"What – he has a steady girlfriend now?" Richard marvels.

"One of his girlfriends, I mean."

Max reappears in the doorway, a pack of toilet paper in his hand, and CB gestures with his chin for him to clean up the blood on the rug. Then, with his hands on his hips, CB takes a few steps, runs a hand through his hair and decides to stretch out on the bed. Richard drops down into the old armchair in the back of the room, while Max, once he's done, throws the bloody paper in the garbage and, hesitating, comes back towards CB.

"Couldn't we take Teta off the chair, so I could sit down?"

CB is staring at the cracks in the ceiling, his hands behind his head. Max sighs, wipes his hands on his pants and then sits on the rug, his back against the wall.

It's like, after so much emotion, Ketcia thinks, he needs a little quiet, a little rest. Personally, I never would have thought we would have ended up here. She always thinks it's too bad to have to resort to violence, but, sometimes, it's true, and CB has said so, they have no choice. The image of Mixon pops back into her head, he got out of the hospital yesterday. Since his parents want him to rest up over the weekend, they're not letting him go out. She again thinks of the strange evening they spent yesterday at Mixon's, when his mother invited all the members of the gang to come to dinner, along with their parents. Everyone came, except CB of course, he doesn't go out of his way for that kind of occasion. After they'd eaten, when they were all sitting in the living room, Mixon's mother got up, crossed her hands and spoke to them solemnly, having apparently prepared a speech: what happened is serious and we wanted to talk to you about it. Especially with you, the other parents. There followed a long, unbearably boring tirade about the decadent morals in modern cities. In conclusion, the woman spent a great deal of time lamenting the decline of faith in the Sweet Lord Jesus.

Seething, Ketcia's mother coughed and said what was on her mind. Was she finished now? Ketcia smiled, her mother had never been one to hold her tongue. Mixon's mother looked distraught, then hurt, then she finally got angry. Yes, now that she thought of it, it's as if Mixon's mother wanted her revenge: there was something else. Our children are on drugs. Their mouths hanging open, every member of the gang turned towards Mixon. Shit, Ketcia had suddenly thought, what could he possibly have told her? Later, visibly ashamed of his lack of courage, Mixon explained that, under his parents' pressure, he'd had to admit certain things, or else he'd have been held prisoner in his own house for a month. Keep an eye on your children, Mixon's mother had added, proud of having regained control of the situation. At home, as soon as she'd hung her raincoat on the hook, Ketcia's mother took her aside: what's all this about drugs?

Ketcia avoided her eyes, weighed the available choices and lied as naturally as anything: no, no, Mom, that woman was just making things up. You said it yourself, she's crazy! Having dropped down into his armchair in the living room, from a distance, her father called: Ketcia, you're telling us the truth, aren't you? And she felt a tickling in her stomach, then she quickly replied: maybe Mixon had been smoking, but not us. When the words left her mouth, she immediately felt bad, CB always says, the worst thing is ratting on other people. Her mother took her by the shoulders and shook her: don't ever let me catch you doing anything that stupid!

Ketcia turns back towards the others: CB and Max seem to have fallen asleep, while, in the dark corner, Richard is struggling to stay awake. Teta is looking at her with sad, sleepy, begging eyes. You're really barking up the wrong tree, she thinks, if you believe that just because I'm a girl, you can soften me up. It's true he looks pitiful, though: a clot of bloody snot has dried under his nose and his T-shirt is covered with scarlet red spots. She forces herself to think of Mixon, his arm, his bandage, his haggard face. Outside, things are pretty quiet, the two boys who were playing hockey went home quite a while ago. She looks at her watch: an hour has passed, she can't believe how time flies. She rotates her head so she doesn't get a stiff neck. Now, the breathing and different-sounding snores tell her that all of them, including Teta, are asleep. How come she's not sleep? When she sees the police car quietly park in front of Teta's building she suddenly understands why CB asked her to keep an eye on what was happening outside. She claps her hands: they all jump, swear and get up staggering.

"The cops are here!" she shouts, forgetting to speak Créole.

"I knew it," CB says, rushing towards the window.

Teta starts screaming his lungs out and, for a long moment, panic stricken, they all freeze, their eyes staring. CB finally jumps towards him, goes behind the chair, covers his mouth with one hand and squeezes his stomach with his arm, like he's trying to empty it. The Latino chokes, coughs and stops shouting. CB orders Max to bring him a dirty T-shirt, which he puts on Teta's mouth, before knotting it energetically. Then he comes back to the window.

"What are we going to do?" Max asks in a trembling voice. "Shit, this is getting fucking serious."

CB doesn't answer, he's watching the police officers walk towards Teta's building.

"You think we should let him go?" Max goes on. "Have we waited long enough? . . . It's getting heavy, man."

"No way," CB orders in a loud voice, without looking at him. "We have to finish what we started."

"Buddy," Max insists, "the cops are outside. This isn't funny. What if they decide to do a complete search of all the neighbouring buildings?"

"Shut the hell up, you coward! . . . I'm ashamed of you!"

CB looks at Max in disgust, glances at his watch and, in an authoritative tone says: "We have no choice but to wait for Flaco to call."

"Completely naked?" you asked.

"No, no," Carmen replied, "don't be silly, it's just a figure of speech. She was wearing a bathrobe, of course, it is the month of April. What were you thinking?"

"You should know," Roberto pointed out, "that your mother is incapable of telling anything without feeling like she has to add something. With her, everything is possible, a tiny spider can suddenly be the size of Godzilla."

"You stay out of this, please!" Carmen said. "To the best of my knowledge, I'm not talking to you! Anyway, you didn't see it. You were snoring when it happened."

"She came out onto the balcony in her wheelchair," you said, "and then what?"

165

"Well, I was getting dressed before I came to make breakfast," she continued, "when I hear shouting. No, wait, it wasn't really shouting, it was like screaming. I go over to the window, I open it and that's when I saw her on the balcony. After that, it was like she was talking to herself, she was saying things in Creole, I think, I didn't understand what she was saying."

"Okay!" Roberto interrupted her. "Now your story doesn't make sense anymore."

"She didn't fall out of her chair, she was just there near the balcony railing, but she kept waving her arms around like this . . . It was like she had a stomach ache or something. People were stopping on the sidewalk, but then they'd just move on again. One man just kept on walking, without even looking at her, like nothing was going on. I couldn't believe it. . . ."

"You should have called the ambulance right away," Roberto said. "You don't let something like that wait. It could explode."

"That's what I was going to do, Roberto, I told you. But once I was in the living room, when I picked up the phone, I saw the ambulance pull up. Someone else in the area must have called. And there is another reason why I didn't call sooner, I was waiting for Cléo to come out onto the balcony."

"He's probably not even home," you said. "On weekends, he always sleeps over at one of his friends'. But what do you think was wrong with his mom?"

"It's hard to say. I don't know any details about her private life. All I know is what you tell me. You're in a better position than I am to explain things. Although, I did bump into her two or three times this week."

"You did?" remarked Roberto. "You didn't tell me that. . . ."

"Yes. She works in a factory on Boulevard Saint Laurent too. She told me that in the beginning it was okay, but now she was suffocating from all the dust at work. If I remember right, she said she didn't have the strength to keep working. The last time she even said she was thinking about going back to Haiti."

"Marcelo, maybe you should call Cléo before your cousins get here," Roberto suggested. "He could probably use some company right now, with his mother being in the hospital and all, it can't be easy for him."

"It's just that we don't see each other much anymore," you explained. "We're not such good friends anymore."

"Really?" Roberto asked in surprise. "Did you have a fight?"

"No, I don't know. Sometimes I even have a hard time explaining to myself what happened."

"For once," Carmen offered, "I agree with your father. You should call him."

"You think so? You really think so?"

"Of course! The least you can do is call someone when they need it. It can also give you a chance to start over again."

"He's probably not even home."

"Don't make me ask again," Carmen insisted. "Go on, do it."

Remember, Marcelo: you'd gone into the living room, you'd picked up the receiver and you'd dialled his number without much hope. When you heard his "hello," you said to yourself: is that Cléo? Since you hardly spoke to each other anymore, his voice seemed to have changed. You hesitated and, fearing a refusal or a bad mood, you simply said: how are you? It took him a little while to answer, as if he hadn't yet decided whether or not to talk to you. Yeah, he was okay. And is your mother getting better? In an apathetic yet intrigued voice, he asked: did you see her on the balcony? My mother's the one who saw her. And he said, she's okay, she's going to be all right. Remember his little devil-may-care smile, Marcelo. Why? Then, just to make a little conversation with you, he added that he'd been at Carl's when everything happened, that his Haitian friends were the ones who'd told him. She'd taken too many tranquilizers, that's all. A heavy silence followed, during which you thought you heard confusing conversations over the in-and-out sounds of his breathing. I'm telling you, he added, there's nothing seriously wrong with

167

her. You sure you don't need anything, Cléo? No, it'll be okay, thanks. It's not the first time she's done something like that. Okay, I just wanted to know if you needed anything. No problem, Marcelo. Bye, bye.

You hung up and you remained motionless for a long time. Why was Cléo talking to you like that? Why did you have the feeling he was mad at you? Because, yes, there was some resentment, skilfully camouflaged by feigned indifference, that surfaced in the inflections of his voice. At that point, you swore you'd never talk to him again, then the image of Carole in her wheelchair, with arms outstretched, came back to you and shame burned your cheeks. What were you supposed to think about all this? Hey, champ, what are you doing? someone shouted at you, putting an end to your reflection. Enrique and Toño, your two cousins, had just burst into the living room, after slipping into your apartment without knocking. Boy, you're looking pretty down in the dumps, Marcelo! Toño commented. It was nothing, you just hadn't got enough sleep, that's all. Shall we go? You put on your windbreaker, you asked your cousins to wait a minute, then you went to say goodbye to your parents. They asked you what Cléo had said to you. You see, you did the right thing by calling your friend, Carmen approved. Yes, Mom, you were right.

Outside, it was chilly, and Enrique energetically rubbed his arms through the sleeves of his windbreaker: you have no idea how eager I am for summer to get here! Remember: Enrique and Toño, twin brothers, had emigrated to Canada the previous August and, since they'd moved into the neighbourhood a month ago, you'd seen them almost every day. They thought of you as their little brother, and the speed with which they took you under their wing surprised you and made you happy. Anyway, continued Enrique, as far as the weather is concerned, there's no place like Chile! What do you know about it, Toño retorted, since the only places you know are Canada and Chile. Enrique gave him a dark look, but then he softened, as if he'd thought better of it.

168

You strolled down Légaré acting silly, then you ran across Van Horne and Kent to avoid the cars. On the sidewalk, two girls with sparkling eyes and tight pants passed you. Enrique was quick to whistle, his eyes riveted to their asses as they rose and fell with each step: hey, look at that! Not bad for Asians, eh, Marcelo? Surprised, you didn't answer. Tell me, do you have a girlfriend? Give me a chance, I'm only in primary school. And Toño wiped improbable sweat from his forehead with his forearm and said impatiently: yeah, he's still too young. His face beaming, Enrique put an arm around your shoulders and hugged you both: what are you talking about, guys? In primary school in Chile, he already had lots of girls after him. They'd come by the dozens to knock on his door! Wasn't that true, Toño? Lots of times, it even ended with terrible fights. And when girls fight, they don't fool around, they pulled hair and everything. Here, at the Polyvalente, all he had to do was sit on a bench and they could be sure he attracted them like a magnet! It was simple, he wreaked havoc wherever he went! Grinning, Toño noisily cleared his throat: are you sure you aren't exaggerating just a little? How can you say such a thing! Enrique said, offended. He'd seen them during breaks, hadn't he, there were always two or three of them orbiting around him? Toño sighed: yes, but you're in grade ten and you're always going out with girls in grade seven or eight. How do you explain that? Enrique's face closed up, then, his voice thinner under the effects of increasing irritation, retorted: what does that change? They're still girls, aren't they? It was better than what you were doing anyway, stuck with the same chick since you'd come to Canada. And a Chilean on top of it all! At least he was exploring, he'd tried girls who were Lebanese, Vietnamese. He was adventuresome! Toño exchanged a knowing look with you and shrugged his shoulders in a sign of amused powerlessness.

You entered the underground parking lot at the Plaza Côte-des-Neiges and, a few steps later, you noticed that two boys with jet-black skin, both wearing faded T-shirts, were coming towards you, laughing loudly. In passing, Enrique lowered an icy gaze on them, as he bit his tongue, and the Black guys, astonished, immediately stopped laughing. Did you see? Enrique asked. What? You asked with a nod. You don't see that those guys were laughing at us. You went through the revolving doors into the mall and, as you went past a hair salon, Enrique said: the other day at the Polyvalente, when I told a Québécois kid I lived around Côte-des-Neiges, you know what he answered? Huh, you know what? He answered: You mean Côte-des-Nègres, that Black alley? There's nothing but immigrants around there. Can you imagine? Enrique energetically shook his head, as if smoke was going to start coming out of his ears, and he added: anyway, one thing's for sure, the neighbourhood's filling up with dirty Blacks faster than you can count them! Toño turned around: man, you're an ass, you're so prejudiced! Then Enrique got mad: we know why you're always defending the Blacks. It's because of your Jamaican friend Andrew. Let me tell you something, they don't need you to defend them, there's enough of them as it is. On the escalator, he was now leaning towards his twin and from time to time he poked him in the chest with his index finger: you know what the teacher said to us after that fight between the Italians and the Latinos? Eh, you know what he said? Please stick with your own people. And to that, just for you, Toño, I'd add: defend your own kind before you defend others!

Remember, Marcelo: in front of the chrome turnstiles of Zellers, you quickly felt something wasn't quite right, that Enrique was getting dangerously angry. He turned and stared at every passerby and, when you asked him a question, he'd answer without looking at you: what? what did you say? Okay, said Toño, I'm going to the sports store downstairs, I think they have soccer balls. We'll look at the prices and we'll meet up back here, near Pick-Nick. He disappeared behind the tables where dozen of boys in basketball clothes were devouring hotdogs, but he came back a few seconds later, tapping his finger against his temple: look at

170

the quality and the brand of the balls, too. Yeah, yeah, Enrique answered, exasperated. When his brother had gone, he started looking around, as if he was looking for someone, and then he leaned towards you: listen good, little cousin. You stay here, he said, articulating each syllable meticulously, and if you see anything unusual, you meet me in the store right away. Enrique was already walking away when you held him back by tail of his windbreaker: I don't understand. If I see what that's unusual? Enrique stared at the elevator in the distance as if it was the other end of the world and, with a discouraged grimace twisting his face, he grumbled: use your brain once in a while, Marcelo. Don't be *huevón*! And he went through the turnstiles, as you stood there swallowing your saliva with difficulty and wondering: what should I do? Should I stay or should I go?

After five long minutes, Toño reappeared. The balls were either monstrously expensive or of poor quality, like they were made out of plastic, but you couldn't really tell. All the better to screw you, kiddo, Toño added. Three times more expensive than in Chile, can you imagine? Now he was nervously tapping his foot, and he kept checking his watch. Then you saw Enrique coming towards you at top speed, slaloming through the multicoloured crowd. Time to go, guys. He wasn't kidding. Toño, humming a meandering tune, asked him with a nod of his head: so, did you find anything? I hope you had better luck than I did. But Enrique was already heading for the door with long strides: you deaf? He just said it was time to go! You fell into step behind him and, once you were outside, in silent agreement, you all began to run as fast as you could. Once you made it to Rue Barclay, Enrique slipped like an eel into the lobby of an apartment building, and you followed him, pushed by a sort of automatic reflex. With one hand against the wall, a grimace of pain twisting his face, Toño kept repeating, shaking his head: tell me it's not true, tell me you didn't do anything, Enrique, tell me it's just a joke . . . With lightning speed, Enrique pulled down the zipper on his

171

windbreaker, dropped his pants and, pulled a deflated ball out of his T-shirt and underwear. Victoriously, he waved it under his brother's nose. Toño remained silent, furiously running one hand through his hair. If it makes you feel any better, Enrique said, it's not the best one they had. Now Toño was looking him up and down severely, squinting: you're really an idiot! What's your problem? Why do you always have to steal? You. . . . you. . . . He didn't finish his sentence, he lowered his arms and turned toward the glass door. Remember, Marcelo: thunderstruck, you were thinking that you'd been right, in front of the department store, to think what you'd been thinking.

VII

When Flaco gets home, and stops in the living room doorway, Carmen is dozing under a grey poncho, and Roberto, sitting in the armchair, his back straight, his arms crossed, keeps his eyes riveted on the TV. Earlier, on the bleachers in Parc Kent, he'd seen his father surrounded by his friends, at the finals of the Coupe Allende as well. When the crowd stood up to give an ovation to a player who had just scored a goal, their eyes met and he thought for an instant that his old man would turn his head, but after a few uneasy seconds, he waved his hand vaguely. Why the hesitation? Was he ashamed of him? For months now, he's only spoken to him to ask for the salt at dinner, to tell him to make his bed or turn down the volume of his music when he shuts himself up in his room. One day, from the hallway, he overheard part of a muted conversation in the kitchen between his father and his Uncle Juan. Roberto's voice had become ironic: relationship? what relationship? I prefer not to talk about it, Juanito, believe me, there's not much to tell. Flaco sits down on the arm of the sofa at Carmen's feet, while Roberto, determined to ignore him, continues to stare at the screen. Prisoners are digging a tunnel by handing buckets of earth from one man to the next. Carmen stretches, yawns, opens her moist eyes and blinks. She sits up suddenly, looks worried and mutters something he doesn't catch. She repeats: "Was Teta with you?"

"No. I haven't seen him all night."

She tells him that Señora Eugenia has called several times. After Mass, Teta was supposed to come over to see him then go right back home for lunch – but he never came home. Does Flaco have any idea where he could be? Flaco's heart panics, and, for a moment he imagines the worst: a sliced-up body, blood, haggard faces, tears. *¡Pobre Teta! No, Dios mío*, let him be safe. He glances at his father who seems hypnotized by the movie.

"You really don't know where he could be?" Carmen insists.

"No, Mom, I swear. We were all at the park. We told him to meet us early in the afternoon but he never came and since he's always making us wait, we got fed up and left. We figured he'd meet us later."

Carmen tells him that Señora Eugenia, gnawed by fear, finally called the police. The old woman is sure something bad has happened, she had all sorts of premonitions that left no room for anything good. He knows what the old woman is like. Who knows if her worry is justified or not. But she's all worked up!

"She also mentioned stolen leather coats," she added. "What's that all about?"

Now, Roberto turns and looks at them.

"Leather coats? What leather coats?"

"She said she found a bag full of coats with drawings of panthers and English words on them."

"I don't know anything about it. I swear to you."

"That's what I thought. I said to her: listen, Señora Eugenia, I'm not stupid, I know our children aren't saints, but they're not the kind that would steal either . . . I bet Teta's probably with a girl while she's worrying to death."

The last sentence's questioning intonation is not lost on Flaco.

"Even we were wondering where he could have been," he offers. "Yeah, maybe he is with a girl, it's possible. I'll call Señora Eugenia."

He steps over to the little round table where the phone sits and picks up the receiver, which he wedges between his shoulder and his ear.

"Oh yeah, I almost forgot," says Carmen. "You got another call. Someone named CB, if I remember right. He wants you to call back. He said it was urgent."

¡Putamadre! Teta's slashed, demolished, purple body flashes in his mind again. A crust of dried blood under his nose, his T-shirt torn to shreds. He bends his knees, unplugs the cord and takes the phone.

"Who is he?" she asks.

"Hmph!" he says, dropping one hand, "just a friend from school."

He goes down the hallway, locks his bedroom door, and collapses like a pile of bricks onto his chair. He wraps both hands around his head and lets out a long breath through his mouth: he can't believe it! They went to church with him just to make sure he didn't get kidnapped, and that's exactly what happened. How the hell did they do it? He plugs in the phone, but he hesitates between just dropping the whole mess and calling the old woman. He knew when they all got together in front of Lalo's building, that it was a mistake not to wait for Teta. He should have insisted they stay there until Teta showed up. Lalo was the first to urge them to leave without him. Then, since the others didn't want to miss the beginning of the first game, they decided to clear off. He dials the number, it only rings once before a trembling voice answers.

"*Buenas noches, Señora Eugenia*. It's Flaco."

"*Dios mío* . . . Is Teta with you?"

"No, señora. He didn't come meet us at the park."

A long wail comes down the line, then she begs God's mercy in returning her son to her. The old woman is short of breath, as if she were asthmatic,. He tries to calm her down, but he also admits he doesn't know where Teta is.

"I've been tolerant enough with you all. Now stop lying to me and tell me where my son is."

"Listen to me. I don't know. And that's the absolute truth. I'm as surprised by all of this as you are. But I think I have an idea where he might be."

"Tell me right now, *niñito!*" she begs. "Or I'm going to have to tell the police all about the coats! Don't force me to do something like that, Flaco, don't force me to do it!"

"Calm down and listen to everything I'm going to say. I need you to trust me, do you understand? I'm asking you to give me till one AM. If you don't hear from me by then, you can tell whoever you want whatever you want. You have to give me that much time to keep this situation from blowing up."

Flaco hears her moan and cluck. He adds in a sweet tone, "I'm sure nothing's happened to him, that he's safe and sound."

"That's not what I think, Flaco. . . ."

At the other end of the line, sniffles punctuate the silence, and the old woman gives her nose a good blow, but a whistle continues to accompany her breathing.

"What do you mean?" Flaco asks.

"I see all kinds of things I don't like, Flaco," she sobs. "I see shadows, a lot of red, and it's all a bad sign. I'm afraid. Very afraid."

"Calm down, señora. I'll bring him back to you before one AM, I promise. But you have to trust me. You have to."

The old woman erupts in a frenetic fit of tears that sounds like a tumultuous laugh. Little by little, she gets hold of herself.

"Of all Teta's friends, I've always liked you best, Flaco. You've always been good to him. You're a loyal young man."

"I treat my friends as if they were my brothers, señora."

"Don't disappoint me, please, don't disappoint me."

176

"You won't regret this, Señora Eugenia. I give you my word of honour."

Half-heartedly, still sniffling melodramatically, she tells him it's okay, she accepts, she'll wait for his call. Flaco comforts her one last time, then hangs up. For a good minute, he's in such a state of confusion that as he stares at the alarm clock on his nightstand, he's conscious that, one by one, the seconds are slipping away. He gets up, staggers, runs his hands across his face. Now what? He stands there, unmoving, for a long time. He goes towards the dresser, pulls out the top drawer, takes out the condor and shoves it in his pocket. He looks into the living room: his father is in there alone, still absorbed by the movie.

"Can I talk to you?" Flaco asks.

For a moment, Roberto pretends not to hear, then he levels his black eyes on him. Flaco sits very close to him, on the couch. They watch each other intently without speaking. Flaco looks into his hard face, his hollow cheeks, his straight nose, his drooping moustache. His eyes are overly narrow: is he just tired or is it a sign he's on his guard? Roberto picks up the remote control and lowers the volume on the TV.

"Listen," Flaco begins. "I don't know how to explain this. But I have to talk to you about something that's going on. It's about Teta."

Roberto follows his hand movements with suspicious attention.

"I think I know where he is. But I don't know what to do. I feel like I'm caught in a trap and I want. . . ."

With a gesture, Roberto stops him, clears his throat.

"I want you to understand one thing. You may not have to explain as much as you think to me. I know more than you think."

Flaco looks taken aback.

"You're surprised? What did you think? That I was never young?"

177

His eyes suddenly lose their tired look.

"You think I didn't know you were lying before about the coats? You can hide a lot from your mother, but not from me, Flaco. Don't forget that."

"But that's why I came to talk to you."

An annoyed look hardens Roberto's face. Then for several seconds he blinks his eyes as if thinking intensely.

"It doesn't work like that, Flaco. Don't you know that? I don't even know who you are. If you want to know, you're like a stranger to me now. You think it didn't hurt me in the beginning? But to tell the truth, I'm not even mad at you about it anymore."

He smoothes his moustache.

"You wanted to live your own life, put up a barrier between you and us? Well, go ahead, see it through now."

"But, Dad, that's just it, I want things between us to be like they used to be."

"Today, because you're in a jam, you're coming to see me. No, Flaco. You're an adult now. You're going to have to make your decisions on your own."

For a long moment, Flaco is silent, flabbergasted. Ready-made sentences, full of desperate sincerity, pop into his mind, but he can't bring himself to utter them. Roberto grabs the remote to shut off the TV, stands, and heads towards the living room doorway. Already in the darkness of the foyer, he stops and slowly turns around.

"I'll give you one piece of advice, Flaco. Just one. If there's any possible way, avoid a bloodbath."

Then, lowering a finger at him, "I know that's how bad it is now."

He shakes his head, purses his lips and disappears into the darkness of the hallway. Flaco feels like he wants to cry but then, after a moment, his sadness makes him angry and it takes all his strength to hold back his tears: now is not the time. He goes out quickly, he needs some fresh air. Outside, he takes a few steps,

178

realizes he's shaking, his teeth are chattering. He crosses the yard, passes under two streetlights and goes around one building: okay, there's light in the windows on the second floor. Climbing the stairs, he hears the cheerful voice of a TV announcer and a shower of applause. He raps on the door three times. The wide smile of a little boy appears in the narrow space the door has opened: what do you want? You're here to see my sister, right? Out of bravado, the boy opens the door a bit, he's wearing blue pyjamas covered with all kinds of trucks. And he says, I don't have time to play, Diego, I'm not kidding around. Is she here? And the little boy answers, I don't know, maybe, and he gives a high-pitched laugh. Steps approach and Paulina appears. She gives the boy a little tap on the bum: go on, go on, children your age are all in bed by now!

Flaco slips into the foyer, tells her he has to talk to her. She runs her fingers across his face, you're all pale, takes his hand, what's wrong? Come on, let's go into the kitchen, he answers. They go past the living room, Flaco nods hello to Paulina's parents, and her father, taking drag after drag off his cigarette, waves at him, *hola, pibe*. In the kitchen she turns on the lights and the yellowish glow from the naked bulb, suspended over the table, is reflected off the greasy walls. They sit diagonally across from each other, she observes him and continues to caress his hands. When he finishes telling her, he arches his eyebrows into a point: what does she think? She pulls back her hands, gets up and looks deeply into his eyes: he knows what she's going to advise him to do. Is she sure? Yes, Flaco, it's the only thing to do. What else is there? Right now, he sighs, he's not sure of anything. No, he's sure of one thing, he needs her. Really. Once again she covers his hands with her own and squeezes them, a kind smile on her lips: of course, he can count on her. First he has to go get the bag of coats at Teta's he explains. The problem is, since he has to get them without the old woman knowing, he needs someone to distract her. She tells him he can count on her to help, and she says it with such spontaneity that he wraps his arms around her. They go back to the living room and Paulina steps over to her parents: I'll be right back. *¡Un momento, niñita!* says her mother snapping her fingers. Where are you going at this hour? I'm going out, not for long, Mom. But it's late, Paulina. Come on, just fifteen minutes, please. Let her go out, the father intervenes, points a pistol-shaped finger at Flaco, and winks his goodbye. Bring her back safe and sound, *pibe*. I promise, Flaco smiles, and he thinks: her old man really likes me.

When they get outside, they hurry across the street and step into the building where Teta lives. When they get to the third floor, they inhale deeply trying to calm their breathing, and Flaco hides on the stairs while Paulina rings the bell. Señora Eugenia's slow steps make the floor creak, she asks who it is, unlocks the door when she hears the answer, and Paulina flashes a charming smile: *buenas noches*, she's come to keep her company for a little while. She heard what's happened. The old woman's sagging face smiles weakly: that's so nice of you, *niñita*! Of course, come in, and the door closes. Since it's taking Paulina quite a while to come back to let him in, Flaco finally sits down on the stairs. The fluorescent tubes above his head go on and off unexpectedly, buzzing like a regiment of furious wasps. Finally, Paulina opens the door a crack, just barely enough for him to get in. Flaco slips into the darkness of the entryway, and she whispers to him: there's no danger, she's in the living room. To be on the safe side, Flaco removes his shoes, carries them in his hand, and heads for Teta's room, while Paulina goes back to the living room to start up a conversation with Señora Eugenia. Without turning on the light, he goes straight to the closet, which exhales a nauseating odour of old socks, and sticks in his head. The bag doesn't appear to be in there. He rushes to the dresser and pulls open all the drawers, but nothing. Under the bed? Not there either? In the four corners of the room? No luck. *¡Putamadre!* That's all he needs!

Suddenly, he hears steps: it's not possible! He stretches out on his stomach under the bed, the door opens and a bright ray of light slices the floor. Someone turns on the light: Flaco? He recognizes Paulina's running shoes, standing there before him holding the garbage bag. It was in the kitchen pantry, she whispers. He jumps to his feet and opens the bag: the coats really are in there. It's okay, he grabs the bag, swings it across his shoulder and heads towards the entrance, followed by Paulina. At the door, as he's putting his shoes back on, she tells him she's going to stay a little while longer. They kiss on the mouth and for a moment she holds him back. He frees himself and she asks, in an evasive voice: and now? He gives her a sorry look, then his face closes up and he doesn't respond. Anyway, don't be a hero, okay, Flaco?

At his place, everything's dark, his father's probably gone to bed. In his room, he puts down the bag, takes a couple of breaths, sits on the chair at his desk and, having made a decision, picks up the telephone.

You were beginning your second warm-up lap, jogging side by side with Akira and inhaling the cool morning air, when you quietly forked off towards the back door to the school. You crossed the silent, deserted gym, and you pushed open the door to the boys' washroom. You rushed towards one of the urinals holding your crotch with both hands.

"Who's there?"

You looked all around: strange, you couldn't see anyone. Who could it be? When you finished going to the bathroom, you pulled the lever, water ran through the urinal, and you took several steps towards the place where the voice had seemed to come from.

"Cléo, is that you?"

Some coughing sounds could be heard, then a voice spoke as best it could, "Hi, Marcelo. You're not with the others?"

"I had to go to the washroom, but I made sure Serge didn't see me."

"Don't you think he's a pain with all his rules?"

"He doesn't want us to waste any time. You know how serious the competitions are for him."

You noticed a thread of bluish smoke rising from the stall where Cléo was.

"So," he asked. "What's new with you?"

You told him about how a few times you'd gone out with your cousins, who, older than you, were teaching you all kinds of sports like soccer and table tennis. Then he opened the door and came forward holding a cigarette between his first two fingers. He was wearing an oversized T-shirt marked Public Enemy and thick-soled basketball shoes, with thick red laces that went all the way up to his ankles. He started to cough, lowered his eyes, then leaned one hand against the wall.

"Well," he said, "lately, I've been taking it easy."

He went back into the stall, threw his cigarette in the toilet, flushed and came back towards you.

"Now I know that I used to just be a little twerp. Do you remember my first day at this school? The first Phys. Ed. class?"

In a neutral voice, you answered yes, you remembered.

"It seems so long ago . . . Today nobody would dare give me a hard time."

"Can't argue with that," you commented, "you're a real tough guy now."

Your statement hit its mark: Cléo gave a lazy laugh, a laugh you'd never heard from him before, Marcelo.

"You know what," he remarked, "you're the only guy I couldn't beat up."

"What do you mean?"

"I don't know. You're too good a guy."

"Too good?"

"Yeah, everybody likes you, you never try to pick fights."

"Maybe I'm tougher than you think."

"Maybe, but I don't think so. And I know you well enough to know, I think."

The conversation turned to what you were going to do for the summer, then to each of your families.

"My mother?" Cléo asked. "She's doing better. The other day, with some girlfriends of hers, we went out to eat. It was the first time she'd been out of the house for weeks. You know, really, it would take a miracle for my mother. . . . Sometimes I think she'll never really be all right. She's a depressive."

"A what?"

"A depressive. My father says that's someone who doesn't like anything anymore, and who always has strange ideas in their head. You get it?"

"What kind of strange ideas?"

"You know, dark thoughts, like they're sick of living. Anyway, I'm going to try to get a job this summer. That way, I'll be able to buy what I want without always begging my mother or waiting for my father. I'm going to buy a Super Nintendo, like yours."

"If you want to play, all you have to do is call me and come over. You know that, don't you?"

Cléo smiled and nodded his head: "Yeah, I'll call you."

At the time, remember, you said to yourself, "Yeah, yeah, so you say."

"Anyway," you cut things off, "I have to go. Otherwise, Serge is gonna have a fit."

Together you headed back towards the schoolyard. The students were sitting on the asphalt all around Serge. When he saw the two of you, the teacher broke off what he was saying.

"Where were you two?"

"Just in the washroom," you answered.

Serge put his fists on his hips, sighed in exasperation and stared at Cléo.

183

"For the past three weeks, you've been showing up late. Would you like to tell me what's going on?"

All heads turned towards Cléo who then craned his own neck and went boo! like he wanted to scare the others.

"Cléo, I'm talking to you!" said Serge.

"What?"

"I asked you a question."

"I dunno."

"This is the last time I'll tolerate you being late. I'm warning you."

"Yeah, yeah . . ."

"What's this attitude about Cléo? Don't you care about competitions now, or what?"

"No, no . . ."

"You don't care about them?"

"No, I'm telling you. I'm just sick of doing warm-up laps and exercises. When you're good, you're good. When you're lousy, you're lousy. Even if the lousy guy practises his whole life, he'll never be better than the good guy."

"Yeah, well . . . I'd like to tell you that your little theory is pretty pretentious."

"It's true and you know it, Serge."

"You do ten laps right now. Or else you're not going to the Jeux du Québec. Get it?"

"I can't believe it! All that just because I say what I think!"

"No, Cléo, you don't understand. All that is because you're getting a big head because you can run fast."

Serge had got to him: Cléo was scowling at him, his face was hard, his upper lip trembling. After a moment, loud enough for the teacher to hear, he mumbled, "You can stick your ten laps you-know-where."

Then, his arm outstretched, Serge pointed towards the school.

"To the principal's office, right now!"

Cléo got up, and ambled nonchalantly towards the door. They went on without him by putting Sylvain in his place in the relay race. Serge wanted them to practise passing the baton. Later, during recess, Cléo was able to come back to the group. Spring had come early that year and you'd started playing dodge ball again. Near the end, just before the bell rang, you and Cléo ended up alone, against each other. You threw the ball furiously, but neither one of you would die. Recess was over, but there was no winner.

Cléo came towards you, "Not bad, buddy. Your throws are really good."

"Don't worry, Cléo. You're still better."

"Oh, yeah, I wanted to tell you something. Everybody calls me CB now. You can say it in French or English, I don't care. But you have to admit it sounds cooler in English."

"Whatever you say."

All around you, there was a rush to line up.

"You shouldn't have given Serge such a hard time. He was really mad at you."

"Don't worry. He likes to win so much he'll end up coming to me. Remember what I said."

You stared at him, amazed.

"That guy," Cléo continued, "has no right to talk to me like that. Saying I think I'm someone I'm not. I'm not going to take that. I never had to pay my dues cause I'm a good sprinter. Anyway, you can be sure, he's not going to push me around like that again."

Without saying goodbye, you separated and each went off to join his own line.

"We've been waiting for you to call for hours," CB states, trying to control himself. "We were starting to think you didn't care about Teta anymore."

"What do you want?" Flaco asks. "What have you done to him?"

185

"What have we done to him? Oh, we've just been sitting here playing Monopoly with him for hours. What do you think we want?"

"Let me talk to him."

"Let's get something straight, Flaco. We're the ones who have a hostage, we're the ones who set the conditions."

Flaco decides not to answer.

"The police came earlier," explains CB. "This situation is getting pretty heavy, as you can see. So you'd better not be a smart ass. I want a clean trade, you understand?"

"I want the same thing."

"Two pairs of sneakers, a watch, a knife and Teta, for the leather coats. Does that work for you?"

"Yeah, that works."

He notices unusual eagerness in CB's voice.

"The exchange will take place in Parc Kent at the top of the hill, between the baseball diamond and the running track. At exactly midnight. Okay?"

"Okay, but on one condition. I want to talk to Teta."

"What? You don't trust me?"

His voice betrays a suspicious hesitation. Yes, he's hiding something, but what?

"I want to talk to him. I insist on it."

"Ask me the questions and I'll tell him."

"Put him on or the deal's off!"

A long moment goes by during which CB seems to be weighing the options he has before him.

"Okay, but you talk to each other in French and we listen on the other line."

Once again, Flaco prefers not to contradict him: he knows they'd listen even if he said no. He hears steps, then Teta's voice: shit, he's groaning when he talks.

"What's wrong with you?" he asks.

"Me? Nothing."

186

Teta can't talk. Thoughts are racing through his head. He remembers the codes they set up in case of emergency.

"Teta, tell me one thing. Did the Canadiens win yesterday or not?"

"They lost, Flaco."

"How many goals did the other team score?"

"Three."

He's been punched in the face three times.

"Any breakaways?"

"None."

He hasn't been stabbed.

"And the trade they announced with the Bruins?"

Suddenly confused noise comes through the line, sounding like someone trying to grab the phone out of Teta's hands, then the receiver hitting the ground.

"You think I don't know what you're doing?" CB growls. "You want me to tell you? If you're straight on your side, nobody will get screwed. And another thing, your little friend here only got a few scratches compared to what you did to Mixon."

He paused as if he was hesitating about adding something else.

"You attacked him five against one! I'll remember that, Flaco. It was so heroic of you. Really heroic. What can I say, you're a man."

"I didn't attack Mixon, for your information."

"I'm not so sure about that. Besides, at this point, it's not really that important anymore."

"Do you really think I'd do something like that?"

"I think you'd do anything at all. You're a coward. The only time you strike is when you've got your gang around you."

"How long have you known me?"

CB doesn't answer, then he laughs in strange, exaggerated, throaty way.

"That's another problem of yours. . . ."

". . . ."

"You think too much about the past, man. You're obsessed with it. Get this into your head: as far as I'm concerned, I don't know you and I never knew you. All I know is you're against my gang. Can you get that through your thick skull?"

Flaco doesn't really know why, but the effect of all this brings him back down to earth, violently. An attack of sadness veils his thoughts.

"There'll be four of us," CB goes on. "Me, Ketcia, Richard and Max. What about you?"

"Four, too. Don't worry."

"I don't want any low blows. Understand?"

"Nothing sneaky. Same goes for you."

"See you later."

Flaco sighs like a locomotive and, in a daze, starts playing with the phone cord. Just who does CB think he's dealing with? A coward? He's going to have to go through with it, either you're a man or you're not. He looks up at the flowered wallpaper and sees Paulina's worried face: no, the cops are not the solution. He has no choice but to be loyal to his gang. Yes, after the exchange, they'll let Teta go and the nightmare will be over. He calls the members of his group, wakes up some of them and tells them to meet him at quarter to twelve, in front of his place. With their knives, just in case.

Outside, the cold wind stings his face, and the rustling of the leaves frightens him. He follows the sidewalk, with the bag on his back, and turns his head at the slightest sound. He stops in front of a sewer drain and puts down the bag. He takes the condor out of his pocket, weighs it in his hand for a moment, and with a disgusted pout, throws it in. He waits for the splash, but all he hears is the drone of the wind in his ears. Suddenly he rushes to the grate and gets down on all fours. *Dios mío*, what has he done? Through the spaces in the grate, his eyes peer into an unfathomable black hole. What did he do? What a jerk he is! He lifts his head and sees the thin chain hanging from one of the crossbars.

With a trembling hand, he retrieves the object and examines it at length, as if he'd never seen it before. The condor has lost one of its wings. *¡Putamadre!* For a long time, he tries to find the missing bit of metal by feeling around on the metal grate and on the asphalt. But with no success. He gets back up, worriedly looking around in embarrassment, and stuffs the condor into his pocket. He sees Lalo and Pato hurrying towards him, then Alfonso crossing the street.

When you came out of the house, Enrique, sitting on the hood of a car, flattened by the heat, jumped off and landed on both feet: what were you doing? He came towards you tapping the tip of his finger against his watch, I've been waiting for you for fifteen minutes, and he stood motionless, his hands on his hips. A friend wanted to know if I felt like going to the movies, you explained with a shrug. What did you expect me to do? Hang up on him? Not that friend you used to have . . . what was his name again? You know, the Black kid? No, not him. He was talking to Akira, a Japanese kid. Japanese, eh? Did he have any sisters? No, he was an only child. Too bad, that's one nationality I've never tried, and Enrique licked his chops. You laughed and your cousin became serious again: did you eat? Yeah, by himself: his parents had got into another fight. As usual, they'd closed the door to their room so you couldn't hear. I bet they were fighting over stupid stuff again, right? Yeah, it was all because your father had told your mother her *caldo* was cold. Enrique laughed sardonically. Fighting over cold soup! he said shaking his head. He thought it was pathetic. No, he'd recently decided he was never getting married. Anyway, it was old-fashioned. You just had to ask Toño what he thought. Even Mr. Intellectual-and-All-That said marriage had no future.

Lazily, you went down Linton towards Victoria. It was a sunny Saturday afternoon, with a blue sky and small, bright white clouds. You were both wearing long T-shirts that covered your

189

shorts, Enrique's had a picture of a Ferrari, yours had the Power Rangers. Earlier this morning, Enrique had called to see if you felt like keeping Toño company at the video store where he'd been working for a week, because he was bored all alone. You'd immediately said yes, what else could you do: you were so jealous of Toño because of his job. You thought your cousin was lucky, because now he could buy almost anything he wanted: sports equipment, music cassettes, clothes. When you heard about it, you even thought to yourself: and what am I doing here with my newspapers? You'd talked to your mother about it, but she didn't share your worries at all: you know what your problem is? You compare yourself with your cousins too much. Don't forget, they're a lot older than you are. You're certainly not going to start working at eleven years old!

On the way, in front of an unpaved driveway, you bumped into some Latino friends, all wearing black shorts, high white socks that came up to their knees and cleated shoes, and you shook their hands enthusiastically. They invited you to join them for a soccer match against a Portuguese team in the Parc Vézina. But Enrique stiffened and tried to look important: not today, *compadres*, they had things to do. At the corner of Lavoie, Enrique filled his lungs as if he were out in the countryside, and sighed: if the weather was like this all year round, Montreal would be a cool city. Poetically, he added, a melancholy wind sometimes rose up within him and homesickness sometimes haunted his nights like a ghost, my friend. He remembered the delicious Santiago summers, *ay, ay, ay,* when the girls in miniskirts made you walk around with a hard-on all day. Again, he licked his chops, very slowly this time. Because the most beautiful girls were where, eh? With their golden skin, their round asses, and their angelic little faces? In slow motion, as a joke, he pretended to punch you on the chin: I know you know the answer, champ.

You crossed right in the middle of the street, without looking left or right. On the sidewalk, you walked past a sagging mattress

– with a visible yellow circle right in the middle – and some gar-bage bags that were giving off a rotting odour that made you nau-seous. Enrique held his nose and started walking faster, you did the same. About your Black friend, your cousin said, a few metres farther on, he'd seen him at the Plamondon station, stretched out with his friends. Cléo? you'd asked. Without answering, the other boy stared at the end of the street, took a breath: I walked past them and they squinted at me, as if little jerks their age could scare me. I didn't say anything, I was in a hurry. Then, from a dis-tance, they started shouting: Latino this, Latino that, I don't re-member what. You can be sure that next time I'll teach them a lesson they'll remember for a long time. You know in Santiago, I did karate for three years. Suddenly, he came to a stop, bent his knees, got into an attack position and sliced the air as he let out a sharp cry. But you know the rules, he went on, the demonstration completed, you can only use your karate when someone attacks you.

Just before the intersection, Enrique motioned for you to stop and hide behind a van. Observe, *compadre*. Isn't she just a tiny bit magnificent? Stretched out on a lounge chair on the second floor balcony, with her shirt open, a young girl, with her eyes closed, directed her face towards the sun. She's Argentinian, Enrique said enthusiastically, her name is Gladys. After a few seconds of stupefied contemplation, Enrique bit his fist: so, what do you think, champ? And you said, she's pretty, all right. Pretty? said the other boy, amused, and he sniggered. That, *compadre*, is not pretty, she's an *hostie de pétard*, as the Québécois say, she's fucking hot. Enrique took several long breaths, like a swimmer preparing to dive in, then, relaxed, he stepped towards the balcony, and you followed him: hola, Gladys, *¿qué tal?* The girl sat up, blinked her eyes several times, then offered you her most beautiful smile: *¡hola, Enrique! ¿Cómo estás?* You know me, he puffed out his chest, his smile so broad it looked like a grimace, I'm always great! He introduced his

191

little cousin, Marcelo, and Gladys said, hola and you replied hola. Do you live on Rue Linton, too? Yeah, just a little farther up, and Gladys, who was now fanning herself with a magazine, frowned slightly: that was strange, she'd never run into you. Do you go to Saint-Luc? Enrique coughed slightly: let him finish public school first.

There followed a long exchange between Gladys and Enrique. They asked about such-and-such a person who went to such-and-such a school, then they took turns sharing information about future parties thrown by mutual friends. After a little while, from the darkness of the apartment, there appeared a young girl in a navy blue dress, with chestnut brown hair that fell to her shoulders. Gladys slipped one arm around her waist and hugged her: she wanted to introduce her little sister. I didn't know you had a sister, Enrique said in surprise. You both said hello and Enrique whistled: I see you have some competition, Gladys, for the title of Prettiest Girl on the Street. Isn't she pretty, said Gladys, examining her from head to foot. And top of her class, too! But she's not interested in boys yet, she's too young. In any case, she was going to protect her from vultures like him, Enrique. And the four of you laughed joyfully.

Remember, Marcelo, Enrique nudged you discretely, while you, still in shock, couldn't keep from following her slightest movements with fascination. That first time, from those very first instants, you'd noticed her big light eyes, sometimes gentle and frank, sometimes sly and mischievous. What's your name, asked Enrique. Paulina. What are your names, she asked as she leaned on the railing. Enrique told her his name, and you pronounced your own and, strangely, those three syllables gave you the feeling they described someone else. Then, was it your imagination or had she really repeated your name in a low voice as if she was trying to memorize it? What school did she go to? asked Enrique. She pointed to a brown brick building on the corner: her public school was called Roberval. He had a super idea, Enrique bragged, why didn't they come with them to visit his brother Toño at the video store? What did they think? Gladys gave a start: I didn't know your brother worked at a video store. Yeah, you know, the one on Victoria. Okay, good idea, she answered hurriedly, I'll get dressed and we'll be down. You want to, Paulina?

Enrique and Gladys walked in front of you, as, at Paulina's side, you couldn't keep from glancing sidelong at her profile when she was looking straight ahead. How long had she been going to Roberval? you asked, and you gave a long fake yawn to hide your unease, your stomach was all turned upside-down. She'd hardly been able to answer before you jumped on her with another question: how long had she been in Canada? Who were her favourite actors? What group did she listen to most? What sports did she like to play? Not so fast, she interrupted you, she couldn't answer all your questions at once. And continuously, obsessively, you kept a close eye on her turned-up nose, her light lips, the beauty mark on her cheek. ¡Ay, ay, ay, Marcelito! The rustling of new sensations. At the time, as you felt a familiar confidence settle over you, you thought Toño was right when he said it was easier to talk to Latin American girls.

When he saw you coming, Toño came out from behind the counter, looking delighted: okay, here we go, he'd buy them all a Coke! What did they say to that? Okay, good. You stepped close to the shelves against the wall: most of the boxes advertised Hollywood movies dubbed in Spanish, though every once in a while, there were the old Mexican melodramas your mother liked, with Dolores del Rio or Jorge Negrete, Venezuelan action movies, and comedies starring the indescribable Catinflas. Enrique showed you the foosball table at the back of the store: why didn't he play a game with Paulina? And she said, good idea! How much time did you spend at the foosball table that first time, Marcelo? Three, four hours? From time to time, you'd look up at her quickly, and that would give her the chance to score a goal: I told

193

you not to let me win, Marcelo. And you were fascinated by the way she said your name.

In the meantime, since the twins' parents were going to visit family in Toronto, Gladys, sitting on a stool between the two of them, was trying to convince them to have a party at their place the next weekend. I think it's a good idea, Enrique stated, because with Gladys, we're sure to get all the Latin American girls from Saint-Luc. Don't exaggerate, she contradicted him. Then the conversation turned to the Jeux du Québec, which were taking place in three weeks at the Centre Claude-Robillard. And, at the foosball table, you were surprised, you thought they were only for primary schools. No, no, Enrique specified, Toño was on the grade ten relay team. Really, Gladys said, looking over Toño's athletic body with admiration. Tall and strong as he was, that didn't surprise her at all, and she laughed nervously. Hey, are you still going out with the same girl, she ventured. You looked up at Enrique: he was furious with her. This wasn't the first time you'd been present at a scene where a girl preferred Toño over him. As a distraction, Toño turned his head and asked you, though he'd posed the question before: which event were you representing your school in, in the Jeux du Québec? And you answered, the relay team and Paulina said, Really? She was on the long jump team. You'd certainly see each other there.

Around three o'clock, when he realized Gladys had eyes only for his brother, Enrique got up with stiff movements: bye, everybody, he was going to go hang out with his friends. Half an hour later, now realizing that Toño was only replying to her advances in monosyllables, Gladys got up and waved at them: don't come home too late, eh, little sister? Remember, you'd spent almost the whole afternoon drinking Coke and playing foosball, a game which, until then, hadn't really interested you. When he wasn't serving customers, Toño was absorbed by a novel he was reading as he balanced on the stool behind the cash register. After many hesitations, you let go of the levers and summoned up your courage: would you like to go practise for the Jeux in Parc Kent some day? Her face turned serious, then she smiled discreetly: yes, okay. You left the video store, as twilight extended its domain and an attention-grabbing wind blew. At the door to her building, you said goodbye to each other and, as you moved away, she came running back down the stairs: she wanted to give you her phone number. You searched your pockets, crap, you didn't have a pencil. No problem, you'd memorize it, you reassured her. You repeated it out loud several times. Anyway, if you forget it, you know where I live, it's apartment two. With a kiss on each cheek, you went back up Linton. Continuously repeating the number to yourself, you barely answered friends who shouted hello. When you got home, you conscientiously wrote it down on a piece of paper. That night, you hardly slept a wink, and the next morning, you woke up with a terrible headache. You went into the bathroom to wash up, and, with a frown, your mother stopped you in the hallway to examine your face: *Dios mío*, Marcelo, are you sick? You're so pale! It looks like you've just seen a ghost!

VIII

The lights around the baseball diamond go out, darkness settles on Parc Kent and Flaco takes advantage of the gloom to make the sign of the cross. He watches everyone who walks down Côte-des-Neiges, he will not be surprised by the Bad Boys. A breeze offers its coolness and rustles the straggly bushes, and he glances behind him one last time: the tip of Lalo's cigarette is glowing brighter, Pato is firmly seated on the garbage bag, one hand beneath his chin, his elbow on his knee, and, beside him, Alfonso yawns so widely he could dislocate his jaw. Earlier, since his parents won't let him out after eleven, he escaped through his second-storey window. Flaco pushes up his sweater sleeve: it's ten past twelve, where the hell are they? Hearing steps, he turns around and sharpens his gaze: a couple walks slowly by, arm in arm. At the same time, a sugary tune can be heard, carried by a nasal, Asian voice, and a few cars, following one behind the other, thunderously disrupt the calm street. Lalo steps over to him and, without looking at him, exhales the smoke from his cigarette. He says: "What if they decided not to come? What if it's a trap, eh?"

It's true, how else can this lateness be explained? Lalo blows little smoke rings and, seeing that the other boy offers no reply, goes back over to Pato. Flaco checks his watch, examines Côte-des-Neiges's dimly lit sidewalks, then, again his watch, then Côte-des-Neiges. Finally, there they are, they're walking past the Provi-Soir: counting Teta, there are five of them. After the swings, they cut across the park, go around the baseball field, climb the hill and stop nearby. Richard and Max, their eyes full of spite, are positioned behind Teta, holding him firmly by the arms. Where do they think they are, in an action movie? In the semi-darkness, it looks to him like Teta's face is stained by a black-and-blue mark distorting his cheek. All this time, CB, two steps away, is being a smart aleck: his sniggering reveals his pink gums. Suddenly Flaco turns on his flashlight: none of the Bad Boys has brought the items for the exchange. He clenches his fist.

Flaco hears steps behind him. Two Black guys are coming towards them with bouncing, rhythmic steps. When they come to a stop, he recognizes their dark-rimmed eyes, their large lips, their features carved into bone and ebony: Carl and his big brother. *Putamadre*, it's a set-up! No, his intuition wasn't wrong, CB came with reinforcements. For a year, the two brothers have been living in a one-bedroom apartment and are now head of another gang, the Panthers. Physically, compared to Carl, Flaco measures up, but the other one, despite his neck being strangely crammed into his shoulders, is like a refrigerator, both taller and wider than they are. Flaco has heard stories about them that would make your hair stand on end: armed robbery, intense drug trafficking, corruption of minors, pimping – the list is long and impressive. Disheartened, Lalo stubs out his cigarette and whispers, in a broken voice, "What are we going to do?"

Again, Flaco doesn't reply, concentrating as he is on staring into the whites of CB's eyes. Calm down! he repeats to himself. No time to panic. And above all, no false moves. CB steps forward, his face crossed by a triumphant irony.

"I'm disappointed in you. Very disappointed. I'm amazed how easy it is to con you."

197

Flaco continues to look at him, without moving even a centimetre.

"We even brought Mixon with us so he could watch the show that's going to take place in his honour."

Indeed, the injured boy, his arm in a sling, is standing proudly off to one side. Amused, CB turns towards him, "So, Mix', which one shall we bump off first?"

"You're not going to do that, are you?" Carl's big brother interjects in an effeminate voice, "No, CB, please, don't bump them off!"

All the Haitians laugh heartily, except Carl's brother, who begins to click his tongue, his little eyes shine because he is fever-ishly drunk, Flaco notices. Though a shiver of terror is rising from the pit of his stomach to his chest, he thinks, thinks, and finally says, "We don't have time to fool around. We came here for an exchange. Is it still on, or was that just bullshit?"

CB points his thumb at Flaco and calls to Carl and his brother, "Did you see that, guys? What a man! Now that's the voice of a leader!"

And he releases a big laugh and, as he tries to keep it going, he momentarily loses his balance.

"I think you're the one who's going to get the first taste of it," he adds, becoming serious once again.

Curling his finger at him, Flaco signals for Pato to come over. Pato brings over the garbage bags and he immediately hands them over to CB.

"What an idiot!" exclaims the leader of the Bad Boys, tossing the bag at Ketcia.

Then, rolling menacing eyes, Carl's brother takes out a knife and pops open the blade. All the others, Haitians and Latinos both, imitate his action: the blades sparkle in the moon-light, arched and thin as freshly clipped fingernails. The Hai-tians surround the Latinos, tighten their circle little by little, and, impassive, Carl's brother lets out a huge burp that provokes infectious laughter. Above the sound of their hilarity, Flaco again hears the sound of the Asian's sharp tremolos. He feels pressure upon his arm and immediately turns his head, his heart in his throat: Alfonso is hanging on to him, his face pleading. Suddenly, Carl and his big brother take to their heels, go over the metal fence surrounding the running track and disappear behind the bleachers. The others, as if dazed, turn towards the hedge-lined hill: four uniformed men are rushing towards them. Instantly, two of them climb over the fence and take off after the brothers. CB tries to run for it, too, but one of the officers grabs him by the leg and topples him to the ground, immobilizing him with a knee on his chest. The police? What's this about? Who . . . The other officer undoes the holder on his right hip, removes his revolver and orders everyone, in a powerful voice, to lie down flat on the ground. And he's not going to say it again! All of them, their hands in the air and their heads pointed down, comply. In the meantime, the corpulent officer, his face red as a lobster, is holding CB's wrists and pushing down even harder on his stomach with his knee.

"Fat pig," CB says indignantly, "I can't breathe."

"Stay still or I'll break your arm."

Freeing his hands, CB lets fly with punches that hit the officer in the sides, as the cop struggles to keep him under control. A long time goes by, during which Flaco, with his ear against the grass, watches them battle without blinking. Losing his balance, puffing like a locomotive, the officer shouts to his younger colleague: "Come help me, dammit!"

The younger one is still pointing his revolver at them and wiping the dampness from his free hand on the thigh of his pants.

"If I turn my back on them, they might jump us, don't you see?"

The fighting between CB and the officer intensifies, their blows more brutal, more rapid. Flaco hears their grunts and sharp, little cries. The officer snorts excessively and bursts out laughing, half amused, half disgusted.

"Christ! The little brat won't give up!"

"Stop hitting my butt, you disgusting pervert!"

"That's right, that's right! I love you too, my handsome little Black friend!"

Then, coming out of nowhere, the knife pierces the officer's stomach four times. The movement is quick and clean: the blade goes in and out, in and out. The return movement makes an unmistakable gurgle: his eyes glaring with pain, the officer opens his mouth wide and tumbles head first onto CB who pushes off the body and tries to stand up, letting out a frightened moan. On his knees, his face gripped by a tremor, he raises his hands as if to surrender, murmurs a series of confused words in Creole, and then the shot is heard. For a moment, his body remains in the same position, as if balanced, and his face looks both stunned and afraid. Then he drops down and rolls onto his right side. Flaco's eyes return to the young, motionless officer, with his cap pulled half-way down his forehead: the barrel of his gun is still smoking. In the distance, a dog barks, whiningly, as if the shot had hit him.

With one hand, the officer takes out a walkie-talkie while, with the other, he continues to hold his revolver. His voice breaking, he repeats three times loudly and clearly that one of his colleagues has been stabbed. Around him, the ten teenagers, flat on their stomachs, their hands behind their backs, follow his movements without budging. The dog has again fallen silent and the park is as quiet as a cemetery. At last, sirens, coming from all directions, pierce the night. Three police cars stop with squealing tires on Rue Appleton, several uniformed men and women get out and rush towards them. As they begin fitful conversations on their walkie-talkies, they stand everyone up and handcuff them all. As soon as the ambulance arrives, two men in shirt sleeves get out, pushing gurneys. Flaco feels a cold hand on his forearm indicating he should hurry up, then, at the police car, the same hand touches his neck and lowers his head. He inches his way to the end of the back seat, turns towards the window and stares at the ambulance's red lights. Barely aware that Lalo is being pushed in next to him, he tries to convince himself that what just happened is nothing but a dream.

How easy it is to remember that morning and its creamy light, Marcelo: for the children you were then, it was, literally, the most highly anticipated day of the whole school year. You'd spent part of the night tossing and turning in your bed, and you'd gone into your parents' room to wake up your mother, who, sullen and with tousled hair, had agreed to make you a hot chocolate. Still, the warm milk and the long lecture had got you nothing but a stubborn headache, sleep hadn't come to envelop you until several hours later. The next morning, when the alarm went off, you didn't budge – your mother even had to come and shut off the ringer herself, she'd told you later. When you opened your eyes, you felt a light wind on your ankles: your mother had pulled the covers all the way down to the bottom of the bed, and she was shaking you by the shoulder. Now, sitting there on the platform, next to Akira, you felt torn between the desire to sleep and the excitement of the competitions.

Early in the morning, in the finals of the grade five 500 metres, Cléo had pulled off a perfect start, getting a good distance ahead of his opponents after only twenty metres. Even so, it wouldn't have taken much for another Haitian boy, this one from Quebec City, equally fast, to beat him out at the finish line. Still, there was something unbelievable about it: Cléo was the fastest ten-year-old boy in the province. His prediction had come true, quite easily it appeared. Serge had indeed come and made up with him, his tail between his legs: they weren't really going to get angry over such a little thing, were they? You'd overheard Cléo telling Carl what had happened when they'd talked: according to him, it would have taken just a little more for the teacher to get down on his knees and beg.

At noon the sun, round and bursting on that humid June day, seemed to halt in its exhausting course at its zenith. The Centre Claude-Robillard, full to bursting, was decorated with crepe paper and balloons, and, in stands set up here and there, university students served orange juice and plastic cups of milk, as they distributed posters about the food groups. Most of the students strolled around the track in tank tops and shorts, since they weren't allowed to go topless. Girls in bathing suits, on the other side of the cement platform, were sunbathing, glistening with coconut oil, dark glasses on their noses. You kept looking for Paulina. Why wasn't she with the others from her school, on the bleachers? Crap, maybe she'd got sick? Still, the night before, when you'd both practised for the last time before the Jeux, as she perfected her technique, she'd achieved her best results in the long jump. At lunch time, you went to wait for Enrique and Toño at the edge of the track and you went upstairs to the cafeteria. Enrique was just there to keep Toño company, his relay team hadn't qualified for the finals that morning. Next year, Toño had said, a good sport, shrugging his shoulders.

Late in the afternoon, Serge motioned for the grade five relay team to come down and warm up. You and Akira stretched your thigh muscles, lying out on the grass near the pads for the high jump, when you heard a voice chanting your name. In the middle of the bleachers, leaning over the metal railing, Paulina, on her toes in her running shoes, was waving her arms at you: ¡buena suerte, Marcelo! Remember how your heart beat like a drum when you waved at her. Cléo came up on you from behind, turned on his heels and fell to the ground on his hands, ready to do a set of push-ups: that your girlfriend? And you, presently stretching your calves, frowned with your whole face: no, she's just a friend. How that remark had made you clench your teeth, Marcelo! Cléo stood back up and, maintaining a

surprising rhythm, ran in place for quite a while, lifting his knees
higher and higher: I didn't know you were interested in girls
now! You didn't answer and, since it was one of the few times
where you bumped into each other, you talked about what you'd
been up to, but that time, remember, you did it more to be po-
lite than out of real interest. Cléo, standing up very straight,
with his legs spread, started doing waist rotations. He was still
having problems with his dear old mother. She'd stopped working and was living on social assistance, so now she spent the
whole day hanging around the apartment with the drapes
drawn. But, most of all, Cléo made clear, she hardly ever talked
to him any more: he reminded her too much of his father, she
said. To tell the truth, lately, he'd only had one thing on his
mind: getting out of the apartment. Going to live with his father, maybe. Suddenly, without giving you a warning, he again
turned on his heels and sprinted, as if his behind was on fire, to
the other end of the track.

In the bleachers, where shouts and applause rose up in
waves, students waved banners bearing the names of their
schools. One of the organizers of the Jeux, a ruddy, corpulent
man, decked out in a straw hat, gave a long whistle: runners, it's
time to take your marks. Remember, Marcelo: since your team
had had the best time, you'd got one of the centre lanes, the
fourth one. You delicately placed your fingers on the starting
line, the official raised the starting pistol and the explosion rang
through the stadium. As usual, the crowd's encouragement was
immediately transformed into a lion's roar. As you entered the
turn, you noticed you were already ahead of the runner in lane
five, and that boosted your confidence: you went faster. You
closed your eyes and, even though the taste of blood had risen
in your mouth, its effect on you was calming. After a moment,
you heard nothing but your own breathing, the beating of your
heart, your steps, and the droning of the wind. When you
opened your eyes coming out of the curve, you almost stopped,

thinking you'd made a false start: no one was on your heels and, the deserted, desolate track seemed to take on gigantic proportions.

Just when Akira, his eyes half closed, took hold of the baton, was it your imagination?, an expression of fear passed over his face. But he ran like a shot, like you'd never seen him run before. You stood still, the opposing runners closed in around you, and you began again to hear the cheers and the laughing that Akira's comical way of running drew from the crowd. Near the end of his run, he was at least ten metres ahead of his nearest rival, and, as he came out of the turn, Yuri, the baton in hand, his blond hair exposing his rounded forehead, had doubled the lead Akira had gained.

Under the growing ovation, Cléo grabbed onto the baton and once and for all lost his opponents. His head surged forward as if someone inside him was trying to go even faster. The distance was so great that the organizers, who were usually quite jaded, actually looked up. On its feet, the crowd was frozen like a stone statue, and silence like a threatening cloud passed over the stadium. Cléo cut through the finish line, and thunderous shouting split the June air. He came to a stop, his hands on his hips, still breathing hard. Catching him unaware, Serge jumped on his neck, excited as a child. Soon there was such a crowd, strangers were hugging you like they'd known you forever.

Then, remember the photo, Marcelo: since you didn't fit in the frame, Serge, euphoric, asked you to squeeze together. A little more! But without pushing! You still have that black and white photo, now yellow and wrinkled: Akira, with a serious face is staring into the lens; Yuri is pensively looking at the ground; Cléo is looking for someone outside the frame; and you, looking bothered, have your eyes closed. No one was smiling. It doesn't look like a victory, Marcelo.

After the medal ceremony, when you went back up into the bleachers, Paulina came to congratulate you and she sat between

Akira and you. But, to your great chagrin, the four winners were asked to please go to the locker room at Serge's request. You took a shower and put on clean clothes, finally ready to leave. But Serge, moved to his very core, red as a rooster, climbed on a stool and spoke in a confused way, repeating three times in a row how proud he was of you. Then he finished with a convoluted ode to teamwork that bored you to death, anxious as you all were to go out and meet your friends.

As you left the locker room, you noticed Paulina and her cousins waiting for you. You got the customary pats on the back and Enrique asked you to show him your medal. Houaououh, *es bonita*, and he pretended to bite into it: don't worry, champ, it's just to be sure it's not made out of plastic. Now that you're a great athlete, Toño teased you, were you going to start turning your nose up at them? And you said, no, you jerk, don't be stupid. Despite her disappointment in the long jump, Paulina's light eyes were sparkling when she met yours. You were on your way out of the stadium when you noticed Cléo waving at you from the other end of the corridor, near the vending machines. Half-heartedly, you waved back at him. In the company of Carl and the others, he was walking in the opposite direction, and twice you saw him turn around. But you soon forgot his insistent looks.

Beneath the gaze of the monitors which, for once, is indulgent, the students flow slowly into the gym, almost lazily, like a wine stain spreading across a tablecloth. Though it's almost the end of the school day, no one is running or shoving, and they're certainly not joking or laughing. Everyone in the school knew CB, and across the faces float expressions that are sometimes distressed or horrified, sometimes indifferent. As usual, the director appears late, building up the crowd's impatience. They discreetly pull on their neighbours' sleeves, and ask in low voices: is it true he got shot by a cop? That he stabbed another cop? How many were on the Bad Boys' side? What about Latino Power's? What were they doing in the park so late at night? Why were the two gangs fighting?

With their backs to the wall, surrounded by Mixon, Richard and Max, Ketcia is sick of avoiding the other students' indiscreet looks. Yes, she has puffy eyes. Feeling her legs grow heavy, she lets herself slip to the floor and concentrates her attention on a point on floor. No, she's never cried so much in her life. And so what? Most of the students only knew CB's façade, she may be the only one to know who he really was. Despite herself, last night's interrogation parades in front of her eyes once again. With their morale at zero, intimidated by the slamming of the police station doors as the cops moved from one room to another, the Bad Boys couldn't help but expose precious information about Carl and his brother, to the point that the police are sure to get their hands on them soon. It looks like they've been searching for them for four months already, for the armed robbery of a convenience store. At the end of the interrogations, to everyone's surprise, both gangs were released, on the condition they appear before the Youth Court in exactly one month. Between now and then, each of them must, every three days, meet with a police officer, a social worker and a psychologist for rehabilitation. The outcome of the shooting: the police officer died at the hospital from his injuries, while CB, who was shot very near the heart, died at the scene.

When Barbeau appears at the podium scattered boos and whistles ring out, but they fade almost immediately. This time they're acting up more to make fun of his affected manners than to communicate any real discontent or frustration. The director has no need to look stern or to clap his hands to impose silence. After his usual long introduction, he expresses his most "sincere sympathy" for the Bastide family, and for the family of the police officer, Guy Phaneuf, too. In addition, today he is feeling "deep sadness" and "indescribable bitterness." He hopes that the events will offer "everyone here today" something to think about and that from this day forward the students will understand the "disastrous consequences" of racial gangs. For anyone who feels the need, the school psychologist and nurse will be available to discuss the shock that can be caused by such events. Also, he wants to warn them: in the upcoming days, the media, indiscreet as always, will undoubtedly come ask them questions. They must tell the truth! he booms. Give them "the exact time"! They mustn't forget, they are each responsible for their school's image! Do they understand? He stops, visibly pleased with his tirade. Additionally, and he agrees this is unfortunate, such events force the administration to undertake supplementary measures to avoid any similar confrontations occurring at the school in the future. That's why, beginning next week – they made this decision for everyone's well-being – metal detectors will be installed at all the entrances to the school. A wave of protest spreads, but there's still no real, rowdy heart in it.

Already Ketcia has stopped listening. She feels exhausted, tired of going over and over what happened last night. During the night, when she tried to get some sleep, she convinced herself, for a good half hour, that CB rose like a zombie and took off after his attackers. More clearheaded now, no longer pretending just to make herself feel better, she's certain of one thing: an unjust act of barbarism was committed. After CB's death was announced at the police station, the thought of revenge ate into her. But this morning, staring into the whites of her eyes in the mirror, she could see it wouldn't do any good. No fight, no murder, no fleeting dream would bring CB back. It's so strange: she feels like she's aged terribly in the space of one night. In the bathroom, her features seemed more severe, more oval, as if a Haitian mask had been placed over her face. Come hell or high water, she's sworn to go on fighting: the story of the Bad Boys will not end here.

Flaco, withdrawn in the back of the gym, in the middle of Latino Power, stares into the distance as he chews on air. He's thinking about Lalo, who will have to appear in court for stabbing Mixon, and trying to fend off a growing sense of guilt. Then he sees Roberto's disappointed face at the police station: like there was a chance you'd take my advice, he says sarcastically. Also, painfully, he remembers how his father refused to talk about it later in the car. He's tortured by a pang of anguish for a moment, and he sees Paulina step out of the crowd and come towards him.

"Hi," she says quietly.

He turns his head away.

"You still want to talk to me?"

His first reflex is to tell her to go the hell away. But, deep down, he knows he's happy she's come to see him.

"You can stay if you want," he mutters, feigning casual detachment.

The principal is interrupted by a few boos, and two monitors back a handful of students up against the wall. A long stretch of time goes by as Flaco feels the weight of Paulina's eyes on his burning cheeks.

"How are you doing?" he asks, without looking at her.

She sighs, places a hand on his shoulder.

"Listen, Flaco. Are you going to stay mad at me like this for a long time? It was really the only thing to do. And you know it, too. . . ."

"I told you, you should have warned me before you called them. I thought I made myself pretty clear, didn't I? You know I've never wanted you to get mixed up in our problems."

"You have to understand me, Flaco. It had got much too dangerous. I was scared to death. Imagine what could have happened to you if the police hadn't shown up. . . ."

Since he hasn't been listening to what Barbeau's been talking about for several minutes, Flaco is surprised to suddenly see him gesticulating emphatically. Again, as has been happening frequently since last night, his thoughts plunge into a well. It's always the same scene: late for a class, he rushes up the stairs and

208

comes face to face with CB smoking a cigarette, his elbow on the window ledge. Flaco is overjoyed: oh, man, he's so happy to see him, he can't imagine. He wants to talk to him, they have so many things to work out together, doesn't he agree? Then he feels arms slipping around his waist and hugging him tenderly. He opens his eyes and breathes in the fleeting perfume of her chest-nut hair.

"It's over now," she whispers. "You're going to be able to move on to something else: move out of your house, the neigh-bourhood, like you wanted."

His eyes mist up, he has a hard time seeing.

"Don't worry, I'm here."

He rubs his eyes and contemplates her well-formed lips, her straight teeth. He wants to ask her to come with him, tell her that without her, his plan to write is meaningless, that she is the most precious thing in the world to him. But he settles for hugging her back, and he drops back down into the gaping well. CB, still standing, meets his gaze and lights up with a smile: just like that, he asks mockingly, he has a lot to tell him? He's told him before, but he'll tell him again: you're too sentimental, Flaco, you're too obsessed by the past. And he can't get over seeing him there: maybe I am, buddy, I'm sentimental, naïve, anything you say. But you know what? I don't care. What matters to me is that you're here. And CB takes a long drag on his cigarette: okay, I'll listen to you. But watch it, just because he was listening, it didn't mean he agreed with him. He bursts out laughing and the metallic, reso-nant sound is distinct in Flaco's ears. A stream of white light co-mes in through the window, outlining CB's shape, and Flaco feels someone hugging him very tightly again.

You stretched out your arm and you grabbed the can of Coca-Cola and, your throat parched, you took a long drink. Since early June, the days were following one after the other, splendid and restful, just like this one, and you went out on the balcony for a breath of air and to say hello to your friends, or just to watch what was going on on Rue Linton. Laughter cascaded down from the balcony above you, then came an indiscriminate exchange in a language you didn't understand but that you often heard. It was the three brothers of Indian origin who lived on the second floor: they enjoyed spending the afternoon on the balcony soaking up the sun like lizards, as well. You would have liked to have known what made them laugh, yes, you would have liked to have someone tell you a good joke.

You'd been on vacation for three days. You were now going into grade six, but you were dreaming about the day when the big doors of high school would be opened to you. That was when life really started, Enrique, condescending, constantly reminded you. You'd got good grades and your parents had given you your freedom for the summer, but in return you had to clean your room every weekend and take out the garbage on Mondays and Thursdays. You deserved it, Flaco, you'd worked hard all year, your father said to you one day in your room, tousling your hair. You couldn't keep from smiling: since your cousins had bestowed that nickname on you, Flaco, Skinny, even your father had started calling you that. Oh, yeah, he'd added, about the trip to Chile, they were putting it off until next year. Your grandparents were going to be disappointed, but they didn't really have much choice. They didn't have the money, Flaco. But don't worry, we'll at least go to the beach in the U.S., where the Québécois people I work with go. They called it Old Orchard.

It wasn't until the second police car parked, with one tire on the sidewalk, just behind the first one, two buildings to the left of yours, on the other side of the street, that you came out of your daydream. Remember, the second car had stopped facing the wrong way. The officers got out pulling up their belts and went into the building lethargically. Soon, an ambulance appeared and stopped with its bumper against the police car's. Pushing a gurney, two men with beards headed towards the building, too.

The police, ambulances and firefighters came and went so often in your street, that dazed as you were by the heat, you only paid vague attention to the scene. Probably another domestic dispute that had turned ugly.

You saw the three Indians from your building cross the street and join the growing crowd on the other sidewalk. When the police officers came back out, they stuck to them like flies. One was answering the onlookers' questions, but after a while, he made an abrupt gesture with his arm and, in a deep baritone, ordered them to move along. A tall Black man came out of the building and rushed towards the officer. He was constantly running his hand down his face, through his hair. When the police officer moved, he followed, opened his arms wide and continued to talk to him. Then you noticed Enrique in the crowd. You called to him, your cousin trotted across the yard and approached the balcony.

"What happened?" you asked.

"A suicide."

You looked up at the building.

"It's your Black friend's mother . . . Cléo's mother."

You started to say something, but you were speechless, unable to articulate. The words got stuck in your throat, Marcelo.

"Looks like she hanged herself, man. In the bathroom."

Enrique shook his head. Then, as if he was talking to himself, he added, "What a day to commit suicide."

Now you were looking for Cléo, but all you could see was the tall man pacing back and forth with long steps, his back curved, gesturing desperately. And then you understood: it was the father. That was the first time you'd seen him.

"Your friend's got really lousy luck. Imagine: your mother kills herself and you find her hanging from the shower curtain rod. What do you do? . . . Hmmm? . . . What can you do?"

You turned your head towards him and he answered himself: "Nothing. You take it. That's all . . . *Así es la vida.*"

A growing number of curious people came out onto the

balconies or stood in the building entryways, with their arms crossed.

"To do a thing like that," Enrique continued, "you really have to be desperate. The way I see it, there are just two reasons to commit suicide. All the rest is just variations on the same two problems. Either you're having trouble in your love life or you're in the hole, financially."

But you'd already stopped listening to your cousin because Cléo had just come outside. He zigzagged forward, his arms swinging, apparently surprised to see such a crowd in front of his building. He sat on the grass and started to swing his head back and forth, back and forth, then he buried it between his knees. His father sat next to him, sweeping his eyes across the activity going on all around, put an arm around Cléo's shoulders and held him close for some time. You got up, having decided to jump from the balcony, but you saw Carl and his big brother rushing towards father and son. They chatted quite a while, occasionally bringing a hand to their forehead and shaking their head. The paramedics came out with the body hidden under a grey blanket, hurried it into the ambulance, and one of them stepped over towards the little group. Cléo and his father got into the vehicle. The police officers dispersed the crowd. The ambulance sped away.

"I'm going home," Enrique announced. "We'll do something this afternoon. Okay? I'll call you."

Your eyes followed your cousin as he trotted away like a soccer player. Despite the heat, a shiver went down your spine. You felt excluded, disoriented, crushed. Why, why? Suddenly your name rang out, your mother was calling you. In the kitchen, you sat down in front of a plate laid out with little fried *empanadas*. You let your mother know you weren't hungry. What do you mean, Marcelo? Have you started eating junk between meals again? No, Mom, and you told her what you'd just witnessed. *¡Madre mía!* she shouted, covering her mouth with the towel she used to dry the dishes. What could you say about such a thing? In any case, she'd seen it coming. *¡Pobre niñito!*

You went into the living room, dropped down in the chair and put on the TV while you waited for Enrique's call. An episode of *The Flintstones* was just finishing. During the first set of commercials, even though you were making an effort to think of other things, you remembered the day of Cléo's birthday, when Carole had spoken to you in Spanish. Remember how it had surprised you. She'd immediately won your confidence. You spent a good part of the afternoon channel surfing, then you finally called Enrique yourself, but he'd gone to help out Toño at the video store. A headache was starting to make your temples pound when the phone rang: it was Paulina! It was the first time she'd called since you'd given her your number. Did you have any plans for today? And, happy she'd asked, you answered, no, not really. Did she have anything in mind? And she said, what did you think about going to the pool? Why not, you said with some hesitation in your voice, because you were happy she'd called and everything, although you didn't really feel like going swimming. Really, do you want to? she insisted. Yes, really, you reassured her, torn between the dark thoughts that were worrying you and your burning desire to see her. Gladys, her sister, was there already. In five minutes in front of your building? Okay, see you there.

You stuffed a bathing suit and towel any old way into your backpack, you went downstairs and sat down on the top step to wait, as the sun beat javelins down on you. When she arrived, you were breathing like a chicken on a rotisserie. You kissed each other on both cheeks and you walked side by side as the dense humidity made your joints swell. On the corner of Kent, you stopped in the middle of the sidewalk and confided to her that you really weren't feeling very well at all. She asked you about it, arching her eyebrows, and you explained what was wrong. She cried out in astonishment and then it was her turn to keep apologizing. She suggested you go to the park and you agreed, though your voice felt strangled. You walked silently over to a bench. After you told her all the details you knew of Cléo's mother, you felt the sadness slowly leaving you, like a spirit that was tired of living in you. She looked at you and occasionally brushed a hand across your hands, your knees, your cheeks: she was glad you'd told her. You felt better when you talked to her. You now had a friend for life, she assured you. She took your hands without embarrassment and squeezed them, and, for a moment, clearheaded, you wondered if you loved her. You didn't really know, you only knew you couldn't do without her anymore, even if you had to settle for just having her as a friend. She asked you what you wanted to do and, with a weak smile, you said, we can go to the pool now if you want.